The Mires

The Mires

a novel

Tina Makereti

HARPERVIA

An Imprint of HarperCollins*Publishers*

HarperCollins books may be purchased for educational, business, or sales promotional use. For information, please email the Special Markets Department at SPsales@harpercollins.com.

harpercollins.com

Originally published as *The Mires* in Australia in 2024 by Ultimo Press, an imprint of Hardie Grant Publishing.

FIRST HARPERVIA PAPERBACK PUBLISHED IN 2025

Designed by Yvonne Chan

Library of Congress Cataloging-in-Publication Data

Names: Makereti, Tina, 1973- author
Title: The mires / Tina Makereti.
Description: New York : HarperVia, 2025. | Identifiers: LCCN 2025006284 (print) | LCCN 2025006285 (ebook) | ISBN 9780063399365 paperback | ISBN 9780063399389 ebook
Subjects: LCGFT: Novels
Classification: LCC PR9639.3.M245 M57 2025 (print) | LCC PR9639.3.M245 (ebook) | DDC 823/.92--dc23/eng/20250602
LC record available at https://lccn.loc.gov/2025006284
LC ebook record available at https://lccn.loc.gov/2025006285

---

25 26 27 28 29 LBC 5 4 3 2 1

He tohu maumahara ki a Moana Jackson

And, for the children who show us
how to see

Because every rock
every river
every mountain
as it is in your country
has a name and a story
and those stories are still there
in spite of all that has happened
waiting for us to hear them
if we care to take the time to listen

—Moana Jackson, Yorta Yorta Woka, 2018

Ask the god to open the house of your chest
wide enough that your enemy may enter

—Tusiata Avia, "House," *Fale Aitu | Spirit House*

Ko au te repo, ko te repo ko au

The Mires

What a Swamp Knows

A swamp knows more than most people about most things. It's our nature, for within the damp and nebulous borders of swamp, water carries messages, stories, and even gossip. Swamp is connected to all waterways, of course. All of them, from pond to stream to river to sea out into the many oceans of the world, and back. Always out, and back, the collective breathing of all the waters flowing through all the channels of the earth. Hence, a swamp in Kāpiti, on the west coast of the lower half of the North Island of Aotearoa New Zealand, knows more than she probably should of the fortunes that have been won and lost on Old Ford Lock near the junction between Regent's Canal and Hertford Union Canal in London, England; or the precious waters collected in gnamma holes in Goomalling, Western Australia, by the Ballardong People; or the Southern O'ahu aquifer, the principal source of drinking water for 400,000 people in Hawaii, contaminated by the jet fuel of the occupying American military. And a swamp knows more than this, for there is nowhere our waters do not connect: the drains and gutters that run along your concrete footpaths, the pipes and taps of your houses, the flush of your toilets. We know your secrets, hear your arguments, wash your bodies of their sweat and sex and blood. Swamp runs beneath everything, especially in places like these, even though you have drained and paved and dammed us. Even though you pretend we no longer exist. We are too old and deep and vast to trouble ourselves with the impermanence of your wood and concrete and steel. Just watch how we rise after an earthquake, reclaiming the land with our wet.

The earthy trickling channels of swamp are like the roots of trees that spread and connect and communicate. People have just discovered that this is what trees do, that in fact trees are more sentient than you have heretofore understood, and that they share information with each other underground, via their root systems, and the fungal mycelium networks they share. Or should we say that people have recently *re*discovered this understanding of trees, since people have known this for eons, and then forgotten it, then learned it again, then misplaced the knowledge. People are forever in the act of coming to know something and then losing themselves in or from that knowledge, forever going through enlightenments and dark ages, then collectively forgetting their history. Swamp doesn't forget, but looks on in amusement when humans do it again, when humans forget so wholeheartedly that they can't even see the ones who haven't lost their knowledge, or their connection, to all that is. These few are disregarded, sometimes ridiculed, until things come round again. And things always come around. Or at least they have until now.

One

WAIRERE

Dharug Country, Sydney, not long ago

Keri had chosen to do things the hard way all her life, so it was no surprise that she gave birth to Wairere alone. Others were supposed to have been there: the midwife, the assistant midwife, and her mother, but it was 3:15 a.m. when she called them, and everything was calm, and everyone thought she'd be okay for another couple of hours. First babies aren't born quickly, everyone knows that. But Keri's contractions moved from thirty-minute intervals to ten-minute intervals in an hour, and before she knew it she was heaving on the toilet, thinking she might die before anyone reached her. They said they'd come at six, and it was only 4:30 a.m., and she couldn't make it to the phone to call, just to her knees by the bed, where she was overcome with the need to push. She tried to hold back, but she didn't know how, and the pushing alleviated the pain. The pushing was like all heaven's angels gathering around her uterus and squeezing with their heavenly fingers, and she wasn't even religious. She visualized a flower opening like the birthing video said, even though she didn't believe in that hippie shit. She didn't care what she had to believe to make the pain subside. She was a sea anemone, she was a mud goddess in a slaughterhouse, she was a gunslinger racing a train on a half-wild horse.

Maybe she was delirious, or maybe it was the movie marathon she had just watched that evening, when she was still ignorant and pregnant, not really the woman she had imagined herself to be after all, but some innocent child. Now that Keri was half woman, half amphibious animal birthing itself onto land, she understood that she was entering the darkness from which it was necessary to draw life forward. She was going in to clasp her child from the embrace of the gods who inhabited the world on the other side of life. She was become something else, something powerful and mad: Kali, Medusa, Hine nui te Pō. Of course, it made sense as soon as she said the name to herself: the Great Lady of the Night, Mother of the Dark. Fierce and fearsome. With nobody else around, she could let all these ancient and imaginary selves flare into being, if only for that sweet moment when the pain drove her right out of her mind.

Then the contraction subsided, and she was back, realizing she didn't want something to happen to the baby even if she lost herself, so she found the phone and made the calls. But no one arrived until after.

After the birthing of the head left her wide-legged and two-headed, an unfledged hydra.

After her daughter slipped full-bodied from between her legs, slick and seallike.

After she lifted the babe into her arms, curled in a warm, wet ball, and found herself gazing into eyes that came not from darkness, but from before the dark existed.

The midwife and the assistant midwife and her mother arrived to find Keri wrapped in her quilt on the floor, the baby sucking on her fist, eyes firmly shut against the lights they switched on to assess the damage. Her mother set about cleaning up the room. The midwives set about managing the birthing of placenta and stitching the places Keri had torn. The baby didn't cry and Keri didn't speak, except to answer the midwives' questions. For some time after that, at least until the umbilical cord had fallen off and for two or three weeks more, Keri could still see the place beyond and behind the dark whenever she gazed into her daughter's eyes. But then the baby began to focus more on the world she now inhabited, and her eyes developed a regular, this-worldly brown color. Though when she fixed people with her stare, they inevitably felt like she was staring into their soul, and what she found there was perplexing.

Te Ātiawa lands, Kāpiti, sometime in the near future

You will find me in the meeting point between open seas and solid land, in the seam of sky and earth, between what you think you know and what you don't. The creatures that flock my way exist here too—waterbirds and land-migrating fish—metamorphic, amphibious, mythical. And that is where Wairere seeks me, whenever she is troubled, like today, all held-in tears and shoulders hunched until she gets away from the house. She takes a deep breath at the corner and looks both ways, not really seeing but instinctively avoiding fast-moving objects—cars, people, scooters, dogs, planets—then moves as quick as she can without running, going over the fight again and again in her head, even though she can't quite pinpoint what it was even about anymore. She was right though, wasn't she? What did she even say? It seemed right at the time. At the time, her mother was being bossy and judgmental, like she always is, and Wairere had had enough. It was unbearable. And she'd told her, tried to make her see what it was like to be on the receiving end of her constant nagging. You don't see anyone else, Mum, she'd said, *Mum* in that condescending tone, you're such a bitch, you know, *bitch* in a way that gave away a little too much of the embarrassment and daring she felt about swearing at her mother, as if that was a big deal. It wasn't a big deal, and her mother *is* a bitch, so she doesn't know why she sounded so unsure when she said it. Where was the justice in any of this? Although, as she walks away from the house, anger rising out of her pores like steam from a bull's nose, she still can't really place what the argument was about, apart from her mother always telling her what to do, and always thinking she's right, and not leaving her alone.

But no one is ever alone, are they? And if you were to witness Wairere now, you would see a young person, neither child nor woman yet, embodied in that in-between state that shifts like afternoon cloud moving over the bush-covered ranges to the southeast: shadows falling in continuous movement, interspersed with sudden bursts of sunlight, wondrous even though those small hills might seem insignificant and plain, a little bit distant, a little bit mysterious, perhaps even uninteresting to an observer not paying proper attention. And indeed, Wairere is not alone, she walks in the footsteps of all the people who have walked this place before her, whether their feet left their mark below the concrete or upon it, and is always accompanied by the birds and lizards and insects, and of course the stones and earth and fern, flax and mud.

Wairere doesn't think of that now, she just waits for the wind to rinse the fury off her. She knows well enough that at some point her pacing will leave it behind, and up ahead she'll find me. The locals call this place the estuary, though Wairere prefers the idea of swamp, not pretty but a little treacherous, as full of sludge that'll suck you down as it is of native plants and pretty birds. Wairere is in love with the idea of being alone with the world. She loves all the many things the world is made of except for humans and their havoc, so as she walks she also lets a fantasy play out in her head: all humanity wiped out by something like the plague they've just had. Yes, another plague, this one cleaner and quicker. The still-burning coal of her fury doesn't allow her to care about the loss of life, not at that moment, or even the practicalities of so many dead bodies, and especially not the fact that she doesn't actually want everyone to die, at least not the ones she loves, and she'd be quite sad if they did.

The imagining is too delicious, and besides, it's just a fantasy. So, her roaming self, alone in the world and free. Peace then, and access to everything. She'd have enough to go on for some time alone, living in the nicest houses, raiding the supermarkets as needed, letting everything grow up around her wild and free, no humans to fuck it up. Like that classic old movie *Zombieland*, but without the zombies.

And so she finds she has cooled to smoldering by the time she reaches Old Swamp Road, and tonight we have something special for her. See the slow dawning on her face as the sound comes into range—the chorus of trills unlike anything she has ever heard—the sonorous chirping of a thousand watery throats floating toward her on the same wind that has taken the anger from her. Frog song—each small fellow urgently calling for love, bursting for it, humming, vibrating, expanding as great as air and as his amphibious skin will allow, each singing his own particular pitch, trying to drown out his competitors, to make such heavenly sounds that his prospective mates will have ears only for him. Wairere moves toward the damp heart of her destination and becomes still, finally, listening in wonder.

She stays for some time, but even one who disdains her own kind can become self-conscious standing on a suburban street at dusk, so eventually she pulls herself out of her trance, and heads along the boardwalk. A girl-woman like this is given to dramatic swings between agonies and ecstasies, and by the time she is a hundred paces into swampland, Wairere has forgotten the anguish that twenty minutes earlier had caused her to mentally obliterate humankind. She'll be cold and distant later, of course, when she returns home, and her mother will feel hurt when her attempts at reconciliation are rebuffed, but there will be no fire and bloodshed in the process.

Secretly, the longer she walks, the happier Wairere becomes, for now ahead of her are those forest-clad ranges, and the clouds dancing over them, the cirrus and cirrostratus wisping in painted patterns behind the lower, faster, fluffier clouds as the sun shares its last glowing embers. And to the east, dense cloud threatening rain, though the immensity of that darkness is thrilling rather than worrying. Wairere is lifted above herself by the contradictory feeling of being both fuller and lighter. Perhaps this is what it feels like to be a singing frog. And if she looks to the west, past the thick, sticky heads of flax flower, the tufted tops of tī kōuka, the dense thicket of replanted spinifex and native seedlings, she can see the sea. She can hear it even when it's obscured, as she can hear the gulls and the occasional pīwaiwaka or pūkeko who check her out before flitting away.

Old nimbostratus is ready to offload—she can feel the change even before she smells it—it won't be long before the downpour, but Wairere is reluctant to quicken her pace. It's as if the singing of frogs is inside her now, the ecstatic, heaving, sighing urgency, the *need*—isn't the world so fresh and full and soaking wet? And where is my love, where is she, and where are my little babies? Eggs and semen and kicking and bubbles and joy! And soon the squirming, quicking tails. Suddenly it's as if Wairere is in the reeds, half immersed in water, so full of frog song and love she finds herself.

It has always been this way with Wairere. Sometimes, it seems to the outsider as if she disappears inside herself. Some might see only an insignificant child, or a dull teenager, but even those paying attention will find it difficult to place just what has happened, because though her physical form is present, it is clear, as her mother, Keri, has often observed, that the girl is elsewhere. There is danger in this for Wairere. She can never be quite sure whether the experience will be good or bad. For a long time she thought everyone could do it, until one day she asked her nan how to stop it when she felt others, you know, inside her. *When you do what?* Nan asked, her eyes wide. And then she kept looking at Wairere funny and asking her about it, even though Wairere didn't have the words to say more than that. That's not what it is, anyway, she thinks now, perhaps it is more like she becomes them, fleetingly, like she moves into their space.

Sometimes it's animals, sometimes it's less animated things, like trees or mud. The worst is people. You don't ever want to feel what's going on inside another person, not if you can help it. It's so confusing, so dense with thought and word and feeling, all scrambled together. And she is beginning to see the pattern to it, the necessary conditions that make it occur. A certain friction in the air, sometimes emotional, sometimes atmospheric—family arguments, or threatening weather.

Tonight, it is the singing of frogs.

And so, the rain comes.

Two

KERI

At home there is a plate waiting for Wairere: sausages, mashed potato, lettuce, and carrots chopped up in sticks. A pool of tomato sauce. She changes out of her wet clothes and gathers her plate to eat on her knees in front of the TV, where her mother and Walty are already in a post-dinner slump, watching cartoons. Wairere stopped eating meat years ago, so Keri makes her vegetarian sausages now, the ones that are all the same despite the packet saying there are different flavors. Wairere hates vegetarian food—specifically, she hates vegetarian food that is pretending to be nonvegetarian food. It's like brown people trying to be white, or maybe like white people trying to be brown, she said to her friend Felicity, or perhaps that's a whole different Old El Paso Stand 'N Stuff Taco Boat Kit. And then she laughed to herself, even though Felicity looked puzzled.

But since she has insisted on being vegetarian and having her mother cater to her needs, she can't say anything. The other reason not to say anything is that vegetarian options cost a lot. Keri freezes one packet to last three weeks, and she and Walty eat the cheapest sausages so that Wairere doesn't have to eat dead animals. Wairere may get annoyed with her mother, but she still feels guilt for almost everything her mother has to do, and say, and sacrifice so they can eat.

She was eight when she stopped eating meat; her first tactic was to keep it in her mouth until Keri gave up fighting with her and told her to spit it outside, where the cat appreciated her sacrifice. That cat always loved you the best, Wai, Keri said when Ngeru died, but that was 'cos she got a whole extra feed from Wairere pretty much every night. Still, before Keri relented, they had to debate it, as they did with all things ever since Wairere was old enough to nod or shake her head.

"Why won't you eat it? You need protein."

"It feels like it's decomposing in my mouth."

"You're eight years old. How do you know a word like decomposing?"

"School."

"Can you just eat it? We don't have anything else in the house."

"If an animal crawled into your mouth and died, would you want to chew it up and swallow?"

"You're being very dramatic, Wairere."

"No, I'm not. You're making me eat decaying life. The animals are screaming."

At which point Keri looked at Wairere like *she* was decomposing, and left the table. What she didn't know was that the animals were sometimes literally screaming, at least to Wairere's ears, or mind, or however that particular sense that gave her too much access to the feelings of others worked. But Wairere's insistence won. Keri never bothered to give her meat again.

Such as it always is with Keri and Wairere. If Keri were to take stock of how often she won any argument with her strange eldest child, she wouldn't be surprised to find how rare it was, for she had noticed Wai's unworldly stubbornness from babyhood. Baby Wai was known to refuse the breast at any sign of disharmony or stress, and since her father was more than a little useless at being supportive, or even being around, Keri was often stressed and fighting with him. Poor Baby Wai would cry from hunger, or so Keri thought, but not eat, until Keri resorted to the bottle and banishing the man. Teenage Wai is little different, though she has learned the value of a meal. They have been to the foodbank too many times for anyone in the house to waste a mouthful. Now Keri tries other tactics, any way to connect with Wai, any way to make friends.

"Saw the new neighbors today," she says.

"Oh?" says Wairere. Now that she's calm, Keri can see Wai wants to humor her, and she can also see that Wai couldn't be less interested. Even so, her daughter tilts her voice so that it sounds like she might care. This moment of effort is so touching to Keri that she wants to grasp hold of it, keep talking so that they can stay in that space—of *trying*—for a bit longer, even though she's aware she might be pushing it. "It's a family, so that'll be nicer than some of the ones we get."

"Yep."

"Pretty little girl, running around on the lawn. Reminded me of you in your fairy dress-ups when you were that size." Keri looks meaningfully at Wai, hoping she'll receive the compliment as it is intended, but Wai can't see the memories that flit across Keri's mind: a wide-eyed cherub with thick, dark hair, chubby limbs sprouting from layers of faux tulle and satin, stomping around in ladybird gumboots. The fiercest, grumpiest fairy princess at any birthday party. Keri feels a kind of sickly love at the image: a child so beautiful and vulnerable and somehow sad, even when she was happy. She has to stop dwelling on it.

Wairere stares back at her mother, the silence having carried on a beat too long.

Keri looks away and sips her drink. "I think they're immigrants. I mean, the majority of our neighbors are immigrants, but like, newly arrived. From somewhere interesting. That's cool, huh?"

"Sure, Ma. By somewhere interesting, do you mean somewhere brown?" Wairere says.

There it is. She's tried too hard. Teenagers can smell weakness like wolves seeking prey. But so what if she does mean that? "Maybe I do. Maybe you can, you know, learn about their culture, the neighbors. For an assignment or something."

"That's a bit inappropriate, don't you think?"

Keri stares, then realizes her mouth is open and shuts it,

deliberately. Her teeth make an audible clunk as they knock together.

"They're not a sideshow or a school project."

Ah. Now she's being separated from the herd. Taken down. Or maybe she's being forced to see she's part of the herd—all the other adults who think these things. "But I didn't mean—don't do that, Wai. You know that's not—"

"Got you, Ma. Whatever."

Keri eyes her daughter. How do they manage to be so clever and so scathing and so hurtful and so vulnerable at the same time? She wants to laugh. She wants to send Wai to live with someone else. She wants to wrap her arms around her daughter and rock her like a baby. Instead, she sits. "Now I feel like an idiot."

"Yep. I think I'm going to do my homework now. Night night!"

Keri mock swipes the air as Wai passes. "Little hōhā." That girl, she thinks, always ten steps ahead and tripping over her own toes. She feels a bit uncomfortable about what she said now, but she meant it. It *would* be good to know these neighbors, and knowing more about their world would help that. Maybe the assignment idea was wrong, but Wai isn't going to make friends just for the sake of it. And it would make a nice change from Mrs. B, who is about as far from somewhere interesting as a Pākehā lady can get, which is quite far.

Since the most recent lockdowns, something in Keri has changed. She has never gone out much, since the kids, she supposes, and they never had much money for going away, even going home to the lake. She barely sees the other mums at school. She has started to think about what it would take to make a community out of this neighborhood, like they did back in the day. Why not actually get to know the people they live beside? How strange is it, she thinks, that they all live so close together, in this series of flats, and barely know each other's names?

Later, as the night deepens, Keri tucks her babies into their beds, even Wai, who has fallen asleep in front of her battered laptop. Keri lifts the laptop carefully and places it on the side table, so that it doesn't burst into flames in the bedcovers, which is what some online article told her had happened to another teenager in a bedroom far, far away, but not far away enough. Everyone so connected, with more hazards for parents to manage, she thinks, and it can't be good that this laptop is secondhand, that its fan makes a heck of a noise as it tries to cool the machine down. How many times has she told Wai to use it on a flat surface? She's reminded again, as she is every day, that the only thing that keeps them alive, really, is her vigilance against all the little things that might destroy them. It would only take one small slip for their thin walls to come crumbling down.

She moves to the kitchen table, takes out her lessons. Tonight it's te reo, real junior stuff, possessives: *tāku, tā tāua, tā tātou; tōu, tō kōrua, tō koutou*. She's done it before, but whenever her reo learning gets interrupted, she has to go back almost to the start, otherwise she finds she's missed something crucial. She's making slow progress at two courses a year, Māori studies and history, but at least she's working toward something. When Walty's a little older, she'll go back to uni full-time and get it finished. Maybe get a teaching diploma. Wouldn't have been able to get much done in the past few years anyway, with all the floods and the latest round of outbreaks, so the glacial pace isn't a big loss. All she's hoping for in the meantime is a better understanding of where she is and how she got here, in a wider sense. But she can't help thinking all her study might only take her so far.

What Keri finds out depends very much on the questions she asks, and it's surprisingly difficult to know what the right questions are. For example, Keri thinks that their flat is on solid ground (it is) that has always been solid (it has not). Their home is surrounded by streets, roads, other houses, and gardens. Trees, parks. When it rains, the water is drained away through concrete pipes. So dry. So firm. A nice suburban area, with the sea two kilometers to the west, some hills inland, and a couple of streams that look more like ditches filled with rain. To the north, an estuary, with man-made ponds and walkways, replanting in progress. What Wairere thinks of as swamp. Because all of it *is* swamp, all of it is me. What Keri doesn't know is that swamp once filled the area up to the center of her living room, that it was so watery in her neighborhood, she could have reached over from her couch and scooped up a feed of eels, my waters were so thick with them. That her ancestors who lived in these parts moved around by waka, not path or road, paddling from one food collection camp to another, visiting friends or family ten kilometers away without their feet ever touching land. Keri doesn't know to ask about swamp because I am nowhere to be seen. But I'm still here, on the fringes, or underground, or in Wairere's dreams.

Three

SERA

A small city in a Mediterranean country, just before it became uninhabitable

Sera wasn't scared. She'd watched her sisters' fearfulness. She'd heard the stories. She didn't know why, given the tales that circled her, but she was confident. Relaxed, even. What she did know was that fear would cause her to tighten where she should be soft, hold her breath when she should release. Somehow, she had faith. Not so much in the god her people worshipped, but in something older, something more feminine, something, possibly, heretical. And even that didn't worry her.

Pregnancy had given Sera a deep calm, and because of this she knew herself to be blessed. It must be acknowledged, Sera had needed some convincing before she allowed herself to get pregnant. The fires had been an aberration at first: a single heatwave in a decade, a series of record temperatures that surpassed 104 degrees Fahrenheit, 10,000 acres of forest taken out by one blaze. But by the time Sera married Adam, the heatwaves came many times a year, and the accompanying fires threatened homes and crops almost monthly in summer. Food and land became scarce, clean water scarcer. Everyone continued as if ignoring the problems would make them diminish, and people got hungrier, and angrier.

She'd always wanted children, but she refused to bring a baby into this situation. She spent too much time caring for her father and procuring food and water for the wider family to even consider it. While Adam worked, Sera kept her eye on the information that came through social media and underground news, always attentive to the thing that would keep them one step ahead: a truckload of canned food, a new well with fresh water on the other side of town, rumors of a good air-conditioned shelter or pool to wait out the next heatwave. But parents have a way of influencing their grown children.

"Sera," her father said on a rare good day when he was lucid. "Listen now. You're a smart girl. A modern woman. You know so very much. But you don't know this. Babies are hope. If you don't choose hope, you will become weak, and you cannot live in this world with that kind of weakness. To live in hope is the radical choice, little one."

The radical choice. What nonsense. Everybody hoped. It was as common as the children who continued to be born despite everything. Hope wasn't the thing that ensured they had food and shelter and safety. That was pure quickness and vigilance. She kept them prepared, the whole family, and how could she do that if she let her guard down? No. She loved her father, but hope wasn't something she could dwell on.

After her father died, as the wider family observed the rites and ceremonies, Sera leaned on her husband, letting go of her vigilance for the many days of ritual. When the time came for them to return to life, she found something in her was broken. She had been surviving, she had been willing them all to survive, but her father's death was like a circuit breaker and she could no longer return to the ways of the time before. She closed her father's house at the end of the mourning period, after five days of cleaning and sorting, and faced the street. It wasn't as it had been when she was a child. She knew the damage her hometown had sustained would likely never be fixed, but the world was a big place. They would go on. They had to go on.

What if she let herself hope, what would that look like?

She walked the five blocks to her own house, and in the time it took to make that short journey, Sera began to see the space that had been left by her father's death and how it had split everything open for her. Her wily old dad might have been on to something. She realized she could fill this space with anything at all now. She imagined for the first time in many years what might be possible if she chose freely, without fear, without caution or regret. When she got home, Adam opened the door as if he had been waiting for her.

Months later, when she felt the baby move, calm enveloped her. Her focus went inside, and nothing, not food shortages, or storms, or even the fires, could get her blood pressure to rise. She became as fat and steady as a buddha, serenity in the smile she bestowed on all who saw her, and people did come to see her, because it was a marvel, this oasis of peace she created around her. Nothing was sure, not even a bottle of fresh drinking water on a hot day or meat and vegetables at the market, but Sera was sure of her body, and even five minutes in her presence was enough to bestow a moment's wonder and warmth in a life.

The truth was, she couldn't do both—live fully in the world they were faced with, and be a safe vessel for her child, so she chose the latter. She indulged in a kind of benevolent insanity, if insanity meant ignoring reality, ignoring the terrifying possibilities that lay before them. They were on the brink, but while Sera was growing a child within her, she gave up worrying. She let Adam take care of everything for the first time since they married. She didn't question him, even when he stored the rice in the container that leaked, even when he forgot to lock the storage locker and they lost some supplies to thieves. She would not worry, not until the babe was upon the earth, because she knew, somehow, that she'd spend the rest of her life worrying after that.

And when the contractions came, she still wasn't scared. What would be would be. Maybe it was the exhaustion before and the exhaustion to come that held her in this moment. Her body would do the work it was designed to do. She focused on the breathing, and she focused on that pinpoint of joy that would soon become joy incarnate—a squalling, mewing child of their own. And eventually, when the darkness and pain became so intense that she did feel scared and she did think it could all go wrong and she did wonder if she might die, she let all those feelings come in, and she was back to herself again, so far beyond serenity, she already couldn't remember what that had felt like. Finally, she told her husband and the attending midwives—her aunty and her eldest sister—of her fear, and all three felt relieved, because this was normal, and while it was nice to be around someone so calm, it was also alarming, given they had very little to be calm about. Sera was back in the world, and Aliana came roiling out on a tide of red, her skin hot and flushed to match.

When Aliana cried for the first time, it was piercing, high-pitched, and painful to her mother, who would do anything to quieten the distress that could generate such a sound. Instinctively, she placed the baby at her breast, and from then on thought obsessively of how to keep this child safe and fed. Sera felt pity for the man who might stand between her child and safety. She felt so powerful that she might walk through fire and not get burned, drink oceans and not drown, squeeze men until they wept blood tears and exhaled their last breath. And she would need all of that for what was to come.

Te Ātiawa lands, Kāpiti, sometime in the near future

Next door to Keri, a family awakens in swampland for the first time. They have traveled by water and air and overland to be here; they have traveled through years made up of minute capsules of time stretched into painfully long seconds and minutes and hours, weeks and months and long, long days; they have occupied a small number of the waiting rooms of the world, which grow more numerous by the day. Their displacement, once unusual, once something to feel pity for, once a reason to be kind, is now so common that humans facing their predicament are routinely ignored or vilified. The family doesn't like to dwell on the worst things that are possible for them, because those worst things happen too often to too many, but occasionally, occasionally the best happens, which is a new home, a new country. Peace.

Except, this is not the best thing. The best thing would be a different world in which the home they can make a life in is the home in which they grew up. The best thing would be a choice.

Still, fortune has smiled on this family. A quiet neighborhood, a house, what seems like solid ground. Outside, so much green. The house is small, and it smells of old damp, but it is clean, and the carpet looks almost new, and it is comfortable under their socked feet, or when they kneel, as a family. This is what Sera notices on the first day. They have beds and fresh linen, gifted and set up by the refugee support volunteers, and even though she feels out of place here, and she misses everything, even the Refugee Resettlement Center where they at least had people like them to talk to, she eventually sleeps the deepest sleep she has had since she left home. In her sleep she argues with everyone she has left behind. *Why Sera,* they ask, and they hold out their hands to her, fingers spread, *why have you gone without us?* She cries with frustration that they cannot hear her, that they cannot conceive of what she has done. Wasn't there an implicit understanding between them? But no, all comprehension is wiped from their faces, and all that is left is anguish.

As she sleeps, she cries with such intensity that she is surprised, on waking, to feel no tears on her face. And then she is worried because she can feel it is late, and Aliana hasn't woken her, and Adam isn't in bed. An awful fear grips her stomach, though she knows instinctively that they are in the house, and in the next moment, she hears them. I got up for Ali, Adam tells her when she enters the living room, I wanted you to sleep. He looks up at her from the floor where he is playing with their daughter, and she feels so happy and so scared at the same time. She wants only the happiness of this moment, only the substance of this reality: Aliana will grow strong under the trees of these streets, playing on the grass that seems so plain. She loves the plainness of that grass, the plainness of this house. It is not a good house by local standards, she knows. It is not what they would have chosen, before. But it is good to simply have somewhere. She can draw a small circle around it in her mind: a floor, a roof, three rooms to live in, four walls to each room, a bathroom. The three of them, together. The solidity of that. The quietness of the street. The abundance of food in the supermarkets. All things she once took for granted in her own country, but it feels like a whole lifetime has elapsed between that world and this.

She'll grow tired of it, she knows this too, she'll grow used to all these things, but can she just be happy in this moment?

Can she just be content? She starts to make tea, and can't resist going through the cupboards again, counting the cans and lining them up, tracing her fingers over the large bags of flour, rice, sugar, the big square bottle of oil. The volunteer said she'd take her shopping at the end of the week, when the government resettlement money would be available, but she'd already stocked their cupboards with some staples. Sera opens the fridge. This is a wonder. Fresh vegetables. Milk. Yogurt. Hummus. Even cheese. Cold and bright. Beside the fridge, there are jars of dried beans and chickpeas along the countertop. Fruit in a basket. She doesn't recognize everything, but she'll find out how they should be eaten, how to cook in this new place, where to shop. It's been a long time since she has had that option: where to shop. The thought overwhelms her. She returns to the cupboard and starts counting again, silently, so Adam can't hear her, but he calls for her anyway. Come join us. He knows she can spiral too easily, and strangely it is happening more now that they are safe than it ever did before. Come join us, love, he says again. Bring tea? Hopeful. She knows it's okay—they're okay, the three of them—but somehow only counting the food calms her. She finishes quickly.

All is well.

And yet.

She brings the tea to the Formica coffee table. Adam gets up and sits on the sofa by the tray, ready to pour. She crouches to her daughter who is lining up blocks and plastic toy figurines, the easiest toys, throwaway items from McDonald's Happy Meals and old Duplo sets. At not-quite-three years old, Aliana doesn't see the gimmick, only a splash of color and a smiley face. Look Mama, she says, proud of her tidy work—she has sorted everything to some schema of her own devising, one Sera can't discern, so she nods and grins and makes an admiring sound, looking to her husband for a shared smile. His eyes are creased in delight, as always. On this she can depend for all things concerning their daughter—they share this absolute devotion to her. It is where they connect and come home, no matter where they are. Lately it has been harder to feel like they are together in all things, and Sera thinks it is she who has been the faulty connection. All her wiring is loose. What do they say here? Lights are on, but nobody is home? She is not home and her lights are not on either. But now that they have stopped moving, she wants to fix the wiring. She wants that so much for Aliana, and for Adam. There is something earnest in him, something that has grown since they have been in this new country. Sera feels like she is lagging behind. Lately, she has been trying to hold in her worries so that he might go on in his hopefulness. He seems to feel free to be himself again, always speaking to strangers with such enthusiasm, practicing his English and picking up local words and local ways. She doesn't know how to follow his example. When strangers speak to her, and they don't often in this country, her tongue becomes stone in her mouth. The most she can manage is a tentative smile. Even though she knows English well enough to respond a little, the words disappear whenever she encounters the need to speak them. People have most often been kind, but she leaves them little choice but to continue on their way.

It's been six weeks since they came to New Zealand, which she has learned has this other name too—Aotearoa—a word that is pleasing in the way it rolls around her mouth, the way it speaks of a whole new culture she knew little about before she arrived. Six weeks is long enough for their old places to have lost their vividness, but not long enough for the new place to have become home. They have been in between for longer than six weeks—it's been years, and in those years she seems to have forgotten what it feels like to trust that the earth beneath her feet will not be taken away. They left their home country only when they had no choice. It's strange to her that this one act of survival has marked them in the eyes of many as criminals—surely it is the most human of acts, to exercise whatever skill and ingenuity they possess to escape danger?

After they eat, Aliana is restless, so Sera takes her to play outside while Adam catches the bus to the library to continue his job search. The library has computers, internet, and the latest newspapers, and they have none of these at home yet. Aliana has wrapped herself in a magenta and green shawl, given to Sera by her own mother when she was fourteen, and one of the few items she has managed to carry from home. Their clothes are still not quite unpacked, and Sera hasn't taken the shawl out for years, too afraid it might be lost or taken. Aliana took the shawl from the final case as her mother was going through it, the little girl's eyes dazzled by the gold threads running through the soft, light cotton. It is not a plaything, but today is not a day for admonishments, especially about things from home. To watch her daughter run with it held aloft, the fabric flowing behind her, eyes bright, is the promise of something she can't quite let herself believe yet. She will, she thinks, in time. Eventually she'll get used to this place, eventually it might even feel like home, and, she hopes, that clench in her stomach will go away. It has to.

After a while, Aliana is distracted by a game involving basins of water and dishwashing liquid bubbles, so Sera gently gathers the shawl from her.

"Noooooo, Mama!" Aliana squeals.

"Play with the bubbles, Ali. I'll keep this for later." She begins to bundle the shawl. "I promise."

"Maamaaa!" Aliana throws her arms into the air.

"Bubba, shhhh. Look!" With one hand, Sera lifts a cup and pours water into the basin, creating more bubbles. Aliana is distracted again and becomes intent on the pouring and collection of bubbles.

"No wonder she wants it, such a beautiful scarf."

Sera is startled. There, where she hasn't been looking, is a woman on the other side of a small stand of bushes. Her voice is low and gravelly.

"Sorry, love, didn't mean to startle you. Pretty little thing, isn't she?" The woman nods toward Aliana. "Don't mind me—I'm out here a lot. Gardening."

Sera smiles at her, but doesn't speak.

"People call me Mrs. B," the woman says. "Or Janet. I don't mind which. 12A."

The lady's sentences are rushed together in a way that Sera can't quite understand. But she knows this means the lady is her neighbor. Her own unit is 12B Pine Street, and it has a garage attached to an identical unit next door. There is one on each side, in fact. The lawn is open to all three places, with small garden plots and strangely nonutilitarian wooden trellises on each side. These interventions suggest boundaries but give little privacy.

She nods, falters, manages a quiet hello.

"Where are you from? Obviously not from round here, eh?" The woman stands back now, squinting as if trying to assess what she sees. Sera tries to understand what is being asked of her. She thinks this is meant to be a friendly inquiry, but it doesn't feel that way.

"My name is Sera. This is my daughter, Aliana." She feels exposed, saying their names. She tells the woman what she can of their origins, though the name her country is given in the English-speaking world is not the name she knows it by, just as she imagines that the ideas that go with that name have little to do with her home as she knows it.

"Ah," the woman says, as if she has heard enough. Then, brusquely, "Well, welcome to the neighborhood. I'm sure you'll like it." She makes as if to move away, but then stops, turns back a half step, looks into the sky. "You know," she says, "it's none of my business, but I hope you know how lucky you are. Heaps of New Zealanders don't have anywhere to live. I know it's bad where you come from, but it's bad here too, and having foreigners come in makes it even harder." She looks at Sera directly then. "Just so you know. Nothing personal. You'll find I'm straight up about things like that. Don't mind speaking my mind. But I'm sure you know you're one of the lucky ones, I mean, just look around!" Then she turns with a wave and makes her way to her own door, through which a dog can be heard barking, and disappears behind it with a clang.

Sera crouches to Aliana's side and helps her in her game automatically, without seeing. She feels robotic, as if she is performing for an unseen watcher. They should stay outside, she thinks, to show that the words have not stung her, that they belong here too, now. If she were at home and a stranger moved into her neighborhood, she would bring them in for tea and treats to eat, and attempt to get to know them, even if they were foreigners. She knows that is not the way here, but she cannot help feeling the bitterness of this welcome. All she wants to do is run inside and pull the curtains across. But Aliana is still happy in the game, so she stays there, pouring cup after cup into the basin, until the bubbles subside and all they are left with is dirty water.

Four

JANET

Te Ātiawa lands, Paraparaumu, a few decades earlier

Richard didn't want to be there, and so he wasn't, even though it had become routine for husbands to be at births. Janet was envious of the other wives, the flowers that turned up at their bedside, the cards and chocolates. Richard had plonked her in the waiting room and left her with a peck on the cheek, and not looked back. Not that she wasn't used to it, or even that it wasn't preferred. She couldn't imagine him in the birthing suite, that glare he always lasered in her direction when he disapproved. He disliked complaining almost as much as he disliked displays of affection.

This way, she could do what she needed to do, and be cleaned up by the time he came for her and the baby. He wouldn't have to see any of the mess and she wouldn't have to hold anything in while the baby was being born. She wouldn't have to answer to Richard's needs while she was in that state. They had both agreed that this was her job in the marriage, to look after him. The babies were extra, for her.

Even so, it would have been nice to have that other type of husband. Had she known what she was getting into when she married him? They'd met when she was working at the cafe. He used to come in with his mates from the roadworks, a quiet voice among their rowdiness. They'd often erupt into laughter when she left their table after taking an order. She'd hear them making comments about her ass. She had plenty for them to comment on, she knew that, and she felt self-conscious about it. When they graduated to trying to slap or grab her backside, Janet did her best to avoid them. But she was frequently the only one on tables. It was when the loudest of them tried to grab her around the waist and squeeze her butt while she was taking an order that things changed. Richard stood and shoved him back into his seat, nodded at her, and sat.

"Don't you ever lay your hands on her again," he said, and all the other men looked away.

With those words, Janet felt as if Richard had laid claim to her. The other men respected him, and behaved from then on as if they respected her too. When she approached their table, Richard made eye contact with her more and more often. There was a thrill in having the attention of this serious, quiet man, as if you had to be a certain caliber of woman to gain his interest. She was already in her thirties, tired of trying to find a partner who had any sort of decency or staying power. So when he shyly asked her out one evening after work, she agreed.

Eventually she found out that his seriousness and sense of what's right extended to other personal boundaries: he was the man and she was the woman and they had clear roles to perform as such. Her job was to be feminine and keep order in the home, and to support him so he could work outside of the home, even though she kept working too, part-time jobs mainly. His job was to provide and to keep order over her and any offspring they had. She soon learned that his edict to keep hands off her applied only to other men: once she accepted him, he felt it was his right to lay hands on her whenever and however he wanted. She soon learned to make herself smaller, so as not to attract his attention.

Giving birth did not allow a woman to be small. While giving birth, a woman filled up the room. So Janet was relieved by her husband's absence more than she was envious of the presence of other women's husbands. He was a good man, really. Traditional, sure, but he provided for her, and his rules weren't unreasonable. And now she would be a mother!

Janet knew it would be messy and painful, this was something that had been passed to her in her mother's and grandmother's stories: medieval instruments, heavy drugs, itchy and painful shaving, separation from the baby, infection, doctors who didn't listen. As soon as she got pregnant, every woman she knew told her gruesome stories about pregnancy and birth. But even though she heard all of this, she still wasn't ready. She had no idea.

The pain surprised her—it was so much more than she had imagined she was capable of withstanding. After fourteen hours, she thought something was definitely wrong. She tried to indicate this to the nurses, weakly.

"You'll be alright, Mrs. Bloom. This is to be expected."

"No," she said, some instinct telling her this wasn't quite it, despite having been led to believe it would all be awful anyway. "Something feels wrong."

"Well, we'll see what we can do."

Nearly two more hours passed before a doctor came to check on why she wasn't progressing.

"Looks like you're finally getting there, Mrs. Bloom," he said after an awkward and painful internal examination, "but we need to keep a close eye on things."

Ten minutes later it was all on. Janet wanted to push and the doctor said it was okay to push, and the feeling was overwhelming and she had no control over the power that coursed through her body, as if its only objective was the expulsion of everything she'd been holding on to for forty weeks. She'd never felt so weak and strong and out of control all at the same time.

Then the doctor told her to stop.

The contractions were coming too hard and fast. How was she supposed to stop?

"There's a problem with the baby's position. I need to turn him. Hang in there, Mrs. Bloom. We'll need forceps for this."

Out came two giant salad tong–looking objects that the doctor wanted to put inside her, alongside the baby's head that was coming out. She had no room in her for that.

Janet wailed, the nurses tried to get her to breathe and pant, and the doctor prepared his instruments. She hated him then, and these witches helping him. She hated her body and being a woman. She hated her stupid husband and his terrible needs. She even hated the baby who would no doubt take everything from her, who had already begun taking everything from her.

But she was more scared of what might happen if she didn't do what she was told.

An hour later, a bundle was placed in her arms and she saw her son's washed, scrunched-up, bruised face for the first time. Her lower half was numb, but it wouldn't be for long. Every visit to the toilet for the next three weeks would be a trial, and she would notice how things had been rearranged down there, so that it didn't feel quite hers anymore. But had it ever really been hers anyway?

She loved the baby. She was sorry she had hated him. He didn't feed well at first and this made her love him more. Poor little thing. She would give him everything, willingly, and she didn't mind at all.

Richard came to visit, and three days later he took them home. He was kind and attentive for a few weeks, even though he seemed uninterested in the baby and wanted things back to normal once Janet was up and about. She did everything she used to do, and everything for the baby too, without complaint. When Richard aired his daily criticisms, that her kitchen was a mess or his dinner was cold or that she needed to make herself more presentable for sex, Janet found herself unable to care.

The less she cared, the less she would do for him, despite his habit of offering her motivational threats. Sometimes he hurt her, but it was suddenly very clear to her that it was never the pain that had made her acquiesce. It had always been her need to be loved by him that had guaranteed her devotion.

After that, it was only a matter of time.

The week Sera and her family move in next door, everything in Janet's life seems different, although she still lives in the same neighborhood where her babies were born. One thing for sure is that she doesn't wait for any man to tell her what to do or say or think anymore. She knows her own mind, and sometimes people don't like how direct she can be. The new neighbors seem nice enough, and Janet isn't offended by the way Sera's dressed, even though others might not like it. Always having to mark themselves as different, these people. She hopes, given time, her new neighbors will integrate a bit more. Look more like Kiwis. If the men really wanted to protect their women they'd tell them to blend into the crowd like everyone else. Much worse out there than one opinionated old lady.

Then again, maybe there's no changing some people.

No, Janet Bloom is old enough and single enough to say what she thinks, which is a privilege she feels she's earned over the years. But look at her now, fretting about it. She always relents afterward, not because she's wrong, but because in hindsight she wonders if she should let niceness get in the way of truth. In the moment, she always feels it a necessity to say what is on her mind: in fact, she makes a practice of it. That's why things are the way they are these days, because people fail to speak up. So she won't say sorry. She has nothing to be sorry for. But a welcome cake is a good way to make up any hard feelings. Even if she was right, perhaps it was a bit of a heavy truth bomb to drop on the poor girl on her first day in the neighborhood. Of course, if Janet were in charge of such things, they'd be making sure their own were well looked after before letting in foreigners. She feels a certain distaste about it—people leaving their home countries, in the midst of war or famine or whatever they've been through. Stay and fight. Stay and clean up your own mess. If they love their culture so much, why don't they stay where their culture belongs? If her own people had up and left every time things got hard, there wouldn't be anyone in the right place, no sense of history.

A cake is the easiest thing to throw together and she isn't averse to doing it, whether the new neighbors are friendly or not. Keep your friends close and your enemies even closer, as her father used to say. It's something she prides herself on too. Important to oil the cogs of civil relationships in the community. And she is willing to give anyone the benefit of the doubt. Perhaps they won't be bad neighbors. Can't be worse than the kids that were in there before, covered in tattoos, playing loud music, revving their cars.

Janet Bloom, although she is only dimly aware of it, descends from a long line of women who were likened, in all the different centuries in which they lived, as much akin to old boots. Tough, leathery, and quite useful. She knows this is how her mother and grandmother were, although their propensity toward boot-like qualities extended to a lack of gentleness and a quickness to kick. What she doesn't know is that all her line extending back more than twelve generations carried those same traits, and that her forebear, great-great-great granny Jane, had been the one to bring her people here via the Atlantic and then the Pacific, in two migrations for the purpose of two marriages. Also to escape poverty and some unspoken situation in Ireland. The first marriage ended suddenly and tragically less than a year after it began: Granny Jane's husband, Angus, lost his footing while installing the roof of their new barn and fell to grievous injury below. He landed on hay, which should have saved him, but the pitchfork with which the hay had been stacked had been left in the pile, and Angus landed in such a way that two prongs embedded in his right foot. He should have been able to survive this too, had one of the prongs not severed his posterior tibial artery, which bled profusely. Angus was helped to his bed, and the bleeding was eventually stopped, but three days later he died from the sepsis that set in.

The second marriage was proposed by mail via an aunt who had married into the Joseph family, the youngest generation of which had begun immigrating to Australia and New Zealand in search of land and freedom. Men far outnumbered women in the Antipodes, so they sent away back home for wives, the hardier the better. John Joseph wasn't an easy man but he was the man Granny Jane got, and she was his equal in almost all their work. Still, he was stronger, and that's how he kept her in line, as well as all their children. The fact that Granny Jane's female descendants all took after her and found husbands who could not outdo their wives, except in one respect, meant there was a lot of marital tension over successive generations, a larger than regular occurrence of domestic violence, and a slightly larger, though not noticeably so, percentage of mariticide.

Our Janet was not widowed, but the divorce saved her from the indignities served up by a man who couldn't stand her opinions or her independence. She doesn't like to dwell on what those indignities consisted of. Without a woman to keep him, her ex-husband died nine years later of heart disease, which was exacerbated by a diet consisting primarily of fried steak.

Yes, Janet is the queen of her domain, has been since the kids moved out, with no one to push her around or question her authority, and she finds she likes life a lot more now. She lives by a code of honesty and forthrightness; much better to live that way, she has decided, for the good of all. No one would ever be under any illusion that she had been unclear, or unfair.

Janet turns her mind to cake. Zadie, her Border Terrier, starts circling her feet as she makes her way from cupboard to cupboard, pulling out bowls and measuring cups and ingredients. She could make a banana cake with the old bananas in the freezer, but she uncovers a mental list of questions she doesn't have answers for. Will they even eat banana cake? Does it fit within whatever dietary rules there are for their religion? Does what they eat depend on whether they've been here a while or not? How is one supposed to know? She's not even sure the gesture will be taken the right way. But she doesn't want to be inhospitable, and she's not one to turn back on decisions already made. The girl might like it, even if the parents don't. She puts together the ingredients, a swift and familiar routine: measures and mixes, preps and pours. A bit of an unknown, these people from places with foreign customs. Maybe, if they become friendly, they can talk about the New Zealand way of life. Maybe she can exert a gentle influence. She's sure they will be interested. After all, why move here if you don't really want to be part of things?

Five

PINE STREET

Well, that'll make the old lady's head explode, Keri thinks. She's at the kitchen sink, muddling her way through the dishes, her third attempt that day. She's been trying to keep up with Walty since 5:30 a.m. and now he's finally passed out on the couch in front of cartoons, surrounded by every bottle of sauce he could find in the fridge. That kid. He's excavated and tasted the contents of every cupboard in the house, but the sauce bottle fixation has lasted longer than usual, despite the mustard and soy sauce concoction he managed to ingest last Tuesday. The new rule is he's not allowed to open the sauce, just play with it. He seems surprisingly content with this, treating each bottle as if it is a toy with a distinct personality. Mustard seems to be male and shouty. Tomato sauce is a racing car.

What does Keri care, as long as he's happy with something.

She's craving coffee and cigarettes and sleep. The dishes will keep, but god knows how long Walty will be out, so she slips out the back door with her cup and vape, leaving it ajar so she can listen for him. It's not like they see everything that goes on between the three houses, but Keri is careful about how much of her life she takes out front, apart from the odd smoke break and the inevitable exits and entrances. They tend to use the back door now for most things, where they can go about their business unobserved, or less observed. Her place, being at the end of the row, has a door that faces away from Mrs. B's, and access to a walkway that goes behind a council fence separating the public path from the surrounding houses. Mrs. B owns her flat, but the others are rented, and there's usually new tenants every year or two. Keri always worries about the new people, what they're going to bring, so she values this pathway she thinks of as her own.

During their four years in the flat, there have been neighbors given to domestics, yelling or hitting, or both. Most of the time, it doesn't get out of hand, but such things make it feel like they're under siege. If Keri wanted that feeling she would have stayed with Walty's father. And between trying to block it out and trying not to feel terrible all the time is the question of calling the cops. She can never quite bring herself to do it, though she imagines she would if it got too bad, if a woman was clearly being beaten, or if children were involved. Keri is thankful it's never been that bad. Mrs. B is less patient. That's how they got on speaking terms, her and the old lady. Nothing like a common enemy to create alliances. She saw how Mrs. B looked at her, that first time, across the driveway after the chainsaw maniac moved out, how her eyes lingered a little too long on the tattoo beneath Keri's collarbone, how her gaze swept down over the kids and away again quickly. But they both needed to vent about the chainsaw maniac, so they focused on him instead, his propensity to get drunk and start up the chainsaw at three in the morning, scaring the bejesus out of them and every other house on the street. They'd woken to the sound as if it were inside their own houses. Mrs. B did the cop-calling that time, so Keri decided she was alright, prejudiced but alright. And as time went on, Mrs. B began to give them things: little jobs for Wairere in exchange for pocket money, flowers or vegetables from the garden, real jams and pickles. Not like they could afford vegetables, let alone good preserves, from the supermarket.

And now, this. A new family in their row of flats, wearing their culture literally on their sleeves. Mrs. B would be laying eggs over it. Probably mumbling about infidels and terrorists in her kitchen. Keri has seen her on tiptoes peeking over the hedge. But that baby—too cute. Even Mrs. B would be a sucker for that little one, she reckons. The old lady is a bit judgy about Wairere and bossy to Keri, but Walty can do no wrong in her eyes. If he has a tantrum, Keri takes him to the other side of the house. Last thing she needs is Mrs. B coming over to see what's wrong, trying to give him biscuits or something. Walty loves biscuits. Walty loves all kai. But Keri is also afraid that Mrs. B might call child services if she lets Walty cry too long, and lately his scream has grown even more high-pitched and dramatic than usual. Keri suspects he's figured out how nervous it makes her. She should probably let the new neighbors know.

Keri has a feeling Walty is stirring back in the house and she still has to get to those dishes. Standing, she takes one last inhale, and sees Mrs. B's back door open. There's the nosy parker, she thinks, laughing to herself because in the same moment she steps back into her own doorframe just enough so that the neighbor can't see her. She watches the old woman descend the steps, holding a cake. Involuntarily, Keri feels a craving—banana cake probably, her favorite, with chocolate icing. Mrs. B brought one over for Walty's fourth birthday. She winces and overcompensates for sore hips with each step, goes around the hedge to the new neighbors' back door, places the cake on the doorstep, and backs away. She turns, and then turns back, climbs the stairs, knocks, then hurriedly rushes down the stairs and away to the safety of her own door, entering and closing it behind her. The new neighbors' door opens and a man with the little girl carried high in his arms looks out. The girl reaches her arms down and exclaims, and he crouches to see the thing that has been left, picking it up with his free hand. Both their faces open in delight—he holds the cake aloft to keep it from the girl's grasping hands, but Keri can hear her squeals of delight. The man looks around, leans out the door as far as he can, balancing his two handfuls, and pulls in. The door closes and still she stands there, paralyzed by something she doesn't want to name, some distress that tastes like failure, and heartbreak, some kind of void between her and her daughter that she doesn't know how to fill. Before the fear comes, she heads back inside, picks up her phone, scrolls, and starts a random search for flights—one day, she thinks, perhaps one day she and the kids could go somewhere, the three of them, just have fun for once. Away from everything. How much would it cost to get them all to one of the islands? Rarotonga, probably. She's heard it has the most affordable flights. Doesn't hurt to dream. She gets a small hopeful thrill from the search alone. Imagine. A smile on Wairere's face for once, and Walty playing in the sand until his skin turns dark brown.

It's the next day, and Janet is in the garden, working along the row, pruning, when she hears about how the cake has fared. She's thinking about fertilizer and whether or not to spray. She never thought she'd be into roses, they remind her of her own mother too much, but the unit came with the row already established, and she couldn't bear to let them deteriorate. Now she revels in the satisfaction of a perfect bloom.

"Excuse me."

She steps back and almost trips over her tray. Zadie pulls herself up from her position basking in the sun and starts wagging her tail languidly at the intruder. The great protector, huh? It's the man from next door. What on earth is he doing, scaring her like that?

"I'm sorry. I'm sorry, did I scare you? My apologies. I wanted to ask, did you leave the cake?"

She can barely understand him, his accent is so thick.

"Yes!" she says as emphatically as she can, enunciating carefully. "It Is A Welcome Gift!" Zadie is sniffing all around his feet and legs, circling him, still wagging. She's a pretty good judge of character, old Zades, so Janet relaxes a little.

"Oh, thank you, ma'am. This is very kind. We did not know if it is safe, but now we know it is from the kind lady next door, we will let Aliana have some." He looks toward the door of his flat, where the little girl is leaning against the porch wall.

"Ali," he calls. "Come and meet the nice lady who made cake."

Janet watches the girl who watches her back. She leans out of the porch and looks at the steps, then shakes her head, looking at her father. She's clutching a pink toy of unidentifiable shape, which she puts up to her face, rubs against her cheek, and then seems to curl her shoulders and arms around herself, looking away. Janet thinks she hears a small sob.

"I am sorry, Mrs. . . ."

"Everyone calls me Mrs. B."

"Thank you for your kindness, Mrs. B. My name is Adam. Aliana is shy—she is not yet accustomed to meeting new people here in our new home, but we thank you."

"Oh, but I have met her. The other day—"

"Ah yes, Sera did tell me a neighbor talked to her. I wasn't sure if it was you. Aliana will get less shy when she has had time."

Janet looks at the girl and feels a tug. Poor wee thing. "Zadie is friendly. Sorry about that." Zadie is now on the neighbors' lawn, very thoughtfully peeing right in the center of it, where the basin of bubbles stood the previous day. "Your girl—Aliana? She can pat the dog whenever she likes. Zadie won't bite."

Aliana is peeking over her stuffed toy, mesmerized by the dog who is now sniffing in circles.

"Thank you, Mrs. B! We will be friends with Zadie, and with you." Adam smiles and nods, as if they will, indeed, be the best of friends.

Janet doesn't think so, but he seems harmless, and kind to his daughter, which says a lot. She nods and smiles in return and he backs away a few steps, making himself smaller, offering a sort of bow. He puts his hand to his heart, nods at her again, then hurries back to his daughter, who is now beginning to whimper in a way that suggests a full-on cry is imminent.

Janet calls Zadie back so that she doesn't follow the neighbor all the way to his door, and returns to her roses. Where is the mother, she wonders. Cooking perhaps, or cleaning. She would've expected the mother to be watching the child. But who knows what the rules are. It's unsettling, not knowing how things work over there. And why isn't he at work? She always does this, she thinks to herself, always makes everyone else's business her business, enough to get stressed about it. It's that sense of hers, of order. Of what's right and what isn't, of fairness, everyone making their contribution. Zadie's contribution, at that moment, is to vomit up a watery mixture of bile and grass beneath the washing line. A sure sign the pleasant part of the day is over.

Six

ORIGINS

You may understand, by now, how the swamp runs through your veins. Our bodies are made of water; one of your gurus might say, drink eight glasses a day. Does the swamp not find a way into your bodies, too? Not surprising then, that we can come at a story through one voice or another, moving around in space and time as we please. Our waterways reach into the past like canals carving a route through a city. So it is that when I tell the story of Keri and Wairere, I also uncover the story of the long line of women who came before them. Women who built families and communities and, sometimes, empires.

Wairere knows many of the stories, and secretly holds them to her chest, but every time her mother has tried telling her about them recently, she has scorned her with sarcasm, groans, or dirty looks. "If your eyes roll back any further in your head, you'll see your brains," Keri says, repeatedly, which leads to more groaning. Wairere doesn't even know why she does it. She's always liked hearing about the grandmothers and grandfathers and all the greats. Felicity told her that if you go back ten generations, you have 1024 ancestors, and if you go back twenty generations, there are over a million, although some of them might be related already and therefore have common ancestors, which cuts the number down. Felicity is always in possession of weird facts, and for Wairere, this particular body of weird facts is the most interesting, especially how the number of ancestors *doesn't* keep doubling every generation, because if you go back far enough, you get to the part where everyone is related and all the ancestors are shared.

She can't seem to help herself around her mother: everything Keri does is annoying. But even if she pretends to not be interested in the ancestor stories, Wairere takes it all in. Keri herself can only trace back four or five generations from her grandparents, and has disconnected knowledge of her other ancestors: their names, but not how they fit into her whakapapa, or, more precisely, how Keri and her children came to be descended from them. It's clear that she's proud of them, but the vagueness of her knowledge means that she can't describe them in any detail as she does with the others, who seem dazzling to Wairere like the painted genealogies, woven stories, and carved ancestors she'd seen last time they'd gone to the marae.

Among the ancestors Keri does know about, there is Wairere's namesake, Kui Wairere, a rangatira who, in the 1860s, led her people to safety away from wars with both neighboring tribes and colonial forces, retreating to their most remote lands on the far side of Lake Taupō, up into the hills, closer to where they kept the old bones in caves for safety. There they stayed until the babies they had taken with them were old enough to have their own grandchildren, some of whom were already well into childhood before the hapū decided to make contact with the outside world again.

"In the intervening years," Keri is fond of recounting, "they grew strong and stocky from a steady diet of pig and deer and manu, sweet potato and corn crops, pikopiko, aruhe, and spring water. The cousins they returned to were exhausted from fighting and colonial diseases and alcohol. But each group was so glad to see the other, they celebrated for days afterward."

When Wairere was little, she would ask what happened after that, but Keri knew only that Kui Wairere was a leader, and that she kept the people safe. She couldn't say what happened after they entered the world again—that's when the record went quiet, as far as she knew, though she understood this quietness echoed through the hills and caves where the ancestors' bones lay, once their descendants succumbed to the diseases and bottles they brought back from the celebrations.

The survivors were soon pushed out of their lands, once the land courts started processing them. It was easy enough to lose everything if you didn't have the means to answer to colonial laws and their imposition of foreign rule, court fees, hearings, taxes. The luckiest married out and migrated to the south or north, depending on the origins of their spouses. Keri knows no more until the adulthood of her great-grandmother, who by then was giving birth to babies in the capital city, and giving them English names like Walter and Lizzie, while her husband labored in the railways. By all accounts, Nanny Mōrehu was a modern woman, who wanted her children to have all the gifts of the Pākehā world, due to the Māori world being left behind, and no one who clung to it surviving too well, by her observation. Like all of their ancestors, Nanny Mōrehu was formidable and a leader, though the Pākehā world gave her little to lead, apart from her family, which became known for the strictness of their dress, the shininess of their hair, and the elocution of their speech. They worked so hard, under the matriarch's watchful eye, that they rose in the world from working class to a more educated and comfortable middle class by the time her descendants were of age.

"I might have been a disappointment to Nanny Mōrehu," Keri says in an unguarded moment while recounting all this to Wairere. "I've never been concerned about my position in society, but if I were, being a single parent on a benefit might be a step down from our Nanny's aspirations and the achievements of my grandparents' generation. They worked so hard their whole lives for what they had. I'm educated, to an extent, but I'm not ambitious like that, not in the Pākehā world." Nanny Mōrehu even went by the name Maisie outside of the family. The woman in the portrait that hangs in the hallway at the center of Keri's picture wall is square-shouldered and straight-backed in a tailored jacket, hair pinned under a burgundy hat at an angle, a sprig of small flowers in the hatband. Her eyes are not piercing so much as compelling, even stern, the lips not smiling nor distorted by unhappiness. But there is something about the picture that has always held Wairere's attention—she thinks the word for it is wistful. She's not sure what part of the ancestress's image gives this away, and she's not sure she's right—maybe it's frustration she sees, or even regret. But it's clear to her, always has been, that Nanny Mōrehu wanted more.

On the other side, Keri's whakapapa links them to Taranaki and a long line of ancestors who fought hard to defend their homes and peace, and were eventually forced to migrate south. Her knowledge of this side extends only to her great-grandparents' names and the places they landed. In one book for her history course, there was mention of many migrations, and Keri was surprised to find their ancestors described as refugees. When she told Wairere this, it changed what Wairere thought she knew about being Māori, the reason she felt so inadequate about her own Māoriness sometimes. Wairere had heard her mother speak of it, but she hadn't really been sure she had a tūrangawaewae—a place to stand—or maybe she did have places like that, but not the feet or legs to stand on. She'd been born in Aussie and her first memories came from there. Her mother and grandmother had spent years there, only coming back for occasional summers. Even though they lived in Aotearoa now, it sometimes feels strangely like Aussie is their real home. Yet she also knows that Australia would never be theirs the way Aotearoa is theirs. They had only ever been guests there. So then why does she feel so out of place now? She knows there are others like her—thousands of them—but that doesn't change how she feels.

It had been a revelation for both Keri and Wairere to find out there were so many migrations in their family history. So many wars, so many moments of seeking refuge, their people displaced over and over again, sometimes displacing others to survive.

"I'd always thought being Māori was about coming from one place," Keri said when she showed Wairere the map of their iwi's migrations. "I guess we're more Māori than I thought we were." Wairere looked at the book and shrugged, but she stored that information with the other things she figured she'd need one day, like the story of the first migrations to Aotearoa, the great explorers who knew how to navigate the whole Pacific by watching the stars and birds and currents, clouds and winds.

The stories Wairere likes best are the ones Keri tells about the people she thinks of more as whānau, or family, than ancestors—people she knew in her lifetime. Walter, Keri's grandfather and Nanny Mōrehu's son, who was a much rounder version of his mother and sister—he had not their angles nor their analytical minds, and his eyes were softer, as was his tendency to indulge both his children and his grandchildren. Koro Walt was known for his smile and his tolerance. He married a woman named Rose, with the same formidable strengths as his mother, though the two clashed as much as they agreed, and sister Lizzie too often took a third position just to be contrary. It was a good thing Koro Walt was as easygoing as he was, for he was forever between the women in his life, being ordered one way or the other, somehow managing to fulfill everyone's wishes at one point or another. It is a credit to him that, whenever he was called on to make a choice, he chose his wife. It so often goes the other way, but Walter's friends might have heard, once or twice, his announcement that he knew what side his bread was buttered on. Rosie was famous for two things: her hourglass figure and her cooking, and although no one could guess which one Walter was thinking of when he mentioned the buttering of his bread, it was widely assumed that he was a well-satisfied man.

Nana Rosie's parents were Irish-Māori and Irish-English, and that's all Keri knew of them, since the Irish-English great-grandfather died in the war, leaving behind a wife and seven children, most of whom were taken in at one point or another by other relatives. Rosie's mother, Harata, suffered a great deal from the loss of her husband and the poverty of single parenthood, which led to more loss when her wider whānau decided it was time to help out by taking the eldest children home with them. At first this seemed a bearable sorrow, since they were old enough to start thinking about how they might make their way in the world, and the relatives had plenty of love, and kai, to spare. Then Harata met Joseph Robertson—a thickset, ruddy-skinned man with a taste for beer and half-caste women, as he liked to put it—and he promised to take care of her for a bit if she would take care of him. Take care of each other they did, and Harata soon learned there were ways to make sorrows disappear that she hadn't previously known about, but such things also made the cares of each day seem less urgent, including the care of the youngest children. When whānau came to visit, they were invariably dismayed by what they saw, and found it necessary to take a child with them when they left. So it was that within three years of her husband's death, Harata was childless, though she remained with Joseph Robertson until her own death at the age of forty-two.

Keri and Wairere know only of the youthful death, not the details that preceded it. The scattered children are family legend.

Rosie had six siblings and four whangai sibling-cousins, and all the good upbringing a mid-twentieth-century Māori girl could be in receipt of: the strongest protocols from both the Māori world and the Pākehā world drummed into her from a young age, since she was the second youngest of Harata's children, and the uncle and aunt who adopted her knew she needed all the tools of both worlds to get by. Despite the care with which she was raised, deeper and more overpowering was the shame Rosie felt at what became of her mother, and the sorrow she felt at losing her mother's attention so young. She could not recognize or name these feelings. Instead, she became the fiercest enforcer of the protocols that had given her life some structure, except two or three times a year when she fell into a spell of absolute exhaustion and lethargy and took to her bed, sometimes for days, sometimes weeks, sometimes months. During these spells, Koro Walt became mother as well as father and nurse, and later grandmother as well as grandfather. In these moments, his sweet tolerance would morph into a steeliness that surprised everyone, but which demonstrated that despite his soft heart, he was never a pushover.

Keri's happiest memories from childhood were the summers they spent at Koro Walt's house, she told Wairere. Even though Nana Rosie was sometimes scary, or sad, or absent, and hard to be around, Koro Walt was none of those things. When Keri clashed with her own parents, it was always Koro Walt she went to. She went to his side many times, red-eyed and furious. He would simply continue whatever it was he was doing: mowing the lawns, fixing the car, reading the newspaper, watching rugby, as if she had always been there. No explanation would pass between them. And later, after dinner and TV and sometimes a beer or two, he'd ask if she was feeling better.

"Talk to your mother, moko," he'd say at some point. "If you don't, she'll blame me." She was always grateful for the way he gave her excuses for doing the right thing—making it seem as if she was doing it for him rather than herself or her parents. "Then we'll go up the creek for some watercress. Might even get a tuna." The way he said tuna, as if he were already savoring the flesh. All the motivation she needed.

Wairere wished she had someone like Koro Walt to go to now, when things got difficult between her and Keri. It had been that way for all of the cousins back in the day, apparently. They were all moko. They gravitated to him like he was a planet. But Koro Walt died long before Wairere was born, back when Keri was only fifteen. He was sixty-four. Maybe her life was a lot more like Wairere's than Wairere would care to say.

"I can't blame him, or my parents, for what happened after that," Keri said after she told Wairere about his death. "But I wish I could. Parents are always getting things wrong. It's the easiest thing in the world to blame them for everything." Wairere couldn't argue with that. She had to admit, but only to herself, that sometimes her mother was right.

Seven

HE COMES IN THE NIGHT

It's after eleven and Janet is in bed, nearly asleep, when she hears a sound from outside and gets that familiar jolt—something awry, some noise outside of the regular pattern. Ever since the children were babies, she's been a light sleeper—it doesn't take much to rouse her. She listens and can feel someone moving even if she can't hear them anymore. A minute passes. Another. Enough time to wonder if maybe it's a dream, maybe she's imagining it. But no, there it is again, someone moving, beyond the door. A cat, maybe? A rapist? And then, the unmistakable: a key in the door, rattling, getting caught, the door swinging open. Her boy. It can only be him. She switches on her lamp, reaches for her dressing gown. Why didn't he let her know? What is he doing here? She's caught between her desire to see him and the rudeness of the intrusion. Inconsiderate, but loving. That's her boy.

No lights on yet. He's trying not to wake her. In between considerate and inconsiderate, then. She moves down the hallway to the kitchen, reaches around and flicks the switch. He is midstep between the living room door and the fridge. Typical.

"Conor."

"Mum! Go back to bed. Didn't mean to wake you."

"You could have texted!"

"Sorry, Mum!" He sweeps in, kisses her cheek. Smells of stale sweat. Maybe something else. His face unshaven. Eyes bloodshot. "Was trying to keep it quiet, see you in the morning. Talk then?"

"You couldn't let me know? I could've made a bed."

"Couch'll do. I'll just grab something to keep me going. Been on the road all day."

He's a grown man. Over six foot, sturdy, but still. "I wish you wouldn't hitchhike."

"It's okay, Mum. Save us some money."

Us? Who is this us? The boy hasn't included her in his plans for years.

"Thought I'd come and stay for a while, pay you some rent instead of whatever slumlord I usually pay it to."

"Charming."

"Come here, Mum." He pulls her into a proper hug. He's putting it on, but she softens anyway. He's trying. He's here. It's been over two years. They exchange a few texts now and again, but they haven't seen each other for that long.

"Well, if you're staying, clean up after yourself. And in the morning, you're going to tell me what's really going on. Don't think you're going to get away with it. You could have called, eh."

"Yes, Mum." He dips his head, already slapping four slices of white bread on the bare bench, ready to slather in butter. Swiftly grabs cheese and tomatoes from the fridge. Salt, pepper.

"Cuppa then?"

"Whoa. That would be amazing. You leave it though. I'll do it."

She moves to the jug. Fills it. Flicks it on. Leans against the bench and folds her arms.

"Honestly, Mum. I can manage."

"Let me get you some bedding for that couch." She's away down the hall, pulling out linen and blankets. It'll be nice. Wouldn't mind the company, even if it's just for a bit. Nice to catch up with the boy. She barely knows anything about what he's been up to lately. In the lounge again, she sets up the sofa bed. He's got more gear than usual. The backpack—the one he travels with—and two other large bags, one that looks like it's got computers or cameras, or something. God knows where he's going to stash it all. There goes the spare room, she supposes, which she wouldn't mind, except for all the stuff that will have to be moved—and to where?

He comes in with his sandwiches, having discovered the miraculous invention known as a plate, sits in her recliner, and extends the footrest. Picks up the remote. He flicks through the channels, runs through the reality TV stations until he hits the exclusive news stations. Janet steps back in distaste. News in the middle of the night; such a barrage, especially the American stuff. She moves to the kitchen, finishes making his tea. Brings it to him and sets it on the table beside her chair, reaching to pat his hair a little.

"Night, son."

"Night, Mum." She closes the living room door, heads down the hall and back to her bed. It'll take a bit of reading to get sleepy again, but that's okay. How often does this happen these days? How often does life surprise her? She pulls the covers up as cozy as she can make them around the book she holds, drifting half in and out of the story, a warmth in her chest.

She wakes late, but smiling. In the living room, the couch has been made up and all his things are in the corner. The kitchen is similarly tidy, but Conor isn't there. No note. No text. He won't be far away, she thinks. He *is* a grown man. But she's disappointed all the same. She had been looking forward. Cooking him eggs and bacon if he'd gone to the store to get some, and grilling him over a long and leisurely breakfast. She has completely forgotten what she has planned for the day, as if his arrival has wiped all memory of a former life from her world. So silly, how the boy can become the center of her universe just by showing up, no matter how long he leaves it between visits. What to do then? She potters in the spare room, surveying her sewing and bookshelf and the exercise bike, all her leftover Enriche products. She should give those away. She barely lasted six months as a sales woman, an investment she knows she is never going to make back. She stands there a minute longer, just long enough to feel overwhelmed, and exits. Let him empty it out if he wants it. She goes through the fridge and the cupboard, makes a list. Just as she's getting organized to leave, he's back. Sweating. Singlet and shorts.

"What on earth have you been up to?"

"Running." He shakes out his legs, then his arms. Moves into the lounge and starts doing press-ups. His breaths come in dramatic, audible puffs.

She feels disturbed, as if the rules of the universe have been turned on their head. "I don't think I've ever seen you do that before." But what did she know. What did she know of her own son?

"Oh, I've been in training for about, I dunno . . ."—puff, puff—"nine months?"

"Training?"

"You know. Fitness training." He flips over and starts doing sit-ups. Has a new tattoo on his arm. A geometric configuration: thick black lines in a sort of square-diamond shape, the lines at the bottom continuing past the diamond tip to cross over and tick up. She gave up counting his tattoos years ago—usually they're emblems he'll regret, starting with the Slayer one at fifteen—he looked like some kid had taken a felt pen to him. Not that she'd comment aloud about any of them. She knows better than to even start. The hair though. It felt so spiky last night.

"A new look too? I used to love your hair long."

"Aw, Mum." The way he says Mum is a drawn-out admonishment. "If I'm gonna stay here, you can't do that."

"Speaking of which, if you're going to stay here, you'll need to clean out the spare room." As if that'll ever happen.

"Yeah . . . I was wondering about that. Where do you want me to put stuff? Keen to get my gear set up as soon as possible."

Gear? "Uh, the garage should do. Chuck the Enriche. I'll sort the books and take most of them to the Sallies."

"Good." He's stretching now.

"I'm off to get the shopping."

"Thanks, Mum." Since when does he thank her for doing the shopping? She wants to like this new version of her son, but as she steps through the internal entrance to her garage, she can't help feeling it's not real.

Conor has her stuff out of the spare room faster than she's ever seen him do anything; what isn't thrown out is given away or packed tidily in the garage. He is almost industrious and methodical, two words she would never have applied to him before. He keeps the spare single bed that has always been in that room under her stash of old magazines and paperbacks, and the desk she used when she thought she was going to have the Enriche business, and sets up his computer and other things. When she sees all his gear laid out, she finds herself surprised yet again. It looks like expensive equipment, and she doesn't know how he could have afforded it.

"It's not expensive, Mum—not by computer geek standards. Can't even play a good game on this lot until I get the updates. It's a few years old now and runs slow if I put too much on the memory, so I've got these hard drives."

"Hard drives?"

"Yeah, for extra storage."

"Storage?" She probably looks as bewildered as she feels. None of this means anything to her. And he still hasn't told her how he could afford it all.

"Yeah. I just started buying gear when I was working at Hallensteins. It's not a big deal these days, Mum. Everybody has almost everything I have here."

"I don't."

"Everyone my age. For gaming. Or working. Or just entertainment. I'm planning to work online while I'm here. Then I don't have to go out and get some lame job that pays me minimum wage."

"A bit of hard work never hurt anyone."

"Yeah, but working for nothing might. Don't worry, Mum—I'll have some rent for you."

"I know you will, son."

She leaves him to his sorting, and whatever he's doing on his machines. On the one hand, they make her uncomfortable—she has his old desktop computer that he gave her a decade ago, but she has no use for it, really. Mostly she finds it a difficult way to communicate. She did it for work, of course—emails and inputting data and whatnot when she was a medical receptionist—but every time they updated anything she felt like she had to start again. She felt like an idiot, actually. She knows she was slow at it. People tried to show her what to do so many times she started to develop an aversion, so the last thing she wants is to deal with computers at home, except for the easy stuff: games, shopping and videos. On the other hand, whatever he's doing on there might be good for him. Maybe he's finally found himself, as they say.

She wishes he'd find himself a girlfriend, is what she thinks as she heads outside to the roses, Zadie trotting behind, because what she'd like is to get herself some more grandchildren. If she's lucky, that's what'll happen next. Boy just needs some confidence, steady work. Eventually he might have to get out of her spare room, but it's nice to have him there for now. So nice to have another body in the house.

Her days follow a very specific routine, even now with Conor back. Cup of tea, breakfast, *Good Morning* on the telly. Then she's outside for her walk with Zadie, and whatever else: gardening, house maintenance, the library, her volunteer jobs at the Sallies and the animal shelter. On days off, her afternoon ritual is a special coffee or hot chocolate, depending on her mood, at one of the local cafes. Can't imagine paying $4 for a cup of tea, so she always gets something she'd never make at home for herself. It's a small life, but she finds enough to fill it, and she's content with it. She knows she's lucky she doesn't have to keep working—plenty of her friends do—as there was money in Richard's passing. Who would have thought the old bastard would come through in the end, making up a tiny bit for all the shit he put her through? He'd fallen out with the kids by then, and maybe he felt some remorse, or maybe it was just to make them wait. He must've known it would all go to them eventually. He'd never said sorry, and she hadn't expected a cent, so the sudden windfall was more than surprising; gave her the means to get the flat freehold, and even though it's not as big and not as nice as what they had when she had a young family, it is brick and mortar and she has a garden that is hers, full stop.

A few times a week, when she leaves the house, she sees the neighbors—the woman with the bright clothes, the little girl with her pretty eyes, Aliana, and the man, sometimes all of them together, sometimes just the man, or just the woman, with the little girl outside. They never let her go unattended. The man always smiles widely, the woman politely, though she looks away quickly. The woman and child never talk to her. At times, it seems to pain them, in fact, to interact, and they disappear quickly. What is the deal with that? So she says nothing, and goes about her business. Funny lot. She tells Keri as much, calling her over as she unpegs her laundry.

"How's that boy of yours, Kerry?"

"He's good. Just napping."

"And your girl?"

"Oh, you know, she's a teenager."

Janet nods the slow nod of those who have been there. Her daughter, at sixteen, leaving the house. Not coming back for a week. She decides not to follow that memory to its natural conclusion.

"Ah well. Long time ago for me. Did you know my son is back for a while? Not quite the same thing—nearly thirty-five! How old does that make me? Too old to speak of in company."

"Oh? No—I, er, didn't know that."

"Nice to be surrounded by young families though. It's good, eh, to know who you're living in close proximity to. I do worry about those new ones next door. They keep to themselves a bit. Friendly, but standoffish. It's—well. You hear things about that lot."

"That lot?"

Janet looks around, just in case. "Refugees," she half whispers.

"Oh. Janet. I don't think you need to—"

"Oh, I know. Shouldn't bring up all that stuff, but you never know, do you? You never know."

"I guess you don't, but, ah, I don't think you have to worry about them."

"Well, how would you know? I've been watching and waiting for the opportunity to get to know them properly. The woman and the child are so timid. It makes me wonder. I mean, the man was very polite when we met, but that could be a cover for all sorts of things."

"Uh-huh. Okay, well, I better get back inside, but I think they're okay, eh? Maybe they just want to keep to themselves."

"Yes. Well. That could be the problem. But maybe you're right, Kerry."

Eight

A BRAIDED RIVER

Sometimes Sera feels like a river with two tributaries: one clear icy mountain water, the other brackish marsh water. She wants to follow the flow of the clear water, but she can't separate it out from the dark. It's as if there are many sharp rocks under her feet, making it hard to find a soft landing.

In those first days in Aotearoa, they had felt a kind of euphoria that carried them through anything difficult. Everyone at the Refugee Resettlement Center shared her disbelief, both in where they were now, and what they had been through. All of them carried their old countries into this new place, in the bags on their shoulders, their clothes and their food, on their tongues and in their eyes and hands, under their skin and between their ears and within the valves admitting blood through their hearts. Old Home New Home. Both of these oxygen to their veins.

New Zealand had its own environmental disasters to deal with, just like everywhere else—she'd heard there was too much wind and the water was too unpredictable—but on the United Nations Environment Program viability index, Aotearoa still sat just below orange. Australia and the US had gone orange as soon as the index was instituted; Sera's home country was red before they even developed the warning system. There were three countries like hers—speeding toward a watery or fiery oblivion so fast the only recourse was to abandon their homes. Each country in a different part of the world: Europe, Asia, the Pacific. A nice spread, at least, somehow diplomatic. They'd said the evacuations would be temporary, just until the land stabilized, though she wasn't sure how they would raise the island nation from its watery bed. It was the reason the viability index had been developed at all, and the reason why victims of climate disaster were at last allowed to claim refugee status. Still, she hopes to go home one day.

When she sees the neighbor outside with her little boy one afternoon, Sera knows she should go out and meet her. It would be good for her and it would be good for Aliana to have a friend. She misses having a community of women: friends, cousins, aunts, grandmothers. She misses the ease of talking with women. But there can be no ease of talking here, she knows. All of her interactions with New Zealanders have thus far been hard work, even when they are friendly. She sits in her living room, with its rust-brown carpet, and its old leather couch, and watches her neighbor through the net curtains while Aliana plays at her feet. Not this time, she thinks, but soon.

She says not this time, but soon, two more times before she finally ventures out, and then it is only because the little boy is riding his scooter up and down the driveway between their houses, and somehow manages to go fast enough to fling himself onto her grass, bellowing as he goes. She is out the door almost as soon as he lands, having leapt up in alarm from her place by the window. Poor boy! She doesn't know where his mother has gone. Outside the boy is flat on the ground, face down, arms and legs splayed.

"Hello? Are you okay?" she calls, reaching her hand behind her for Aliana, whom she can hear following.

The boy doesn't move. She waits for a cold finger of fear to trace her spine, but instead she feels only confusion. The grass is soft. Unless he landed so hard he knocked himself out?

"Hello, little boy? Are you okay?" The child doesn't move. She approaches him, and is about to kneel when he flips over, arms and legs still splayed out, a big grin on his face.

"I got deaded," he says proudly. "Dead, dead, dead."

She has never seen a child so happy about death. She starts laughing, and the laugh continues for so long she finds more laughter at the center of it, a whole ball of wound-up absurdity unravelling. She'd forgotten that feeling—her body giving itself over to hiccupping, inane madness. He rolls again and gets onto all fours, then jumps up, grabbing his scooter from where it has fallen, staring at her curiously. She tries to calm herself, but the look on his face . . . it's hard to hold in the giggle bubbling up.

"I'mda supahero vampire now. The undead Spideyman.

Ptchao ptchao!" The boy extends his wrists in her direction as if shooting from them.

"Oh." She ducks and puts her arms up defensively. "Oh no! You got me!"

She's just about to fall into a heap when she sees his mother running down the steps on the other side of the driveway.

"Sorry!" she calls. "Don't mind him—he's always doing that!"

"No." Sera moves her mouth as if the words she is searching for live behind her teeth. "I don't mind. He's a funny boy." She means it in a complimentary way, but she suddenly wonders if it's an offensive thing to say.

"Yeah, I don't know where he gets it from. I probably let him watch too much TV." The neighbor laughs. "Walty's a good boy, really. Weird, but sweet."

Sera nods and smiles. They both watch the children for a moment. Aliana has wandered out behind her mother and, having abandoned the scooter on the driveway, Walty is picking daisies and dandelions from the untidy edges of the lawn. He approaches Aliana. "You can ride my scooter," he says, offering her the bunch of assorted weeds. She simply stares at him, considers the bouquet, then looks at the scooter.

"It's okay, Aliana," Sera says in their language, bending to her daughter. She looks up at her neighbor. "She doesn't know how," she says in English.

"That's okay! She can take it at her own pace—sorry—Walty likes to make everyone his friend. He'll be bossing her around in no time."

Sera doesn't know what to say to that, so again she nods

and smiles. They both watch as Aliana accepts Walty's flowers and he tells her the arcane rules of the undead Spideyman club while zipping back and forth in front of her on the scooter.

Keri introduces herself. Sera follows suit, imitating the patterns of speech. "I'm Sera. This is Aliana. And Adam is my husband. It is nice to meet you, Keri."

"Oh, you roll your Rs the same way we do in Māori. I have a daughter too, you'll have no problem with her name, Wairere. Though we just call her Wai."

"Ah yes. High school girl? I have seen her in the mornings go to school."

"Have you been living in Aotearoa for long?"

Sera gives a rough timeline, where they have stayed, where they have come from. "And now we are here. This is home now."

"Well, nau mai—welcome. Awesome." Keri nods encouragingly and it is a relief to Sera. "It's nice to have a young family next door. You should bring Aliana over to play with Walty sometime! Anytime, really. We could have afternoon tea, or lunch, with the kids."

Sera is confused for a moment, then alarmed, then smiles broadly. "I'm sorry," she says slowly. "It takes me a moment to catch up sometimes, with my English. That would be lovely, thank you." Words she'd learned long ago: *that would be lovely, thank you*. But a moment of alarm comes at the thought of entering Keri's house, knowing what to say and what to do. And her chest is gripped in another sort of fear: What if this encounter is not as friendly as it seems? Everything has been going so well.

"Cool! Don't worry, it'll be very relaxed. No worries."

No worries, thinks Sera, how nice that would be.

The children continue playing together, Aliana now having graduated to standing on the scooter while Walty pulls her, very slowly, yelling instructions. Aliana watches him with wide eyes.

"He's loud, but he's generous for a four-year-old," says Keri above the yelling.

"I think Aliana likes him," says Sera. The moment is so unusual for them both.

But when Walty decides the scooter should go faster, and Aliana should learn to kick along the driveway by way of him holding her ankle and forcing it in the correct motion, things dissolve quickly. Within moments, Aliana is hiding behind Sera's skirt, peeking out at her tormentor. Walty points at the scooter, ordering Aliana back to it. When that doesn't work, he sits cross-legged on the concrete, scooping his arm in a welcoming motion, cooing, "C'mon, sweetie, c'mon." Keri is clearly embarrassed by his obvious imitation of her own way of coaxing him. "Alright! I think that's it! It's so nice to meet you, Sera."

Sera smiles and says it is nice to meet her too. Keri crouches to Aliana's height. "Do you want to come and play at our place on Thursday, Aliana? Would you like to come over for lunch?"

Aliana only stares.

"That would be lovely," Sera answers, those unfamiliar words coming in good use again. She wants to ask what she should do. Should she bring a plate? Apparently this is a custom in which the guest brings food to the host's house. Sera assumes they name the plate but not the food itself so as to avoid awkward attention on the act of bringing food, which in her own culture would be considered odd, if not insulting. She can't bring herself to say any of this.

"Great, awesome. Come on, Walty!" Keri beckons to Walty, who folds his arms and pouts theatrically. "Bye-bye, Aliana." Keri waves. "Do you want to wave bye-bye, Walty?" Walty sustains his pose for a beat longer, but relents, waving energetically, then stomps off in big steps toward their door.

Keri smiles at Sera again, and rolls her eyes. Sera returns the warmth in her smile. She feels lighter than she has in days.

"I'll see you later." Keri raises her eyebrows and lifts her chin in that characteristic way Sera has noticed Kiwis acknowledge each other, a sort of reverse nod. Sera smiles and can't help but nod in response—she isn't able to do it the other way yet—before clasping Aliana's hand and going inside.

Nine

GRAVITY

Wairere is not like other kids, this is clear to all who know her, but it's surprising how many people her age feel like they are not like other kids, and since the world is an increasingly fractious and fractured place, Wairere seems like an oasis of calm to her peers. Thus, at school she is accepted, if not popular, in all her strangeness. Teenagers see fairly clearly, despite the constant turmoil in their collective environments and collective hormones, and what they see in Wairere is someone who isn't needy in quite the same way they are needy, who is self-possessed in all the ways that matter, who lives somewhere just beyond their reach. Mostly, they leave her alone. Those who harbor too many pretenses keep a wide berth, and those who are interested in more worldly things barely notice her. The strange, the funny, and the abnormally intelligent form a loose group of which she is the nucleus, quite without wishing to be. It doesn't matter what she does, wherever she goes they cluster around her as if she exerts her own gravity. They seem not to notice her desire for silence and independence from the group, and she long ago gave up any attempts to free herself. She's even grown to enjoy the safety she feels in numbers, if only while she's at school. Out of school, she avoids socializing, except for Felicity, who seems oblivious to all forms of discouragement.

Felicity lives around the corner, so Wairere has the great good fortune of accompanying her to school and back again, and therefore receives all the gossip and chatter of the day, and that keeps her from getting too caught up in it. It's all a bit distasteful—sometimes she feels more like an Edwardian nun than a gen alpha teenager—but it would be much worse without all the noise. Even though she often wishes for quiet, she can only enjoy it when she's away from people. Should she be among a crowd when things fall silent, she is likely to find herself inundated with bodily sensations that aren't her own.

Wednesday is her day to walk Zadie and pick up anything Mrs. B wants from the shops, so she leaves Felicity early and heads to Mrs. B's house. Walking Zadie is fine, but going to the shops can be like stepping around landmines—there's so much to avoid in the blank and hungry stares of the other customers. Last time she was there, a woman with dirt-blonde hair carrying a toddler on her hip brushed past and Wairere just about fell over, instantly overwhelmed by a pressure in her chest. Her breath came faster and she felt like she couldn't get enough of it, and there was a pulsing of blood in her skull that quickly turned to tightness. Then the woman was out the door, and Wairere was as normal again, though it took a moment to collect herself. The woman hurried into her car, strapped the toddler in a nonregulation seat, swung out of the carpark onto Mazengarb Road, which unbeknownst to her had been built last century by a crew that included her five-times-removed great-uncle, and drove too fast home, where her boyfriend played on the PS7 and brooded. What he had in store for her was inevitable, and in the meantime the only thing she could do was keep their child quiet with dinner and bedtime. At least she knew what to expect, and that was better than not knowing, and also better than being alone. It was unlikely the dirt-blonde woman was particularly conscious of her decision-making process, just as it was unlikely that Wairere would ever quite know why the woman was feeling what she was feeling, though some things had a certain *tone* to them, and Wairere suspected this was likely due to a mistake the woman was making about what the link between love and pain should be.

This kind of thing can happen to Wairere all day long if she isn't careful—each incident exhausting, and confounding. What use is it, this ability she has? People never understand why she spends so much time alone, or why she seeks the solitude of swamp and sea. All of this is on her mind as she knocks on Mrs. B's door, but Mrs. B doesn't answer as quickly as usual, even though Wairere can hear Zadie bouncing on the other side. Finally the door opens, Mrs. B awkwardly trying to hold it with one arm, while she clicks Zadie's lead to her collar with the other.

"Just the walk today, thanks Wai. I only just got some groceries and Conor is here if I need someone to run out for anything." Mrs. B beams. "I don't know if you've met Conor, have you? My son? Hasn't been around much since you all moved in, I don't think."

Wairere takes Zadie's lead, waiting for the dog to settle before she crouches to pat her. She looks up at her neighbor. "I've heard you talk about him, I think."

Mrs. B begins rattling off the whole story: his arrival in the night, his intention to stay, the rearrangement of her rooms. But while she's speaking, Wairere becomes aware of a looming presence, not unlike a bank of rain cloud. She attempts to ignore it, and then, as it becomes more insistent, to push it away. Mrs. B is calling Conor now to come and meet Wai, and as she does so, Wairere begins to realize that this shift in her awareness might have something to do with the new presence in Mrs. B's home.

"N-no, honestly, Mrs. B, I'll walk Zadie now. Maybe I'll meet your son another time."

"Oh, it would be good for everyone to meet him, since he's going to be here a while. Completely unexpected, but this is quite a change for the neighborhood!"

It is clear that Mrs. B means it is quite a change for her. She's preening, all puffed up like a chicken with a new brood of hatchlings. Wairere's nan used to keep chickens at her little property in Parramatta and there was nothing more exciting than when she allowed a chicken to brood and hatch babies.

Despite Mrs. B's excitement, Wairere detects something discordant in her pride, a kind of sour note that Mrs. B has chosen not to notice. It's better if Wairere can avoid noticing it too, though she knows this is unlikely. Previous experience tells her such things can haunt her for hours if not days.

"He seemed to almost step off the planet after his father died. Spent so long in Christchurch, I didn't think I'd ever see him back up this way."

There it is, a sharp drop as if Wairere is in a car that has just gone over a hill and is hurtling downward, her stomach struggling to keep up with the rest of her. It's not really her stomach though, is it? She sees it more like the fluid inside her body—the way these waters move always tells a story. This one brings nausea. But when tales are told in bodily sensations instead of words, it can be hard to translate. She can only take note: something about leaving Christchurch, perhaps. Something about the unlikelihood of coming back to this place.

"It's nice having someone around. Conor? Can you come out? I mean, he's usually around anyway. Conor?" Once she gets started, it's hard to get Mrs. B to stop.

"It's okay Mrs. B, really, I'm sure I'll see him around."

"Yeah, he seems to be wrapped up in his computer work, so it's just as well."

Wairere manages to hold it together as she leaves. Zadie has gone quiet. She trots obediently alongside while Wairere walks the route they take to the man-made ponds on Kōtuku Drive. This isn't where she wants to be right now: it's too contained, too manicured, the houses too opulent, but the water soothes her and the swamp is only a short walk away. Why does she go around picking up what isn't hers all the time? She's raged about this before, and it never gets her anywhere. Acceptance is the only thing that makes things manageable, but it's not easy, especially at times like these. In this particular moment, she wishes she could ignore what she felt at Mrs. B's door. It's bad, she knows that much, but understanding how bad and why would require her to focus her attention on something that feels oily and slick, polluting. She doesn't want to get too close to it, doesn't even want to acknowledge it's there. But it's close to her home, and that's never happened before, not with something like this, something scarier than the stuff people usually carry around.

Wairere walks, the dog meekly following her lead, until they're both exhausted. When she returns Zadie to Mrs. B, she bolts as soon as the old lady hands over payment. It's rude, she knows, the way she takes off, but that's the thing: Mrs. B, and her house, and all who inhabit it, will be there tomorrow for her to make up for any transgressions.

Sera is stepping out the door when she notices Wairere pass, head down, folded in on herself. She wants to be friendly but the girl doesn't give her the chance—Sera isn't even sure if Wairere sees her at all. Usually she doesn't know how to read such body language. What does it mean in this place if people don't greet her? Is it because they have their own things to worry about, or because she looks different, or because they feel threatened by her in some way? Usually, she feels threatened by them, not because she believes that they mean her ill, but because she hasn't yet figured out how to read the cues. Body language here is both similar and not exactly the same as home. Facial expressions especially confound her. How eyes glide over her face and don't linger. The laughter. More free, perhaps, but also, hides things.

But with Wairere, it's different. Sera knows nothing of her young neighbor's struggle with the world, and she doesn't share any of her peculiar abilities, but when she sees the girl she feels a certain kinship. She doesn't think the hunched shoulders are for her. In fact, she suspects the hunched shoulders are expressing a feeling she herself shares, that in some way this girl understands, that something in Wairere's life is like something in Sera's—a certain outsideness, a certain inability to cooperate with the way things are around her.

They set out for the beach, Sera pushing Aliana in the pushchair, Aliana humming a radio tune Sera barely recognizes and rubbing the soft corner of her blanket on her cheek. They are instantly calmer than they were inside—Aliana always gets scratchy late afternoon, especially when Adam is out. He is at a job interview in Wellington, an hour away by train, which seems so far to Sera now, after years of confinement together, even though they both used to work on different sides of a city that stretched more than an hour's travel in every direction.

Sera takes a deep breath, then a few more. She's trying to force that ease back into her body, despite the fractiousness of the last hour. It doesn't quite feel the right way to relax, but it's what all the experts say to do. She isn't jealous of her husband. She's grateful to be able to stay with Aliana—not that it doesn't get hard, in its own way, but they've never had the opportunity to just *be* mother and daughter, to just live some kind of "normal" life. Walking to the beach. What miracle is this? The clear path beneath their feet. The air on their skin, late afternoon sun making the breeze warm, but not too hot. She observes the plants and trees as they pass, doesn't recognize most of them: there is one that looks like papyrus, some roses, chestnut, but most of it is unknown to her. She must get a book at the library and learn the names with Aliana. The birdsong is pretty, but also unfamiliar, as is the flat, wide layout of the houses, the materials they're constructed from, the brightness of the sky, the abundance of grass.

The path to the beach is only a ten-minute walk. They pass a woman and her children riding bikes, an old lady with a grocery bag, two young men laughing with each other. She feels uncomfortable each time, doesn't know where to look, doesn't know how to read safety in their manner or reveal her own benign intentions. It's a relief to reach the entrance to the beach, signaled by a blue post, the road sounds fading behind them. But here the terrain gets bumpy, and Aliana must get out of the stroller so Sera can fold it up like an umbrella. They follow the path to the dunes, Aliana skipping a little—she already knows what's ahead—and pass a couple who say, *Hello, don't mind Koa, he's friendly*, nodding toward their dog. Aliana freezes and Sera calls to her, telling her it's okay, but she doesn't move until her mother is beside her again. Then it's just them and the wide expanse of sand, the tide out this evening, the water shallow and safe, and there, in the distance, the island.

They stop to take off their shoes and stow them by a log with the stroller, then they venture closer to the water, Aliana stomping her bare feet and curling her toes into the sand. She runs a little way, bounces, picks up an iridescent green-blue shell, some seaweed, a stick, crouches to dig. Sera follows her daughter, and they exclaim at this or that treasure, completely absorbed. When they finally reach the water, they dare to dip their feet in the coolness, Aliana squealing and Sera's laughter a low chuckle in her throat. They splash and stomp, laughing at the seagulls and the black birds with red legs and beaks squawking and hunting along the tideline.

Sera looks to the island, behind it the mountains to the south she can sometimes see on a clear day. It is blanketed in trees, friendly, a sanctuary for birds, she's been told. It has been other things at other times, just as she has. Her feet are cool in the wet sand, she can smell the salt of ocean, hear her daughter's voice pitched high in delight. People pass in little groups, but they don't concern her now. This. This is all they need, her and Aliana and Adam. This gives her something. This place.

She was once so sure, such a fighter. She sometimes wonders if they managed to get here by the pure force of her will alone—the relentless paperwork and phone calls she made every single day they were at the Processing Center. She didn't take no for an answer, and she received hundreds of noes. And now that they are here it's like that part of her is spent, and she's trying to be okay with that. Maybe it's okay to just *be* for a while, in these moments with Aliana, and with Adam when he's home. Maybe learning how to be okay in this new place requires less action, less movement. She has noticed it is just as hard to be still as it is to move, just as hard to settle as it is to keep going. But maybe Aliana needs stillness now, and maybe Sera does too.

They stay there until the sun lowers over the horizon, and then they make for home while it's still light. She feels lifted, more air in her chest. Aliana is sleepy. When they arrive home, Adam has started dinner. He looks up, tension in his jaw, his eyes questioning, and she smiles—it's alright—they're alright. They eat their favorite way, on the floor with music playing. She leaves the door open to the night air. Just for tonight, she thinks. Just this night they will pretend like nothing out there could ever hurt them.

Ten

A WALK IN THE PARK

It's likely that no one other than Wairere has noticed how Conor looms into the neighborhood, since these days most people carry darkness with them, and usually do their best to appear cheerful, to pretend all is well, to make the best of a bad lot. The past few years have certainly been a bad lot, not just for Conor, but for everyone: the wars, pandemics, lack of housing and, for those without enough money to act as a buffer, little access to good food. Sometimes it's easier, collectively, to pretend it isn't happening, even when it's happening directly to them. But in this, there has been opportunity for people like Conor. Where once he was alone in his disenchantment, he now has brothers and sisters, allies, others who confirm what he has known all along, and the confirmation of his knowing brings him relief, if not jubilation. He has returned buoyed by a sense of belonging, something he never found in his mother's house, nor his father's, something that did not exist at school or in work. His mother sees the change in him, and it's a relief to her too, so much so that she finds it easy to ignore any misgivings.

The boys have taught Conor to walk tall, and that's what he does now in his old neighborhood. It feels like a bit of a strut, but he doesn't care. He's been working on himself. He is a strong example of manhood. Johnny and the others have given him this.

He's made a deal with himself: if he completes his training five days in a row, he'll have a night out. He tries not to overdo it anymore, but once or twice a week can't hurt, especially as an incentive to get his runs in. He's been doing a circuit—a big loop from his mother's place, past the high school, alongside the stream where he used to find and torment eels as a kid, then through the church carpark and west toward the beach. He cuts across the golf course, a lot of rich-people houses with wide lawns and high fences, dogs and multiple garages, then down Ocean Road so he can cross Marine Parade and take one of the walkways down to the sea: a good running beach, smooth sand, lots of space, peaceful. He had no time for it when he was a kid, but now he understands its pleasures. Clears his head for the big thoughts. This is where he usually goes over the chats of the night before, any conversations he's had with Johnny especially. Sometimes he ends up arguing with himself, but mostly it's time to get his head straight.

By Friday, Conor is feeling loose and free, running down the beach, as he passes Tikotu Stream. He doesn't know it because there's not much to see now, but it was big back in the day—a source of fresh water and fresh food for the locals. Right beside the stream is the skate park where kids come night and day to ride their two, four, or eight wheels, where parents bring their children to let off steam. There's a man-made pond, a playground, a carpark. Always lots of places to park cars, of course. Public toilets, just like most beachside parks. No one who visits this place thinks about what used to be there—they think only of their fish and chips, ice creams, their phone and how quickly they can get the kids home for a bath. Sleep, often they are wishing for more sleep. The younger ones wish for more money.

They don't see the series of homes, the series of villages—pā—the most recent for Te Ātiawa, who had traveled a long way, fought a number of battles, and intermarried with prior occupants to stake a claim, who could scoop handfuls of eel or kōkopu from that stream, or dig for shellfish so thick beneath those soft sands that they barely had to work for a meal. Te Oraiti, who had grown from a baby to an adult in those strange times between the old days and the new, would visit relatives in Ōtaki or Paekākāriki simply by climbing into his waka and paddling, the Tikotu being connected to all the other waterways that formed a corridor between different pā for ease of travel and gathering of kai. There's no evidence of this now, no sign of Te Oraiti's people, his marriage to Amaia, their five children, the first buried close by. But people who know might see it, notice where the grassy surrounds are heaped up, just so, where the shape of the land might suggest shelter or safety, where the rubbish might be piled, even if excavations have now taken it away, and concrete has been poured. And not far away, in Wellington, a young woman called Amaia is introducing herself to her first te reo class, telling the story of how she is named after an ancestor, though she is unsure about where that namesake lived after the great migrations brought on by the colonial wars.

Conor doesn't acknowledge these ghost marks as he passes, because he doesn't know they're there. Hardly anybody does. It's just shops now, and road, and that nice new building the council built, Gateway to the Island, using the name of the old pā that has gone unremembered for so long, Te Uruhi. Not even old Bill Jenkins' Inn is remembered, the place where travelers more like Conor in complexion stopped on their way to Whanganui along the coast, the first of such businesses in the area. A popular spot due to his wife Pairoke's cooking, their children helping with the horses and the housekeeping.

People are indiscriminate in their forgetting.

And Conor is not so much focused on what's around him anyway. As he runs, he's trying to figure out how to make an impact, how to prove himself. Something elegant, Johnny said, to mark him out as one of the clever ones. No blunt tools, the time for that is over. They have to be clever, to convince people of what they don't want to face. So no yelling and waving literal or figurative flags. His job is to fly under the radar, to have an effect at a deeper level, and to make the enemy doubt themselves. He can do most of that online, and he has been, for six months now, longer in a more casual way. But Johnny set the challenge for him before he left: How was he going to up the ante? In fact, that's why he left—Johnny wanted him in the north. Time to go to the next level.

Tonight though, Conor is due some R&R. After his run, a shower, ironing his shirt, he heads to the pub, down Mazengarb Road, a jaunty walk. His muscles still sore from the workout. He likes the pain. It means he's done the work and he deserves a reward. That's the feeling he carries with him into The Hangman.

There's a thing you must do when you enter an establishment that doesn't know you—kind of like peeing your psychic urine in all the corners—head off anyone who wishes to cause you trouble. Conor pushes his chest out, turns and looks around the room. Eyes lift to meet his and he gives them a good stare. Drink it in, buddy. A little thrill. A tingle in the groin. He surveys, then leans his elbows on the bar. Might as well be wearing a cowboy hat and chewing on a toothpick. The pretty blonde pulling handles calls him love when she asks for his order. He takes the draught on tap, enjoys the view while she's intent on pouring. Nice white T-shirt, doesn't hide much. Looks away when she finishes and asks him for payment.

Then he searches for somewhere to sit. A rowdy group in the corner watching a game. Never been his thing, sport, but easy to pretend like he cares, and something to watch till he has half a beer down. Once he's settled in, it's like he's part of the group. Throws in some inconsequential small talk. Halfway through his second beer, he starts looking for something more fun, sport of a different kind. Middle-aged couples in the corner. Old fellas deep in conversation occupy a booth. A gaggle of women at the center table. He knows how big his balls are now, but he's not sure he actually wants to take on a whole table. That way lies ridicule and ruin. There's always blondie at the bar, though she's got the whiff of a boyfriend on her, all those cute little blondies do.

Two beers in, he needs a piss. A pretty girl at the center table looks up as he passes: big brown eyes, dark hair, pale skin. Maybe he should try when he comes back. After the toilet he heads back to the bar for another beer. Dutch courage. Maybe a bourbon and coke? And there she is, waiting while someone else is being served. He stands beside her, a little too close. She looks at him, annoyed perhaps, or just questioning.

"Sorry!" He takes a step back.

"No, it's okay." She smiles, warily. Still, she's very pretty. "Never know who you might meet."

"Big party." He nods toward her table.

"Yeah. Girls' night." She turns away, a polite close to the small talk. He has to do something to keep her attention, but not overdo it.

"Bit quiet. Shame there isn't a band."

"Uh-huh." She eyes him, the smile gone.

"Sorry. I don't mean to intrude. It's just that I'm from out of town and I don't know anyone, so I decided to just talk to anyone I meet. I mean, I don't usually do that, but, you know, needs must."

"Needs must?"

At this, he blushes. He can feel the warmth rising to his cheeks. So much for his manhood. "Yeah. Uh, something my mother says. God. I'm staying with my mother. I mean, I grew up here, moved away when I was seventeen. Worked all over. Down south. Anyway, life story. It's been nearly eighteen years."

It's the blush that gets her. None of the posturing she saw when he came in. That sweet moment of lost control. So hard to find in men, but it's always when the facade drops that she sees something she wants to know more about. "You haven't been home in how long?"

"Coupla years, and before that only for Christmas, and I hate Christmas."

"Me too."

Suddenly, they're in. They start talking and neither of them want to stop the flow of it. Truth is, she's as hungry for company as he is. She hardly gets out anymore, but when she does, it wouldn't be more than once a month. She thought he might be a bit full of himself, but he doesn't seem to need to say much. She likes his quietness. There's something vulnerable about him, something held in. She doesn't mind a bit of mystery. Like Tabasco sauce on scrambled eggs—gives things a bit more flavor. She knows he's on the make. So what? Maybe she is too.

They go back to her table, and he gets introduced to the five other women. Forgets their names immediately. They all greet him too loudly, make faces and *oooo* sounds at Keri. As soon as the conversation returns to the women, Conor and Keri turn back to each other, talking just low enough to avoid interrupting the others. Keri wants to hold back; she wants to protect her private life from this stranger, but once she starts talking, she doesn't seem to be able to hold anything in. Apparently she has had the perfect amount of wine to make this possible. Conor doesn't seem to mind. There's nothing cool about him. He's a bit eager, and she catches him looking at her breasts, but she's also had just enough wine to welcome it. What's a little flirtation between acquaintances? It's just a game, she's clear about this in her own mind, and by the time she rounds off another drink—the second he's paid for, which is lucky since she can only afford one drink on a night out like this—she realizes she doesn't care too much about who he is. Why not? Why can't she just enjoy the attention of some stranger? She doesn't want a man in her life, not with the kids. Men are too much hard work. Nothing wrong with playing.

The women take turns heading to the loos in twos and threes. Keri makes a big show of pulling her friend Sam along with her, leaning in to tell Conor she won't be long, her breath hot on his cheek. He watches them go, enjoying the sway in Keri's walk. There's something about her that's different than what he's used to with girls. He doesn't know what it is yet, and he's keen to find out. He reckons he might get the chance too, the way things are going, but the crucial moment will be when they leave, and they certainly can't go back to his mum's place. One of the other girls leans in to chat with him. She's solid: fleshy boobs and arms. Not his type, but still, he would. A wave of guilt comes over, fleetingly. Johnny always tells him not to do that, not to lower himself to the base needs of his body. He must be the one in control. That's what the physical stuff is about. Getting some mastery over himself. You can't be a leader of others until you become a master of yourself. Boobs is asking where he works. Nowhere yet, he tells her, just moved back from Christchurch. They compare notes. She would've been a few years ahead of him in school. He's trying to tell his cock to ignore the way her chest wobbles as she leans in. He doesn't even want her, but he's left it so long without female company he can't help the physical reaction. That might have to go into the regimen: more regular sex. Take the sting out of encounters like this. It had gone around the boys that paying for it could be a good thing. Get rid of those physical urges without getting involved. Save the relationship stuff for the right time and the right woman. None of these thoughts help with his current condition though.

Keri returns giggling with Sam, who announces in a voice so loud the rest of the pub looks their way that they're taking the party back to her Big, Empty, House. She is so emphatic about the big and empty part that Conor is sure even the old fellas in the booth are going to get her coded message, but he's all in. It's a ten-minute walk, a loud ten-minute walk, during which Conor and Keri hang back and wander slowly behind the giggling group.

Keri takes Conor's hand and guides it around her shoulders, leaning her head in. It feels nice. She slips her arm behind him and under his jacket, right up to his waist and down again to his jean pocket. Shit, he thinks, he's going to give it to her if she keeps this up. She does keep it up. By the time they reach the friend's place they're making out on the front lawn. The other women turn while waiting for the door to be unlocked, see the two of them, and squeal their excitement at the display in front of them. Then, the door opens and they head inside, making humping motions against each other as they go.

Sam's place has a spare room, so after they have more drinks and a smoke with the girls, Keri drags Conor back there. He's not a great kisser, but what he lacks in technique he makes up for in enthusiasm. She hasn't been with anyone since Walty's dad before Walty was born, and even this fast bruising of skin against skin makes her feel just a little more like who she used to be. Desirable, daring, edgy and—she hates to admit it—human. She knows she is no longer this version of herself, but the illusion feels nice.

He has his hands around her breasts and his erection pushed up against her belly when reality comes back to her, thick and uncomfortable, like a lump of food moving down her throat unchewed. As suddenly as the urge is with her, it's gone. She feels a bit silly. Maybe she is too old for this kind of thing after all.

"I'm sorry," she says, pushing Conor away.

"What?" he asks blearily, his arms out as if they are still encompassing her form.

"Sorry. I can't. I shouldn't have taken it this far. I thought—"

"But, but you—" He hasn't caught up, his hands still hang in the air uselessly.

"Yeah. I'm sorry. This was a mistake." She watches the emotions cross his face like clouds over a landscape: embarrassment, disbelief, disappointment. Then his features settle into pure, cold fury.

"Look," he says, taking a step toward her, frowning, determined.

She takes a step back, and her own hands go up—not too far, just enough to signal a halt. "I'm out."

She moves swiftly to the door and stumbles toward the living room where she can hear the girls declaring opinions about things they won't remember in the morning, talking over each other, cackling, safe. When she enters, they don't even notice. She places herself at the far end of the room, squeezing between two women on the already oversubscribed couch.

Five minutes later, Conor stands at the open door to the living room. He has tidied himself up, and there's no longer any sign of the fury. "Kerry? Can I have a word?" He lifts his hands in surrender. "No pressure."

The women look Conor up and down, suddenly quiet, suddenly aware that something has shifted. Keri looks up from her drink. She's not scared of him, she realizes, she just doesn't want to deal with this shit. She wants to go home to her babies.

"Just one minute," she says, fixing him with the sternest look she can muster. "I'm tired." She follows him out into the hall.

"Look, all I wanted to say is I didn't mean to put you on the spot, eh. I wouldn't have done anything, you know, that you didn't want to do."

She doesn't know what to say, but she's impressed he didn't just bolt.

"Anyway, no hard feelings, but if you're interested, we could give it another go sometime."

"Uh, I don't know right now, okay? Like, I'm really tired. I don't do this kind of thing often and maybe it's not me anymore. Maybe it was the drink or the fact I have no social life. Is it okay if we don't make plans?" She can't imagine, in this moment, the effort it would take. "So yeah, no hard feelings, if you really meant that."

He looks away, then squares his shoulders and looks into her eyes, hard. "Of course."

"And my name is Keri. That's how you say it, you know, the Māori way." Why hadn't she cared about the way he said it before?

She leaves him in the hall and swivels back to the room full of women keen for an explanation. She gives them the short version, impatient to call a car, while she waits for Conor to leave.

He was somewhere else entirely, somewhere open and free, and she was there with him for a sweet moment. It was like all the walls had come down, all the things that usually hold him back, like she accepted him just as he was, like he didn't have to be anyone different. He had felt whole, or like he was on his way to wholeness.

But as he heads out onto the damp early morning streets, he can't locate the triumph he felt less than an hour ago, the pure metallic potency of lust met with lust. It's gone already, and he hates the feeling he's left with, not just inadequacy, but some aching gap he has to talk himself out of. This is why the world has to change. He can see it so clearly. But he can also see where he made a mistake. He thinks of what she said:

Keri . . . you know, the Māori way, and a slide bolt pulls back in his head so a door can swing open. Conor, you dumb fuck! Of course she's Māori. He should have seen it. He just assumed she was pakeha. She looked white enough to him—dark eyes and hair, yeah, but no big nose or lips. She didn't sound like a Māori either—except when she said Māori words, he now realizes. Huh, makes sense though. How is he supposed to avoid the Māoris when they come in all shades of white these days? For some of the guys, it's not as bad as the other races. We colonized them, the boys say, we subdued them. We conquered. Sure, some of them are lippy now, but that's 'cos of all that woke Black Lives Matter snowflake bullshit infecting us from overseas. And besides, if you look at the history, the alternative history no one admits is there, the archaeological digs—they weren't the first ones here.

And anyway, she's obviously more white than brown, that much is clear. And a slut's a slut, like the boys always say. Not like their white ancestors didn't do what they liked with the natives when they were conquering the world. And what does it matter? She was a tease, and he has no intention of seeing her again, so he's off the hook. He's disappointed, yeah, and horny as hell, but he can hold his head up. He took a shot. Johnny is always at him to stop doubting himself. You're a fucking king, Johnny says, and if you believe that, women will impale themselves on your cock just because they can see it in your eyes. So he gave it another go, the perfect gentleman. He knows how to play the game. So what if she didn't go for it? She should be so lucky.

The streets are well lit, but everything at night is a shade of gray, a stark suburbia. If he had the choice he'd be anywhere but here, a place he was never happy. But he has to get the thing done, show some loyalty, prove himself. Then he'll be able to head south again.

Conor crosses the road and heads through the carved gateway to Te Ātiawa Park for the second time that night, where Kenakena Pā once housed many souls, where some of Keri's ancestors once lived and fought and loved, but he doesn't notice, just as no one noticed earlier. One might think the monumental battles and the shattering of the old ways should have been remembered, but no, it's too deeply buried, already so enmeshed in the fabric of things so as to be invisible. One of Keri's friends had thought about netball tomorrow, and another about the softball tournament coming up, their only associations with the park. But it may also be true that they had felt it, some kind of loss, even as they buried the inkling of such things in merriment.

Conor doesn't take a moment to pause beneath the gateway. He tramps through the ghosts who crowd around their fires, reliving meals they'd gathered in the waterways that have disappeared under road and footpath. The boggy ground shifts, a slow wave of mud so imperceptible that Conor doesn't notice it under his squelching boots. He hunkers into his jacket, hands in pockets, his head bent against the early morning wind. A neighboring dog growls at him and barks so viciously he speeds up. The night becomes that barking, as if the whole world's telling him he doesn't belong.

Eleven

NOISE

Felicity doesn't carry a lot of noise. That's the other thing that makes it easy for Wairere to spend time with her. With Felicity, there are no filters, no disguises, no shifting contours. She is what she is, like a rock, or a tree, or a frog, which in Wairere's book, is the most complimentary thing a person can be. Wairere isn't sure Felicity even knows how to lie. She's always saying things other people think are inappropriate, always saying out loud what is supposed to go unspoken. Where other people skirt around her, for fear of being seen and named or just pulled into one of her extensive investigative interviews (for she also asks too many personal questions, and doesn't know when to stop), Wairere feels almost content around her friend's external chatter. Felicity sees her, even though she's not 100 percent aware of what she sees, and because she has no filter, there is nothing under her skin for Wairere to pick up on or shy away from.

When Wairere turned fourteen, Keri asked if she and Felicity would babysit Walty every so often, usually when Keri had work to do, or appointments at Work and Development, or other stuff that Walty couldn't be dragged along to. Very occasionally, Keri goes out to see friends, and the girls have the house to themselves for the evening. They don't get paid much, if at all, but there's pizza and movies and a general sense of freedom, which makes it worth the trouble. Besides, they both like Walty.

And Wairere likes it when Keri leaves the house for anything that isn't to do with worrying about money. She likes how Keri comes back a bit lighter, unwound, her face de-crinkled and open—at least for a day or two. On the day that Keri goes to the girls' night at the pub, Wairere and Felicity decide to take Walty to the park while Keri gets ready. They sit on the swings while Walty tears around the rest of the play area, which in addition to the swings is just a slide and a climbing frame and a sandpit with a big wooden digger. It's the big wooden digger that Walty loves most, coming as it does with the opportunity to get sand in all the pockets and seams and cuffs of his clothes. No doubt he'll leave a trail of sand in his wake when it's time for a bath.

"Where's your mum going?" Felicity asks. She's chewing gum loudly.

"Out with friends. Thank god. She needs to get her sense of humor back. Sometimes she just won't leave me alone."

"What is it this time?"

"Oh, she wants me to do kapa haka for the Culture Fest. I can't think of anything worse."

"Yeah, but you'd be good, wouldn't you, Wai? And Culture Fest is fun. Or at least, the food is fun."

"Nah, I'm terrible. And I hate performing in front of a crowd. Some people love it, so they can do it. But Mum wants me to 'have my culture' because she didn't have it. There are other ways to have our culture."

"Like kai." Felicity gets that look on her face, the one she always gets when thinking about food. "Maybe we can cook something?"

"Mum'll probably go for that actually. And she'll be in a good mood after she has a night out."

"My parents take turns going out, but only to the gym and, like, indoor netball. When they go out for fun they insist on taking me most of the time."

"Do you like that?"

"Yeah. I get whatever I want off the menu. Mum says it's good for my social skills, but then she's always the first one to get embarrassed if I say the wrong thing."

"And your dad?"

"Sometimes he thinks it's funny. Most of the time he doesn't notice. I think I might be more like him."

"I don't know who I'm like. I can't remember my dad."

"Don't you want to know?"

"Not really. I mean, he didn't care enough to stick around so why would I care about him?"

"You might be more like him."

"I can't imagine it. Mum hated him so much she kicked him out."

"So it's not his fault, it's hers?"

"It just is. I don't agree with Mum about most things, but I believe her about him. Not that she's ever told me anything except that he wasn't a good person to have around a little baby. And I've got enough to worry about without a dad. Walty's dad was my stepdad for a while, but we always had to tiptoe around him. And then he started pushing Mum around, so I can't say my experience of dads makes me want one particularly."

"My dad is boring and embarrassing, but I reckon I'd want to know him if he didn't live with us."

"That's because your dad is boring and embarrassing, but also nice."

"Ew. Don't talk about my dad."

Wairere shoves Felicity sideways.

"Waaaiii!" Felicity squeals and jumps out of her swing, running behind Wairere. She pushes her hard, so that the swing hurtles wildly into the air.

"Noooo! Felis! I can't see Walty!"

Walty had been happily digging his pit, but he now looks around, attracted by the squealing. He jumps up and runs over while Felicity keeps pushing Wairere as high as she can go.

"You're flying, Wai!" Walty calls.

"Don't come too close, Walty!" Wairere is up in the air when she says it, and she knows Walty is coming toward them too fast, she knows Felicity doesn't have any younger siblings, doesn't know how to predict their movements. She knows Walty won't be able to see where to stop so that Wai doesn't come crashing into him on her swing. "Felicity! Stop, Walty!"

Wairere sees it all just before it happens. Walty runs under the swing while she's in the air, Felicity's eyes widen in alarm as she realizes he's right in the path of Wairere on the backward swoop. The best Wairere can do to avoid the full force of her body slamming into her brother is to get off the swing immediately, at its full height, before it begins the swing back. They used to do it as kids, but it's been a long time, and never from such a height. Wai sees all of this in an infinitesimal shard of time, and in the following moment, she launches her body into the air, and suspends there for another tiny point in time before she is compelled by gravity to hurl, sickeningly fast, toward the earth. The landing is hard, pain shoots up both shins as well as the hands that have reflexively flung outward to protect her head. The wind is pushed out of Wairere's lungs and she can't breathe for a second that feels like minutes. And then sound rushes back in and she can hear Walty wailing. She wants to run to him but something in her own body needs tending first. It hurts, it really hurts. How did she do this all the time when she was little? She realizes she can bear the pain but she hasn't managed to get enough air back in her lungs, so she concentrates on breathing. She knows Walty well enough to understand that his cry signals shock and minor hurt—it's nothing like the desperate sound he made when he broke his forearm at two years old.

"Wai! Wai!" He is running to her. "You okay, Wai, you okay?" He's bending down, his head sideways, looking at her like a curious puppy, his face wet with tears.

"Yep." She's still trying to breathe, but manages to get enough air in her lungs to speak. "You okay, buddy?"

"The swing hit me!" He points to his forehead where a red welt is rising. "It'll stop hurting soon," he tells himself, then sniffs and wipes the tears with the back of his hand.

"You're so brave, Walty!" Felicity is giving Wairere the same puppy dog expression. "Oh my god, I'm so sorry, Wai. You okay? Anything broken?"

"No—just my—" She takes another breath. "Just my breathing." The pain in her arms and legs is dissipating.

"That was so heroic! You really flew! And you saved Walty from being knocked out, or worse."

"You are da Superman, Wai!"

"Maybe Superwoman, eh, Walty?"

"Superwai-leh-leh." Walty can't roll his R's without them sounding like L's. Wairere imagines some kind of Pasifika goddess, draped in leis. But she doesn't feel super at all, she feels a bit shattered.

"Doesn't matter, eh, Walty?" Wai reaches out.

"Yeah." Walty allows himself to be pulled in for a hug.

When she's caught her breath, Wai gets up and is surprised to find that after the first couple of steps, she straightens out and doesn't hurt at all. They walk to a good spot under the trees, holding hands in a line, Walty in the middle.

"Let's lie down and watch the clouds for a bit. Then we go home." They lie down in a row, swinging their arms and legs as if they're making snow angels, even though it's only grass beneath them. Then they play the cloud game, which is lame at first because there aren't enough clouds and all the ones they can see are wispy, without enough substance to look like anything other than clouds. But it's a windy day, so other, fluffier, dark clouds rapidly come into view.

"Mud," says Walty.

"Sea," says Wairere.

"No, you guys. You have to name something that is an actual shape! Like, cat or horse. I see . . . a nose?"

"That's not an entire thing though, is it, Felis? Not much better than mud. Like, a whole face would be something."

"Okay, um, tortoise!"

"Where?"

"There." Felicity points emphatically and Wai tries to line up her sight to see right along her friend's arm to the point in the sky she's looking at.

"It's a very blobby tortoise. It's kind of cloud shaped."

"Cloud!" Walty exclaims for the fifth time, giggling.

"Oh, there he goes again. Maybe we should go," Felicity says.

"Nah, just a bit longer." Wairere is drowsy and no one really feels like going. It's warm on the grass where they lie—the movement of cloud and wind makes them sleepy.

"What are clouds?" asks Walty.

"It's water, Walty, up in the sky," says Felicity, as if this explains everything.

"Why?" Walty means how, but Wairere realizes she couldn't explain either why or how. She elbows Felicity.

"I don't know. Do you know, Wai? I can't remember what they said in science."

"Something about heat and evaporation?"

"Gases. That's right. Clouds are water made into gas, Walty."

"Why?" It's clear none of these words have meaning for Walty.

"What about Rangi and Papa? You could tell Walty that story, Wai? I mean, it kind of explains things."

Wairere doesn't want to tell the story of the separation of Sky and Earth. They've got a book at home anyway, and Walty has heard it many times. He just likes to ask why because it keeps them talking. "Yeah, there's Rangi's tears falling on Papa, and Papa's tears rising to Rangi as mist, and cloud too, I suppose." But there's something else, far more interesting to her. "What about how our bodies are mostly made of water? Do you think we're part earth, part sky?"

Walty's eyes are round, but then he laughs. "Don't be silly, Wai."

"No, really Walty—we're just like the clouds in a way."

"Nooo, silly." Walty reaches out and grasps her forearm, shaking it a little as if to demonstrate how solid it is. "You're not water, Wai."

Except she thinks that maybe there is something in it—some connection between how the waters of the earth move into the sky and how there are waters inside them. At least, that's how it feels to her. The others continue the game while Wai stares into the sky.

"You okay, Wai?" Felicity raises her eyebrows at Wairere.

She nods. She is. It all seems a bit obvious really, once you think about it, but most of the time they're not thinking about it at all. Maybe it explains how she feels when she's near the swamp. "We could just stay here," she says. "I like it here." But Walty is already on the move. And it must be time to head back. She gets up. "Let's go this way, Walty, past the pond."

Across the road from the park is the artificial pond that captures the waters that used to flow through the entire area. The native replantings have brought with them more birds and insects than there were when it was all lawn and farm, and they can hear the tūī warbling with their glucks and musical trills. They even see a kererū swoop overhead from one stand of bush to another, lifting its heavy body skyward with the most determined and noisy flapping of wings. In another time altogether, their ancestral cousin Tūteroa made a good catch of kererū here, on the heke from Taranaki to Wellington. The whānau feasted that night, and their satisfaction can still be felt in certain pockets of air if one knows how to detect it. All of this sits behind the contentment the kids feel in this moment, even if they aren't aware of it. The air on their skin, the light filtering through the leaves above them, the particular shade of blue in a late afternoon sky.

But Wairere told Keri they'd be back before she leaves, so eventually they drag themselves away from the swamp and head the last few blocks home. People get off buses in their path and dog walkers try to get past with their dogs. It's home time for everyone.

At home, even though he hasn't mentioned his head since the accident, Walty runs to Keri.

"I got bonked!" he says, pointing to the red mark on his forehead.

"Oh, poor baby—what happened?" Keri crouches to look.

"The swing hit me!" Walty is working up a performance now, pushing out his lower lip and whimpering.

"Lemme kiss it!" Keri bends her lips to his head, missing the red mark. He tolerates the kiss and behaves as if it has some magical power to heal. "Pizza will make it better too, eh?"

Walty nods emphatically, bouncing on his feet, immediately forgetting his act.

Keri has left a Domino's voucher and her debit card with enough money on it for three small classics on the table, as long as they stick to the most boring varieties. Luckily, no one minds this—Felicity only eats cheese pizza, Walty ham and pineapple, and Wairere vegetarian.

"If you all ate the same kind, it might be easier." Keri doesn't really care—it's nice to indulge them a bit. "There's something else in the freezer for after."

"You look nice, Keri." Felicity narrows her eyes and examines Keri's outfit. "Very flattering, that cut." Wairere finds the way Felicity talks to her mother, like they're both adults, weird—though she agrees. Her mother looks younger, and she can almost imagine her as someone who isn't just a mum. She *knows* there is more to Keri's life than them, but she can't see it most of the time.

"Lock the doors and don't open them to anyone! The pizza

can be left on the doorstep, just pay with my card online." Keri continues to list off the rest of the safety briefing.

"Yes, Mum. We know! Go away now." Wairere and Felicity push Keri toward the door, but she scoops up Walty, and there is an extended cuddle before she leaves.

"Bye-bye, Mama!" Walty turns before Keri has even closed the door. "Pizza time!"

By the time the pizza comes, they're in pajamas and they've made a blanket fort to watch old cartoon movies. Wairere and Felicity don't mind the kids' stuff—*Shrek*, *Lilo & Stitch*, *Brave*—and they keep watching long after Walty has passed out, his lips still ringed with ice cream from the Goody Goody Gum Drops Keri left in the freezer.

The girls keep watching and talking long into the night. Keri comes in and doesn't say much except goodnight around midnight. She makes them hot chocolate from baking cocoa, the gross kind—Felicity has Milo at her house—and then she goes to bed. She doesn't look as young or as light as she did at the start of the evening. Wairere feels the shift but ignores the feeling that comes with it. She's having too much fun pretending, for once, that she's like any other kid, thoughtless, enjoying what is in front of her instead of thinking about all the things beyond that, using only five senses instead of tuning in to the extra ones that everyone has but very few notice. Sometimes it's nice just to be a girl. But later, after Felicity falls asleep and the house is quiet, Wairere can't sleep. She gets up and paces, trying to slow her breathing, trying not to listen for every sound. As she passes her mother's doorframe, she feels it again, her body loosening as if she just fell from a height, a fluid, disorienting drop. Then the thought appears, clear, as if it has been spoken: something wants in. Something wants a part of them, to have or to destroy, it's hard to say. She sees that it's nearby, this thing, that it doesn't even know itself what it is. She goes around the house again, checking all the windows and doors, and doesn't know what to do, doesn't want to wake Keri, doesn't know how to keep them safe or ever sleep again. Finally, she curls up beside Felicity—serene Felicity who never adds to the noise in Wairere's head—and thinks about the promise her nan made to be there for her. And even though she isn't there, and Wairere is still mad about that, she starts talking to her nan, starts telling her all of her fears, and asking her for whatever protection the dead are capable of giving, and eventually, when dawn light starts filtering into the room, she feels safe enough again to close her eyes.

Twelve

TEA

Keri has had to plan carefully. Make sure her visitors come after a payday so there will be a decent kai. She'd wanted to say more last time they spoke—how nice it is to have neighbors from elsewhere, how great to have neighbors who aren't Pākehā, but it didn't feel right to say such things yet. It wasn't about the non-Pākehāness so much as the kinship they might share, despite their very different origins. Even though she feels good about this, Wai has her simultaneously wondering if it is okay to think such things. Anyway, she wants to extend a proper welcome, despite everything she doesn't know and everything she can't afford. She can at least pull together something nice to eat, with a bit of extra effort. She's even baked scones and cookies—though it would have been cheaper to buy cookies than to bake them, with the price of eggs and butter.

She welcomes them, introduces Aliana to the toy box and Walty's room, tells Walty to give the poor girl some space when she refuses to look at them. Crouching, she whispers to her son, "Walty, Aliana is shy. You need to be gentle, okay? If you can do that, I think she'll be your friend, but you have to be patient."

He nods, and they bring out the library books to scatter between the children in the living room, Walty trying his best to read in a quiet voice, shuffling closer to Aliana at a slow pace, in between each reading. Aliana shows no signs of running away, yet.

"He's a good boy," says Sera, nodding toward the children. "He tries so hard."

"Yes. He's on his best behavior, that's for sure. He's never had a friend next door before!"

Sera smiles and looks around the room. Keri is suddenly aware of the clutter spilling out of shelves and cupboards, which she has tidied away as best she could. Sera's gaze returns to her. "I'm sorry for staring. I haven't been in many New Zealand homes," she says.

"Ah, yeah, well. Maybe ours isn't typical." Keri tries to see her living room through the eyes of a newcomer. Shabby, cozy, perhaps. Messy but not grubby. Colorful—there's that.

"How did you end up coming to Aotearoa, anyway, Sera? I mean, if you don't mind me asking. I'd love to hear the story, if it's not too intrusive? I'm genuinely interested."

Sera hesitates, and Keri is worried she's being too nosy already.

"Let me get the kai. You have a think." She heads back to the kitchen, not knowing how to tell Sera to tell her to shut up if she oversteps some invisible boundary she's not aware of.

Keri returns and places the plate of scones on the coffee table, then the plate of cut-up fruit for the kids, before heading back for the tea. She makes sure the children have their water, then hands Sera a massive mug of tea that she has made with a tea bag and milk. Sera asked to have it the way Kiwis do. She said she'd seen this many times, but never tried it. At home, she explained, they still drank their tea with honey and lemon rather than milk and sugar, in small cups or glasses. That sounds much more elegant to Keri, but she loves her mugs of gumboot tea.

"I might not have enough English to tell the whole story," Sera starts. She looks around the room again, then focuses on the children. "Things had been difficult for a long time—since I was a teenager. Also before that. You have heard about the fires? The water wars?"

Keri nods.

"We had to buy water since I was young. The summers just got worse and worse—eventually the food chain gets, er, damaged. The air was no good. Our waste catching fire." And then it is there behind her eyes. She's looking at Keri now but seems focused on what only she can see. "Winter was too short and then there were storms. We were like everyone else—we thought we'd be okay, and we were for a while. And then . . . once it comes, everything changes, instantly, like that." She lifts her hand, softly snaps her fingers.

"I'm so sorry." Jesus. What has she asked? "That's so hard. I didn't know about the things that were happening where you were, but every year we hear about the impossible heatwaves. It probably all blends into one from here." She laughs nervously, sees Sera's face draw back in alarm, stops herself. "I'm so sorry. I do that sometimes, when things are too awful. I don't know what to say. We should have done more to help, but we were probably trying to deal with floods and cyclones at the same time. Was there really a war over water?" Something would have been going on at home as well, with Walty's father. Keri can't remember anything that happened in the world while they were together. He took up all of her attention. She dips her head. All that time she was sleepwalking.

"War?—not really. There were fights, there were . . . criminal gangs. And the politicians were always fighting about water too. It might have been easier if it was a war. That would have made the enemy clear, but we had no one outside ourselves to blame for what happened. We survived." Sera sits forward, her shoulders tight and high. "We went to government compounds—it took only a few months to fill them. We tried to stay. The space kept getting smaller, overcrowded. Aliana was a baby. We didn't want to leave, but . . . the air was so bad."

"Oh. My god."

"Aliana was sick a lot. You know how you *know* things, as a mother? I *knew* we had to go. I knew."

Keri nods. "Yeah. I think I know what you mean."

"It was terrible, but we were lucky. Somehow we made it out early. It was good fortune or the gods or blind luck. I don't know.

It makes me feel sick to think of it. We could have been stuck there much longer."

Keri feels it, the precariousness of the situation, as if it were her own.

"But I don't feel good that we left so quickly either."

"No. No, you wouldn't." There is a pause. Keri feels like she needs to catch her breath. She watches Aliana, pointing to the pictures in a board book, gabbling the names of animals to herself. Her little hand poised above the book, the plump forefinger so determined in its task. How many like her?

"And then you came here?"

"We were given transit in the UK. All of us were sent to different countries in Europe temporarily until we found permanent asylum. The locals hated us coming in, but there was an international agreement."

"Oh yeah—I did hear about that. Emergency UN resolutions. They think they'll need a lot more, too."

"Yes. Emergency. We were at the processing station for two years, and we couldn't go outside the gates. For our own safety, they said, but when you are locked up, it is prison."

"God. I'm so sorry," Keri says again. "I'm glad you got here somehow." She offers Sera the scones while automatically taking a massive bite of her own, her ferocious chewing a kind of panicked response to her new friend's tale.

"UK couldn't wait to get rid of us. It did not matter that we were legal. But it was good for us. They processed us and we came here." Sera clasps and unclasps her hands, rubbing her fingers together. "I don't know if I can feel it yet."

Keri raises her eyebrows. She can't finish her mouthful. "You mean?"

"Safe, settled. I think we are, but I don't know. Physically."

"Of course. No. But you will. I hope?"

Sera looks at Keri, shrugs, spreads her hands and examines them. Keri waits. What else can she possibly say?

"I would like to know about your life too," Sera says, clearly ready to change the subject. "Do you have a partner or job?"

"No! No partner." Keri laughs quietly, seeing a sudden flash of Conor's neck bent toward her. She shakes off the vision. "And no job right now. I've stayed home with Walty as long as I could. I want him to have me around, you know? But it didn't work out with his dad. Or Wairere's dad. I don't pick good ones."

It's Sera's turn to be embarrassed. "I'm sorry. Was I rude? I don't know how much to ask sometimes. I think you are very brave."

"Either brave or stupid! No, it's fine. I started it. And your husband seems nice. I've only seen him from afar, but I bet you chose well."

"I am very lucky. Adam was an ambulance driver at home, so it was very dangerous. But he is a good man, and he looks after us."

"Do you think he'll get work here?"

"It might be hard for him if he has to retrain to get New Zealand, er, I don't know the word . . ."

"Endorsement? Certification?"

"Certification, yes. But he is looking for a job."

The children are playing with Walty's cars, lining them up and racing them. Walty making all the sound effects.

"Will you put Aliana in preschool? I can tell you about the different ones around here. Walty goes to Little Tikes twice a week, but there's a Rudolf Steiner and a Montessori and a kōhanga too. We kind of missed out on the kōhanga when Walty was littler, so it might be too much for him now. Wish I could give him the reo, though."

Sera stares at Keri, clearly trying to make sense of the jumble of words that poured forth after her mention of preschool. Sera opens her mouth. Closes it again. Finally she says, "Preschool, yes."

"I'm sorry—I've confused you." Keri looks into Sera's eyes then, properly. "Look, I might be clumsy in the way I say things, but I just want you to know I am here to help, or just be a friend, you know? Kiwis aren't very good at *saying* things, in general. We're good at being polite, but we don't know how to do the other stuff. Māoris are better at that. Some of us, anyway. I just say things. And that can be a bit much. But I'd rather say things than not. So the thing I'm saying is, I'm here, okay? If you need anything. You've come a long way. I can't believe you called *me* brave!"

Sera focuses intensely on this speech, and when Keri finishes, she sees tears in her companion's eyes.

"Oh no!" Keri exclaims. And then there are tears forming in her own eyes. "Sorry! I'm a flamboyant crier. And I always pick it up off other people. Just ignore me."

Sera laughs. "We will be friends," she says simply, wiping her tears with the edge of her skirt.

"Yeah. That's right." Keri laughs too. Walty and Aliana are twirling, swinging their arms out and falling in a dizzied pile. "I'll go get the cookies."

She heads to the kitchen. More tea, she thinks. That's enough saying things for now.

Thirteen

SCORCH

The details Sera tells Keri about their journey to Aotearoa are objectively true, but the real events of that life have already faded into a weird twilight of unreality. Sometimes Sera gets lost in that out of the way place. When her mind stays with her body, everything seems doable; with her feet in the sand, or on the lawn, or even on the carpet, when Aliana is in sight or at least within hearing distance, with Adam at her elbow. When she is held in this world by touch or taste or sound. Then she's fine. But her mind is too busy to stay in one place. Circling back in time and over oceans isn't only for swamps.

And it is true that there is a hunger in her for all the places and things that were. Adam has it too, she knows, but he has found his own way through the thicket of grief. The truth is, she doesn't like herself for her inability to let go. She judges herself as weak, and worse, boring. She used to be the one people gravitated to, so strong, so capable, even, at times, serene. She used to be proud of her coping skills. The poster girl for resilience.

But they had to leave, that's what she always comes back to in the end. There is no equation that sees them staying in a city that isn't inhabitable anymore. Living in New Zealand feels like stepping back in time, not because it's old-fashioned or stuck in the past, but because they can breathe here. And people walk around as if everything they have will always be there—the greenness, the air, their families and homes.

Bouts of grief and yearning come at her like a hard slap in slow motion: her face turned away, the slow dawning of shock. It wouldn't be so bad if it didn't keep her away from everything that is here, in front of her, and good—she can see even if she can't feel that her life is so good. So she tries to dig her toes in, to cling to that knowledge, but sometimes she can't resist, and then she is back in the past, trying to conjure the taste and smell of that world. Sometimes she tortures herself with it: what she didn't do, what she could have done. What she couldn't escape.

The time Uncle Balty's housing estate was razed, not by arson or bad wiring, but by a day so hot they had all retreated to swimming pools and movie theatres and cooling centers to wait out the noon heat. They used to go to the river, but it had turned to toxic sludge and was rarely cooler than lukewarm in summer. The fish had long ago succumbed to the heat and added to the stink. No one had died that time, thank the gods, because so few had been at home. Afterward, they had gone with their uncle to see if they could retrieve anything—Adam had the biggest car in the family, which wasn't saying much—but there was nothing left other than the burned-out shells of houses and cars; gutted brick and steel frames standing like charred skeletons. Sera would never forget the sound Uncle Balty made, a kind of choking in his throat that he couldn't control as it became a keening. She'd never heard a man make a sound like that.

From young adulthood, she doesn't really remember a summer without the fires. She was twenty-two or twenty-three the year they survived four heatwaves in a single summer. For ten days in a row, the daytime temperature hit 116 degrees or more. Wildfires spread for 70,000 acres, destroying two towns, roads, farmland, forest. Their city hadn't been in the path of the fire itself, but fire needs a lot of oxygen, and smoke fills a lot of space. They lived under blazing skies for weeks and, in the end, counted 6502 heat-related deaths in three months—the number seared in her memory because she had wondered how that could possibly be true. There was no memorial, no public outcry, no collective decision to change things. They started publicity campaigns for the heat sicknesses: COPD, asthma, heatstroke; buy your air filters, stay inside, breathing exercises, stress reduction, tinfoil on the windows, water in the bath. Protect yourself from The Great Heat, they'd said, as if it were a limited event, as if there were any protection to be had.

She rarely met people who had been displaced by the fires. They just went on with life—surviving the storms that came. Her cousin Linny worked with support services and told her stories, but even she treated each incident as isolated—that's all they could do, she'd said, deal with things case by case. In their city, it was business as usual, each store and business owner stubbornly continuing no matter what. There was nothing dramatic enough to put an end to business, no outward sign that suggested panic was the correct response. She can see, now, how they couldn't have imagined it. Not really. They'd seen it was bad, but they thought they'd all get through, in the end. After all, they'd always been there. They'd always found a way.

At first, the local governments of each district would call a state of emergency only one or two weeks a year, then one or two months a year. People were hopeful these conditions were temporary, and wasn't a little more heat pretty nice really, all they had to do was find ways to live with it? After that there were evacuation *seasons*. In summer, Sera and Adam would go north to the sea, if they could, or to family if all the holiday homes were taken. Eventually there weren't any spare holiday homes, or mobile homes, or tent sites. The permanent evacuations began soon after.

By that time, they had Aliana in their arms. Aliana, small but perfectly formed. Aliana, all their ancestors' dreams in one small bundle. She was a beautiful baby, but she wasn't particularly strong. She was born in spring, and by summer, without a proper house, without clean air filters, the family were exposed. They had temporary accommodation, but it wasn't enough. Sera felt a great swelling of rage at their predicament, a great surge of power: she'd do whatever it took to find her baby a safe place to grow and breathe.

Sera and Adam weren't the only ones. She'd kept telling herself that—we're not the only ones—as if that would make any difference to their survival or anyone else's. Being just like everyone else was not going to save them. What they needed was to become exceptional, but how might they do that?

People were attempting to escape north, and people were attempting to escape all the way south, a journey that seemed impossible given they had to traverse the equator to get there. There were so many refugees moving through all the nations of Europe, so many flowing in and out of each other's countries. Sera and Adam wanted to stay put. They didn't want to leave the family they still lived close to, and they couldn't think where to go anyway—how could they guarantee it wouldn't be worse? But their city, and then their entire district, steadily became uninhabitable. It wasn't like anyone had planned it. How can you plan for such a thing? Even the most stoic of stayers ran away when the fire began to scorch their heels, and when the time came for Sera and Adam, they made the decision to apply for refugee resettlement overseas.

Britain wasn't the goal. Even though it had been one of the cooler countries before The Great Heat, its position in the north made it more susceptible to sudden extremes of temperature, and the government had never been able to raise a system that could deal with those extremes—Britain after Brexit was just too poor to rebuild an infrastructure. But Britain was where they were able to stay while they waited for their claim to be processed. They didn't have much choice—they just hoped to get as far south as they could, eventually. Few other places held the allure of New Zealand—its snowy mountains, vast lakes and rivers, extensive coastline. So much rain. So much air.

The Processing Center consisted of a compound with three large buildings the size of airplane hangars—maybe they were actually airplane hangars?—ill-equipped for human habitation, but at least their size allowed the free flow of air. In each building, there were toilets and showers installed at one end and ready-made units in rows, ranging in size from small to very small; room only to accommodate a bed and cupboard, a shelf and a small refrigerator if you could afford it. No one was meant to be there more than six weeks, but by the time Sera and Adam arrived, most of their neighbors had been there more than a year. Food was dished out three times a day, reliable but devoid of much nutritional value. Health and Safety didn't allow cooking in the units, or even outside them. Residents, or "temps" as the staff called them, were permitted free run of the place, but they weren't allowed beyond the razor wire fences that contained all three buildings.

Adam, Aliana, and Sera were given a unit in the family hangar—single men and women and couples were in the other two. When they arrived they were issued some blankets and sheets, a couple of foam pillows. There was no cot, no fan, and no sink or tap in the room. The bathrooms—four toilets and two showers for hundreds of women and girls, the same for the men and boys—were twenty-one units away. Somehow, Sera managed to obtain one of the few plastic basins that could be taken to their room.

It wasn't comfortable, it wasn't sanitary; there would only

be rudimentary protection from the heat in summer and the storms in winter, but they were so happy those first few nights. They could breathe. The air smelt of too many bodies, of the toilets and also the meal of chili beans or chicken sausages they'd been served, but what it didn't smell of was smoke. They were alive and they had shelter and food.

Those first nights, they slept like they hadn't slept for years, with Aliana between them and the wall. Sera had to curl her body around her daughter to make sure there was room, and they placed her on top of a collection of folded clothes so that she wouldn't get squashed. After three days and nights, the newness began to wear off, as did their tiredness. That was when they noticed the constancy of the noise—not just their neighbors talking, but people leaving their units to go to the bathrooms, children crying, adults sobbing or yelling out in their sleep. After a few weeks, they became listless, like their neighbors. There was nothing to do but wait. It was an awful thing, they discovered, to have no occupation and no purpose.

"We will give Aliana all our attention," Sera said.

Adam smiled. "She will be our occupation."

Sera wasn't sure either of them were really convinced, but they did enjoy lazy afternoons with their daughter, gurgling her first word-like sounds, and soon after, her first giggles as her father tickled her belly with his beard.

But they did find work to occupy them, eventually. Sera made friends with other mothers who needed to find a way to educate their children. There was no unit large enough to hold a gathering, so they would congregate in the only empty corner of the hangar where food was often stored, or outside if the conditions were right. Getting outside was always a revelation, but it was often too hot or too cold, and the hangar was marginally better. When donations of clothes came in, they'd often get books too, so they began teaching what they could: reading, maths, social sciences, history. It depended whether the donations brought in novels or encyclopedias, *Where's Spot?* or *Rich Dad Poor Dad* or *Persuasion*. Sometimes they got paper or crayons. Mostly Sera just liked the idea of reading to Aliana, even though she was still a baby.

Adam found a way to make himself useful as a medic, and he would be called on any time of night or day. They had enough first-aid equipment in the hangar to patch up scrapes, even stitch injuries. He didn't talk about it to Sera, but when he was called in the night, it wasn't unusual for her to find out later it was because someone had hurt themselves on purpose. Sometimes they didn't get there in time. Adam would come back silent, using his shoulders to block her questions. She'd turn to him in bed, facing his back, and place her hand on his arm. It was the only time in their marriage he could not respond.

Sera tried to accept that this was their life, at least for now. Once a month, the toilets got backed up, and the stench was unbearable. Rubbish was taken away only every second week, so if it wasn't sewage it was garbage that reminded them, even with their eyes closed, of where they were and how they were valued. Sera dreamt of overflowing toilets and worried that Aliana would get sick. The viruses and bacterial infections that circulated were beyond Adam's first-aid kit. All he could do was provide electrolytes and painkillers if he had them, which wasn't always. Communications with the outside world were slow, applications for assistance slower. The only thing Sera allowed herself to believe in was the possibility that her letters and phone calls to different refugee and immigrant programs would eventually yield some change in circumstances.

There was a razor wire fence around the Processing Center, to keep people out as much as to keep them in. The gates opened and closed a few times a day to let supply trucks in, mostly early morning and late at night—nobody moved in the midday heat—so anyone who was in the yard taking advantage of early or late cool air would witness the transition. There was a military efficiency to it: protocols for how long the gates stayed open, what Security could say to drivers and vice versa, how close temps were allowed to get. Temps had been allowed a small communal garden in the yard, and one morning Sera and Adam were out weeding the beans and corn, letting Aliana feel and smell the rosemary and mint, when there were shouts and scrambling, the grinding of brakes and the sudden sharp smell of hot tires skidding on asphalt. Everything after that happened quicker than thought: they heard two shots, and Sera saw Aliana's face draw back in alarm, registering shock at the ear-piercingly loud sounds and the fear on her parents' faces. Before she could cry, Adam threw his body over Aliana, pushing Sera down as he moved. She concentrated on breathing, praying that Aliana would be okay, praying that nothing else would happen to them or anyone else that morning. Eventually she realized that the shooting had stopped almost as soon as it had started.

Sera and Adam stayed close to the ground, Aliana squirming and crying between them, while the immediate drama was dealt with. They could hear that someone was calling out in pain, but also that they were being arrested, alongside a couple of others. They couldn't see much from where they lay, but the group seemed to have been after the contents of the truck. Security told Adam and Sera to stay put until the intruders were secured. This took half an hour, by which time the sun had moved until the receding shadow of the hangar almost exposed the family. The ground would be hot within minutes, so they were relieved when they were given the signal to get up. They quickly retreated to their unit. It was already warm in there, stuffy enough to make them sweat.

"All gods, I hate this place," Sera said as she fed Aliana. She rocked back and forth, not sure who she was comforting more: her baby or herself.

"That would be us, though, if we weren't here." Adam nodded toward the door. The wounded intruders were still out there—waiting for the authorities and whatever medical care they brought.

"I know. I know." This was their immediate conundrum. At least they had food and water, however substandard, at the Processing Center. Out there, with freedom, would they even have that? They couldn't be sure they even wanted liberty at this point.

Sera looked at her husband, and said it again: "I know. But this is not life."

"No. It is not life. It is not death either."

They turned away from each other then. How much time did they spend doing this while they were in captivity? How long had they spent speaking in circles?

"They don't want us in this country," Sera said, thinking of the way the processing staff looked at her family, and spoke to them as if they were slow.

"They don't want anyone."

"No. But they especially don't want us. We are too foreign. We look wrong. We don't speak good English. We won't fit in."

"We could fit in."

"But they won't let us."

"We will be processed, eventually."

"But how long, Adam? And what will we become while we wait?"

She was rocking and rocking. Aliana started squirming, so Adam took her, but Sera kept rocking. They had nothing, they lived nowhere, they were nobodies. And this could last forever. She'd heard of it. Generations of refugees. Maybe that would be them. Or it could change tomorrow. Time spiraled out in front of her, dizzying, and she rocked into it, losing sight of her husband and daughter. If only she could stop needing so much, if only she could become nothing. But no, she couldn't stop hearing and seeing and smelling, even in her trance. The toilets were blocked up again, she could smell that from their room.

Adam placed the baby on the bed, placed his hands on either side of Sera's face, and crouched so he could look into her eyes. "My heart," he said.

Her eyes were downcast.

"Sweetness."

She wasn't sweet. She was a lunatic. Not fit to be a mother. She couldn't do this.

"Remember when we met, and we got gelato and went down to the bay, and you dropped it all over your new white dress? It was green. You were so mad and embarrassed at the same time."

"What has that got to do with anything?" Now she was furious too.

"Deep down, I know beyond any doubt that we will have a chance for you to embarrass yourself with ice cream again, and get mad about it. I have complete faith. I promise you, it will happen."

"Idiot." She scowled at him, but she was back in the room again, back in herself. She breathed in, the sickly sweet stench of human filth, but she didn't care. She had survived worse. "One day we will have ice cream by the sea again, and I will drop it on your clothes, not mine!"

Adam smiled. "And Aliana will have an ice cream as big as her head!"

They lived that life the best they could, and Aliana grew strong enough to crawl and walk. Each day they would let her toddle from unit to unit, chattering to their neighbors, as Sera or Adam held her hand. The circumstances of their lives didn't matter to her, she was delighted with each new face, each new pebble on the ground, corncob dolls and hand-drawn books, the odd little school where the women taught their children what they could about the world. The community grew close around its babies, who brought happiness with them even on the dreariest of days. If this wasn't life, at least they had isolated moments of joy.

During their second winter, when dysentery spread through the units, they had to curtail all contact with others. Sera redoubled her efforts to find a way out, checking her application with every immigration officer and governmental official she could find. They'd been at the Processing Center nearly two years when they received news: as health workers, they both fit long-term skill shortage categories, so they would soon be welcomed to New Zealand. They were refugees from long-term ecological disaster, but none of the official channels cared to tell that story. They were taken based on the skills they offered rather than their need, but they were happy to exploit the loophole. They would take what they got, hungrily, gratefully, hopefully, but they knew who they were. They were shadow refugees, leaving smoke and singed footsteps in their wake.

Fourteen

TROLL

When you spend enough time online, it becomes easy to manipulate people. You just have to look for patterns in the way they interact, and eventually you see what is important to them—what, and who, they care about, what they desire, who they want to impress. You watch for a while, and once you see all of that, it's like you know them, but it's not the same as knowing a person in real life—it's like a more intimate version of them, the version they hold inside their own heads and project onto the world. It can be powerful to know that version of someone. Once you see all that they think they are, you can find the gaps, and once you find the gaps, you can take a stick and poke it in the gaps and wiggle it around, so that the person twists and writhes, trying to get away from the prodding. And if you want to, you can knife the gap, to make a bigger hole, to make it bleed. Given time and determination, you can plant a bomb there and watch it detonate. Watch that person's whole life explode, pieces of them splattering everywhere—messy, bloody, shocking. There's something satisfying in that.

There's another way too, not for the fainthearted. Place something rotting in the gap. Send in some bacteria, a phalanx of trolls for example, who you've armed with the right weapons—ridicule and contempt can work like a disease, eating that person from the inside out. Done the right way, this can be even crueler than detonating a bomb, though it lacks the shock value, and can be depressing. Sometimes you want to save them from themselves by the end of it. But it's their problem, isn't it? They let the disease take hold. They shouldn't be online if they can't take that kind of scrutiny, if they're gonna take it personally.

Conor has seen it all, and he's done it all. At first it was just a game—something that raised the blood pressure a little, a hit of adrenaline for each target down. It was just so *easy* to get people going. Like, most of the time he only says what he believes, but sometimes he plays devil's advocate just to watch the target spiral—the more aloof he can be, the more he doesn't care, the better the reaction: blockings, confessions, arguments with whole groups of people that last days. There is no real way to block someone online. It wasn't unusual for him to be in the same argument on three separate accounts, have them all blocked, and still check out the aftermath on a separate account that he uses only for lurking. He's so good at it, so good at getting people worked up, no matter their special interest, that for a while it became an addiction. He couldn't stop going after big names—big in the online context only—and he didn't like having that compulsion. He wasted hours online, and for what? At the end of a weekend he couldn't remember what he'd done with all those hours. One controversy bled into another, and it took a lot for him to feel anything about any of them after a while. Then, he met Johnny.

Johnny recognized him across a few different platforms—connecting his hardcore @conorectal alias with his tame @CBGBs right-wing chat alias. Once that boundary was breached, it took no time for Johnny to follow the conversations outward to more profiles, though he said he wasn't sure they were all Conor at first. Johnny, under his alias @HomelandJ, chimed in on a thread where @conorectal was on the verge of doxxing a lesbian eco-activist who went by @earthdyke. Conor's issue was that he didn't have the info to dox the dyke. *Someone needs to shut her up, and I can tell them where to find her*, Johnny, even though he apparently didn't have that information either. *Wonder what they will do to her*, @conorectal replied, then made some grotesquely violent suggestions. It was theater to him. No one would actually do those things, but he loved the reactions he could elicit. @earthdyke retweeted all of this and their mentions erupted: turns out she had strong Green Party connections, and when MPs started condemning the pair publicly and reporting their accounts, Conor and Johnny went silent. Johnny found Conor on a different platform a few days later, and they started to chat, privately.

@HomelandJ: so you just playin or what?

@conorectal: yeah, probably. Like to make em squirm

@HomelandJ: let me know if you ever want to get serious. There's a real culture war that could use someone like you

@conorectal: really? I'm just fucking with people

@HomelandJ: But fuck with them in the right way and you can get them right where you want them

@conorectal: for what?

And that's when it started. The key, Johnny said, was the disruption of society. Make them see just how warped and fucked up things had got: make them see the need for a different way of life, one that valued traditions, one that took them back to proper values. Anybody could see he was right about the first part: society was fucked. Someone like Conor was the result of a system that didn't give young men a purpose and wasted their god-given power. Conor didn't know about the god part, and he didn't yet know about Johnny's solutions to society's fuckedness, but the problems with everything were as plain as the nose on his face, and he wanted to know more.

It was over subsequent chats that Conor got to see how deep the rabbit hole went: Johnny would send him stuff: videos, manifestos, articles written by like-minded "warriors" as he called them. It was endless. And once he started looking, the algorithms of his online life took care of the rest. He knew this, and yet he couldn't stop looking. There was something compelling about all of it, because deep down he'd always known it was like this. Deep down he'd always known that he was treated like he was expendable. It was as if his thoughts and feelings had no worth because he was a white man in a society that vilified people like him. Deep down he knew all the bleating about black and indigenous rights was a con. He knew they got special treatment—he'd seen it himself. At school, in politics, in the media.

Sometimes Conor wasn't sure about the stuff Johnny sent. Like his spiel about the Jewish thing. Really? That was a bit of a stretch, wasn't it? Though what would he know. Either way he had a lot of time for his new friend. Johnny treated him like he had something special: skills that were actually of use to a higher cause. There was very little Conor had done in his life that had marked him out as useful to anyone. He certainly hadn't developed skills that were remarkable in any way. He had been a mediocre sportsman, an uninterested and unskilled student. He wasn't particularly good-looking and he had few charms for the opposite sex: he worried his hair was thinning, that he didn't have the best musculature, that he might not be endowed well enough in other areas. There must be a reason the girls he met never stuck around.

But Johnny didn't seem to see any of that—Johnny saw the Conor that Conor wished he had enough imagination and guts to bring into existence: a kind of heroic version of himself, and Johnny talked about all the ways he could help bring that Conor into the world. When Conor suggested he hadn't achieved much in life, Johnny wouldn't stand for it.

> @HomelandJ: brother, you just haven't had the right chances yet. That's what this culture does to us, men like you and me—it leaves us on the outside. Because they know what we'd do with the power if we got it back.
>
> @conorectal: yeah I know you're right
>
> @HomelandJ: look how they've got you thinking about yourself. You're a master at getting under the skin of others because you've learned from the best: the government, the communists, Antifa. Do you feel empowered? Do you feel like a strong man?
>
> @conorectal: sometimes I think I do . . .
>
> @HomelandJ: nah that's not it. DO YOU KNOW YOURSELF TO BE A STRONG MAN? Could you shout it in the streets?
>
> @conorectal: no, not really
>
> @HomelandJ: see? But you *are* a strong man—you have what it takes. We have a group that builds men back up again. You wanna join, I'll get you in. You're exactly the type of potential we need.

When Conor showed enthusiasm for this idea, Johnny seemed stoked. They still couldn't meet in person: Johnny didn't disclose his personal details to anyone for security reasons, and said he didn't live in the same city, but they would meet soon. In the meantime, he shared online training programs, and coached Conor in things like physical strength, presentation, dominating a room. Dominating women too, if he just made the right moves.

It was what Johnny said about fighting the culture war that Conor wasn't sure about, at least at first. But he didn't want to seem like a coward either, so he didn't ask too many questions.

@HomelandJ: you know what we are resisting is the Great Replacement eh? You know about that?

@conorectal: sure of course

@HomelandJ: yeah so someone with your skills can help us undermine the homos and the third-world immigrants, take out the pro-choicers. People think it's worst in the US and UK, but those ethno-masochists are rife here. They want us all to "be kind" to each other, meanwhile they're phasing out white people and encouraging the mass breeding of other races. They're getting there too. It might look small, but every time they increase the refugee numbers or open up immigration . . .

@conorectal: yeah I wondered about that

@HomelandJ: see? You *know*. It's a gut feeling. They're doing it right under our noses. At least the States are paving the way for us to get rid of them, and abortions.

@conorectal: does it make that much difference, the abortions?

@HomelandJ: look at the birth rates! It's the white people who aren't replacing ourselves. That's why we have to get rid of the feminists too—the tradwife movement is gaining traction and that's how we're going to fight back. It's our duty to breed our own—have as many kids as you can once you find that woman, or women. I don't have any problem with multiple wives tbh.

@conorectal: dude, I don't disagree but I don't know whether that's me, man. Seems a bit extreme

@HomelandJ: sometimes you gotta get extreme tho, bro, if you don't want to be oppressed. See, that's how they get us. We're not allowed to talk about our own ethnicity, but they can talk all they like about theirs. Man, I'm not a white supremacist! If they're in their own countries they can breed all they like. What I object to is the way they come to our countries and take over, and how our governments let them, even make it easy for them. I'm an ethnopluralist, and I'm fighting this because I don't think anyone's noticing what's really going on.

Conor began to get it, and when Johnny pointed things out—the statistics, the cultural movements, the trajectory they were all on—the reality became clearer. He felt like he was starting to see under the veneer of the polite society that everyone else was living in. The way the government didn't talk about certain policies, didn't pay attention to the graphs that showed the majority of New Zealanders would be Asian or Polynesian in fifty years. It was all there on paper, if you knew how to connect the dots, and he could see where people like him would be at the end of it all. Didn't they have a right to this country that was theirs? This country his people had claimed and named in the eighteenth century—that would be nothing without all the benefits of progress and technology they had brought with them? And there was plenty of evidence that white people had been here longer than that too.

Finally, after months of talking, Johnny invited Conor to something he called the Retreat, though he didn't give him much time to prepare. It was the following weekend, Friday night through to Monday morning, at an undisclosed forest location an hour from Christchurch. Camping gear only. Conor was given coordinates, where he was met by other members of the team in balaclavas, blindfolded, and driven to the retreat.

It was fully weird, but by the time they got him out of the car, placed his backpack on his shoulders, then walked him to the center of a clearing and removed his blindfold, he was excited, grateful even, to finally meet Johnny. He grinned, suddenly feeling shy, of all things, at the bearded man with long fair hair and broad shoulders who regarded him intensely. Johnny was everything he was not: confident, built, stylish. He wanted to impress him, but he knew in that moment that he was kind of a nothing.

Johnny eliminated all his doubts in a second. His face broke open into a wide smile, he stepped forward and gave Conor a bear hug, and Conor was stiff at first, but he couldn't resist the strength of that hug. He leaned into Johnny, felt the muscles of his neck and shoulders relax, tried to return the intensity of the embrace. Then Johnny stood back, patted his arms, still grinning.

"Conor! You're here! I've been waiting for this. And now our group is complete." He introduced the six other men, two of whom, like Conor, had not been before. "Mac here will show you where you're sleeping and the rest of the gear for the weekend, then we'll go over the schedule and protocols."

The retreat was structured around physical activity and intensive workshops. That first night, they built fire and shared food, then everyone introduced themselves and talked about why they were there. Conor had never said so much in a group setting in his entire life, but everyone else had spoken at length, so he thought he should too. He told his life story. Short and uneventful, he thought, but the boys whooped and clapped when he was done and Johnny slapped a hand on his shoulder and told him what he'd said was important. The next day they did military-style obstacle courses, target shooting, historical and political workshops, and personal psychology tests. By the time they gathered around the fire again, Conor was mentally and physically exhausted.

"Get used to it!" Johnny admonished the tired group. "I want you in top condition—prepared to face anything. We could be called on with little notice!"

On the final day, they hunted. Todd had grown up hunting on the West Coast, so he showed the new guys the ropes. Conor had never held a gun before the retreat. They started with target shooting, and he was surprised how easy it came to him. The forestock was smooth and welcoming in his grip, the butt against his shoulder comfortable, solid. He liked the slide and hushed click of the bolt when he loaded the cartridge. He liked the weight of the gun, its heft, the way the power of it would remain quiet, held in, until he determined its release. Now it was time to put their training to the test. He loved the prep, the tracking, the time in the bush. But most of all, he loved the way hunting brought him close to the raw edge of his own life.

When they saw the deer, Conor was overwhelmed with how big and *alive* it was, the power they had to extinguish that life, the way it felt like the hunters and the hunted were in some kind of pact together. He'd never really seen any animals in the wild because he'd rarely been out there himself. A kind of hot joy grew in him all through the day, so that by the time they dragged the deer out of the bush and butchered it, he was as excited as he was repulsed by the gory task.

Todd had made the kill, in the end, but Johnny said they'd done it together. They removed the tenderloins and backstrap for their dinner that night. The rest of the deer would go home with the hunter. Then they built a fire, as big as they could make it without burning down the forest, and painted their faces with deer blood. Someone brought out a bottle of whiskey, and they ate the meat like Vikings, with their hands, juice running down their chins. At some point they started howling and dancing, braying their joy and pain into the night.

Johnny found Conor before the night was done, held him by the shoulders and looked at him. "Conor," he said. "Welcome. This is your initiation. You're part of the Othala Brotherhood now. See this symbol on my neck? That's the rune Othala, or odal, for heritage, homeland, inheritance. That's who we are. We're reclaiming the homeland. And you are our brother now."

Conor tried not to break away from Johnny's gaze, but he felt like crying.

"It's okay to get emotional. That's a good sign." He turned to the group. "Brothers! Let us welcome our new members to the Othala Brotherhood!" Johnny lifted his cup, and a great roar went up.

As the weeks went on, Conor got physically stronger, and his mind got sharper too. He devoured the podcasts and YouTube videos and books with relish. There were late-night calls with Johnny. He began to understand the logic of the movement, the potential of its aspirations. And Johnny wasn't a loose unit. He counseled Conor to be a master of his own emotions and to be choosy about where he showed up online. People wouldn't get it, he said, it would draw the wrong sort of attention. He wasn't like the loudmouth extremists of the world. Johnny's crew wouldn't be stupid enough to project their faces and drum up support for demonstrations that weren't cohesive, didn't go anywhere, and turned the public against them. He had something deeper and bigger in mind than that, and his plans would require total trust and total secrecy. Conor had been chosen, like the half dozen other men involved, and it was important to keep things on the DL until everything was in place. Johnny had even told him to stop the trolling, he didn't need any undue attention. His job was only to watch the hard left and the hard right, the activists, the Māoris, the terrorist radicals—it was important to know what everyone else was doing. That was Conor's job, until told otherwise: to keep track. He didn't know what for, he didn't know what was coming, all he knew was that he trusted Johnny and that Johnny said it was safer for them all to only have a small piece of the puzzle. But Conor was part of something now, something big. Something that might hurt a few people, Johnny had admitted to him, but only in the service of something much greater. That was the way wars worked—there was always some collateral damage. They'd tried everything, Johnny had said, to turn the world on its head. And they'd had a lot of success, even those buffoons who showed their faces on screen, making pacts with outright Nazis and evangelicals. Every little bit helped to destabilize the status quo. But now it was time to get serious. No more pissing about. New order could not be established until they created a vacuum. They were the inner, inner circle of a battle so secret no one else knew it was happening, in a culture war to protect their way of life.

Conor is a member of Johnny's army now, and the army's name is the Othala Brotherhood.

Fifteen

BENEFICENCE

Of the many considerations when designing a Ministry of Public Assistance Work and Development office, the first must surely be blandness: the office should be devoid of all personality, any insinuation of style, most of all any suggestion of intimacy. There must be no toy box with secondhand, semi-chewed toys to be fingered by many children, no symbolic sharing of spit or mucus between the offspring of Work and Development clients. There will be no dog-eared, well-read women's magazines—this is not a doctor's office. Children should be left at home. Clients should wait without fuss until called. This is a workplace, after all. There should be no use of the term "social welfare," with its connotations of charity, poverty, government responsibility, even *socialism*. Work and Development offers benefits for job seekers, not dole bludgers, slackers, single mums, those who don't have the strength or wit to pull themselves up by their own bootstraps, or the enfeebled and infirm, so it is important to give the impression that everyone is working or on their way to work. The office should be clean, featureless, neither too hot nor too cold. There will be a single administrator at reception who will manage the arrival and departure of job seekers, assigning them out to case managers on an ad hoc basis. Ongoing relationships between case managers and job seekers are best avoided so as to make objective decision-making easier down the track. A case manager who knows a client well may be unwilling to cut their benefit by 50 percent should an infraction occur.

Keri runs her hands repeatedly up and down the black metal tubing that attaches the armrest to the seat of her chair in the waiting area. She has already looked through the *situations vacant* cards pinned to the office partition, and is now engaged in a rather boring edition of people watching. Which case manager will she get today? None of them look familiar to her, even though she's in here every few months. From her vantage point she can see most of them, and they can all hear each other. The managers don't smile, but no one raises their voice either. Sometimes one of them stands to go use the copier or consult a colleague. When they do this, she sees more of them: their low-budget office attire: blue shirts and ties and ill-fitting suits for the men; white blouses, cinched skirts, and structured jackets for the women. Occasionally a burst of color in lipstick, scarf, or brooch. Nice shoes or bottle-dyed hair.

The brusque receptionist has gone for a break, so one of the case managers is working the reception. He looks flustered, his tie over one shoulder as he quickwalks to and from the copier. He takes much longer than the receptionist to make copies, and by the time he returns to reception, the line has tripled in size. His next customer is a middle-aged Pākehā man in high-vis gear who leans to one side, bare arms crossed against his chest. Every few minutes he shifts to the other side, looks around, and rolls his head in a half circle. Neck pain. Keri can see it in his posture, the way he can't stay in one position too long. Too familiar. The case manager and the Pākehā man begin a tense discussion over a benefit that has been cut, an appointment that has been canceled, and a vanload of kids waiting outside. The Pākehā man keeps looking out the giant window that Keri sits directly in front of, not that he can see much through the Work and Development logo painted on the other side. After several minutes of back and forth, his voice starts to get louder, he runs a hand through his mullet and puts his hands on his hips. Two new clients arrive and take their place in the line, which now reaches to the door. The case manager asks the Pākehā man to stand aside and wait for someone, then begins to process the others. The Pākehā man runs out the door, then minutes later runs in again to stand at the same spot. Then Keri is called by her case manager for the day.

It's good to be called away. The Pākehā man's frustration has been a distraction from her own anxiety, which has been a bodily sensation in her gut all week, but now she's feeling it in her chest, feeling what it would be like if her own benefit were cut. Everything is so finely balanced on the head of a pin. A few dollars out of place could send her scrambling, but having a 50 percent cut, even for a week? It'd all fall down. It takes all of her will, all of her strength, and all of her energy to keep up with the demands placed on her by the benefit—the community providers she's required to sign up with, the forms she must repeatedly fill out to reapply for the same benefit she is already on, to reapply for support for children she still has, to prove she is not a liar. The time she must spend ringing to declare any casual work she does manage to find, working out childcare arrangements that are costly because they are casual, working out whether that casual work will disadvantage her financially, rendering it an extremely stressful waste of time. If she could find a job that would allow her to work and be a decent sole parent at the same time, she'd certainly take it.

The benefit comes on Tuesday, so that's when the bills come out. Rent takes two-thirds, then power, internet, school fees and associated costs, anything medical, food, transport, clothes. Payday is shopping day, and by the end of it she usually doesn't have anything left. They get their clothes from the Sallies, have no insurances, one cheap prepaid phone each for safety, no money for haircuts or days out or dental care. Wai is supposed to have a computer for school, but since Keri got her a cheap secondhand one, it's kind of useless and slow. Keri got one too for her own study, job applications and the like. She gets them the cheapest internet connection so they have to be careful with how much they use, but it's a life necessity these days: to not have a connection costs them so much more in time, transport, childcare. Even banking in person can cost more. And they both need to study. She tells herself this whenever she has to sacrifice fruit or new underwear to the internet connection.

From Wednesday to Monday, she hopes there are no emergencies. She hopes she doesn't lose her mind and buy them some comfort food or entertainment on the credit card she keeps for emergencies. That credit card has got her into trouble before: once she uses it, it can take her years to pay it back, but she needs it in case one of them gets sick and needs the medical clinic after hours—$100 a pop—or if they need more than the $30 petrol—two car trips for necessities—she budgets each week. Sometimes, she just needs a circuit breaker. When Walty has had her on the go for several days and nights running; when Wai hates her, inexplicably, for whatever reasons a teenage girl hates her mother, probably because everything in the whole world, and yes, it is a pretty shitty world sometimes, is Keri's fault. Sometimes Keri needs a circuit breaker from the shitty world herself, from the stress that infuses her muscles, the clutch of pain at the base of her neck most days, the watery tilt in her gut, the rising tension that moves up into her chest when she wonders how they'll get through. It's the chronic condition of that stress: the way it never goes away, the way survival demands hypervigilance day and night, because one slipup, one over or underpayment, one forgotten appointment, one missed bill, one lapse into frustration, one bout of yelling, one slap, one broken washing machine, one forgotten school trip, one lost assignment, one friendship gone awry, one loose male cannon, one irritated case worker . . . the list of ways she can drop the ball is endless. Sometimes takeaways or chocolate or ice creams for all can give a sweet moment of respite. Sometimes a trip to Te Papa—why not? Why should her kids miss out? Sometimes a night out *without* the kids, JFC. Sometimes those things can make her feel human again, make her feel like she can make it through the next few days or weeks or months. But most of the time she can't afford the twenty-thirty-forty dollars it'll cost to do those things.

The case manager isn't so much hostile as completely aloof. Maybe that's an improvement, and does she really want a case manager who pretends empathy, or even, goddess forbid, sympathy?

"Mrs. Vincent . . ." The case manager's name is Albert Stuntz. She wonders if she is supposed to call him Mr. Stuntz.

"Ms."

"Hm? Right, yes, Ms. . . . Vincent."

"Or just Keri."

"Kerry. I can see you haven't been able to find a regular position yet. The next step for us is to connect you to Pai Community Trust. They have a range of Job Seeking and Skills Development workshops and mentorships." Albert peers at the computer, his eyes darting around the screen as he clicks.

"I've done them before." She'd done so many, and they were often basic and boring, if not just plain condescending. She's pretty sure the grammar and spelling mistakes they insisted she insert to develop her CV did not improve it. She knows she could write more convincing cover letters than their formula dictates. She doesn't need a Job Seeking and Skills Development workshop, she needs a world where a single mother has some work-life-parenting balance. She can't be everything.

"Yes, I see, but there's a new program that Pai Community

Trust have developed since you last worked with them. Perhaps you just need to make your CV more . . . eye-catching, hm? And practice your interviewing skills some more?"

Keri has to consciously refrain from rolling her eyes and swallow the guttural ugh that is forcing its way up from her lungs. UGH, she lets the sound roll around her head, URGGGHH.

And then there is a lot of noise all at once, and Keri wonders for a moment if her inward scream has come out after all, but she follows the sound to a scuffle at reception. The Pākehā man in the high-vis vest is making a kind of mangled cry—she can't tell if it's aggression or he's actually falling apart—gulping and sobbing while trying to yell expletives. He has something in his hand, and in the next moment he's on the case manager filling in at reception, his hand swiftly coming down in the region of the arm, the chest or the neck, Keri can't see, it is all so fast.

"I just . . . I just want . . . I'm a fuckn good dad . . . my fuckn kids . . . fuck."

And then everything speeds up again, Albert is out from behind his desk and so is the other male case manager at the next desk, and they quietly begin to herd the other clients through to another room in the back.

"Please make your way to the safe room, Ms. Vincent. It's important we get to safety now." But Keri can't tear her eyes away from the scene, the only two security guards now attempting to get the case manager who has been stabbed away from the Pākehā man in the high-vis vest. There is blood spreading around a couple of spots on the case manager's shoulder, and he's stumbling a bit, dazed, holding his hand against the flow of the blood. Keri begins to walk toward the safe room, still watching, then stops.

"Please, Ms. Vincent. We can't wait any longer. The police will come to deal with him." Albert looks fearfully toward the Pākehā man in the high-vis vest, who is now standing alone, staring at his hands. He opens the fist that is still clenched around an object and it falls to the floor. Keri sees it is a pen. Then he is out the door. The kids, Keri thinks, that vanload of kids.

"You go, Albert." She says, and he looks from her toward the now empty office. The security guards are helping the wounded case manager through the door to the safe area. Albert follows them.

Keri doesn't think about what she's doing, only that the Pākehā man is headed toward his vanload of kids and he's in no state to look after them. She follows from a distance, watching his hunched walk. He keeps wiping his eyes with his sleeves. As he reaches his van, she gets close enough to talk to him.

"Excuse me," she calls.

He whips around, arms up, ready to defend himself. What was she thinking?

"It's all good! I'm not one of them." She holds her hands up toward him, palms open in a placating way. "I saw what happened. I heard what you said. I just wanted to check if you're okay, and . . . if you need a hand with your kids?"

"I'm just leaving now," he tells her, guarded. "I'm just going to go."

"Yeah, no, I don't think that's a good idea, do you?" The windows and doors of the van are open, legs and arms of various children dangling out. The stereo pumping some Rihanna to keep them company as they wait.

"It's none of your business." He's sweating, his eyes darting around. There's a smudge of blood on his right hand. This was a dumb idea. But still.

"It's just I don't know if it's a good idea to drive, you know, after all that. Maybe sit for a minute and calm down?"

"I've gotta go."

Just keep him talking, Keri thinks, just until he calms down. "Maybe the mum can come get the kids? Give you a minute to think."

"I'm doing this by myself. Their mother fucked off."

"Yeah. It's hard. I'm in the same situation. How many?"

"Five. Two of hers, three of mine. All mine now. Look, I gotta go."

"Dad?" It sounds like one of the younger kids.

"It's okay, Joshua, I won't be a minute." He's jumpy, but he manages to focus on Keri for a moment. "I just gotta get outta here." Then he swiftly runs around to the driver's side, climbs into the van while his children retract limbs and close doors, and accelerates.

The police cars are around him before he makes it out of the carpark.

Sixteen

HINE I TE REPO

The door is locked. And the key's not under the pot in the far corner of the back garden either. Great. Wai's not sure where Keri is, or what's so important she hasn't thought of her only daughter and how this lapse in care means she is now on the streets without anywhere to go. It's infuriating. There'll be something wrong with the car or some other lame issue. Maybe Walty's thrown a tantrum and can't be convinced to go home; sometimes those can go on for half an hour or more. Whatever it is, Wai is never at the top of the list.

She sits on the front step. This is bullshit. She's so furious with her mother. She's so furious that she's never the most important consideration. She's so furious that she doesn't have her own key, that her mother insisted that a hiding place would be better—so she wouldn't lose it at school. Why, for fuck's sake, doesn't her mother ever listen to her? She stands again and starts pacing, kicking the ground. Does a round of check-the-windows, even though she knows they'll be locked.

Near the garage, she hears a familiar squeal. She can see the new neighbors' window is open, a bit of lace netting fluttering out in the wind. The squeal comes again: a distinctive Walty-esque ring to it. Ugh. Perhaps her mother is in there. Perhaps she has forgotten the time. There are few things Wairere hates more than meeting new people, but she's been outside for a good ten minutes and she'd really like to go home. She goes to the neighbors' front door and knocks quietly, everything in her body telling her to avoid disturbing them as best she can. Unsurprisingly, this has little effect. She can hear muffled voices through the door, so she takes a deep breath, and just as she's about to knock again, the door opens. She finds herself face to face with a woman with dark hair in a thick braid coiled around her head, wearing a long turquoise smock. A striped scarf is wrapped around her shoulders in a configuration that Wai finds mesmerizing and complex and impossibly elegant: no one she knows would have a clue how to do something like that, which is just as well because no one she knows would look right in it. The woman smiles warmly.

"Wairere?" She even rolls her R's the right way.

Wairere nods. "Is my mother here?"

"No. I'm sorry. She just telephoned and asked me to look out for you. Please, come in."

Wairere hesitates, but it feels rude not to do what the woman asks. She takes off her shoes at the door, where the family's shoes are lined up in a single neat row.

"Is my brother here?"

"Yes. He is playing with Aliana. My name is Sera. Please, sit."

Wairere sits on the overstuffed sofa. She can hear Walty's voice in the hallway.

"Your mother is stuck at the Work and Development office. Something has happened there. She must wait to speak to police."

"Police?!"

"Please don't be alarmed. Keri is okay, but she is a witness to an incident and they have asked to take her statement."

"Incident?" Wairere can't imagine what her mother has seen that is so bad she has to talk to the police. "Is she in trouble?"

"No. It's okay. I don't think so. And she will be back soon."

"Oh." Wairere is glad the woman is so gentle. It makes it easier to be in her house under these strange circumstances. "Is Walty okay?"

"Oh yes. Walty is very good. We like him. He likes Ali."

As if on cue the two children come charging into the living room, covered in stickers. Walty is wearing an orange tank top and a purple tutu. Aliana is wearing Walty's monster bike helmet, the one with pointy horns in a mohawk row, and a cardboard dinosaur tail that is attached to her waist by a loop of elastic.

"Wai!" Walty runs up and throws his arms around her. He smells like round wine biscuits and orange cordial. There's an orange ring around his top lip. "We're playing dress-ups!"

Aliana, a miniature version of Sera, follows Walty closely, but stops short of hugging Wai. Instead, she stares with the biggest, darkest eyes Wai has ever seen. I know how you feel, she thinks—

the girl is clearly too shy to interact directly. Instead she goes to the miniature table and chairs in the corner and starts scribbling in a coloring book, her hand looping in wide arcs. Walty swiftly follows.

"Just a moment," Sera says, and she disappears into the kitchen. Wairere looks around the house, but other than slightly shabby and spare furnishings, there isn't much to see. It makes their living room at home seem claustrophobic with clutter.

Sera returns swiftly with some biscuits and a tray of tea and juice.

"I didn't know what you would like," she says, placing the assortment near Wairere on a small side table. "I will have tea, but you can have whatever you choose—you are a young woman."

She says this in a matter-of-fact way, as if it is a given someone Wai's age should be treated as a young adult and given choice, not treated like a child as she usually is. It makes her like Sera very much.

"Thank you." Wai reaches for a biscuit and watches Sera pour the tea. "I'd like tea too, if that's okay."

"Sometimes I put cardamom in it. But I haven't today." Sera passes Wai a saucer with a cup of tea.

"I don't know what that is. But Mum has been trying turmeric hot drinks lately."

"What do you think?"

"It looks gross. I'm not going to try it." She's suddenly embarrassed by how childish this sounds. "Mum always wants to try what's fashionable."

"Is turmeric fashionable?"

"Apparently. I don't really know what that is either. Except it's yellow."

"Yes. Very yellow and good for the blood and the mind."

"Really?"

"So they say at home."

That's when Wai smells smoke, at Sera's mention of home. She feels constricted suddenly, as if she's trying to see through smog, and breathe through it too. A hot steam of panic fills her gut. And the urgent need to leave. She doesn't want to give Sera the wrong impression, especially after she's gone to so much trouble, but she has to get out.

"Are you okay?" Sera is staring at her. The panic isn't allowing Wai to mask anything. Even though she knows it's all coming from Sera, she can't say so. It's not the kind of thing you share on first meeting someone.

"Yeah, I—I'm okay—I just had this weird sensation. Maybe I'm getting a migraine or something."

Sera looks concerned, her head tilted to the side. "You should rest. I have painkillers if you want some?" she says.

"No, no, it's okay. Maybe I should just go."

Sera's face drops. "But your mother will be coming here when she's done. She said you could stay here with us."

"I'm sorry—I'm—"

"You will stay a bit longer. Rest."

Despite herself, Wairere feels compelled to obey the older woman's instructions. She's so sure and firm. The smoke has faded for the moment. It's bearable. And the tea might help.

“Okay. Thank you.” She does her best well-behaved-teenager smile.

“I am happy to meet you, at last,” says Sera, taking her own biscuit. “We see Keri and Walty a lot, but you are always at school.”

Wairere nods and keeps chewing.

“I saw you the other day coming from Mrs. B’s. We were going to the beach.”

She’s not very good at small talk, but Wairere finds something to say. “You like the beach?”

“Oh yes. The beach is a miracle. It washes away all the worries in the world, going there with Ali. She gets covered in sand, we both get wet, but it’s the best feeling. As if nothing else matters.”

“Yes.” She knows exactly how Sera feels. “The beach helps clear my head too, and the wetlands.” She never calls them wetlands, but being around Sera makes her want to speak more proper.

“Wetlands? I don’t know these—I haven’t seen them yet.”

“I usually call it swamp. There’s some man-made ponds too. And a walkway through it all with native trees and plants. You get to see a lot of birds there. Sometimes eels and fish. Heard frogs recently.”

“Frogs?” Sera suddenly seems far away, and Wairere feels it before she sees it, that fire again. Not something frogs could survive. The urge to leave returns to her feet, but now she also wants to hear what Sera has to say. Her mother was right: this neighbor is more interesting than the usual.

"I love how wet Aotearoa is," Sera says, her accent making her pronunciation of Aotearoa almost perfect. "Where I come from, there's never enough water. There used to be, but we messed it all up." Wairere is suddenly desperate to change the subject.

"There's a Culture Fest at school," she says. "You should come. Actually, you could do more than that, if you want to. Different communities are bringing food, or dancing or whatever."

Sera is immediately back in the room, focusing intently on Wairere. "Will you be bringing food, or dancing?"

Wairere visibly shudders. "No. I try to avoid crowds. We might make something though. Fry Bread maybe? If Mum can afford the ingredients."

"Perhaps I can help."

"Or you can make something from your country?"

"Perhaps." Sera considers her then, and Wairere wonders how she appears to this tall, inquisitive stranger. "You are a good girl, Wairere."

"Sometimes."

"No, you are. I see it. I see other things too."

Wairere suddenly feels hot. What has she seen?

"Please don't be alarmed! I should have waited until we are friends."

"It's okay," Wairere says, "I think."

"Yes. It is okay. Please don't take it to your heart. Sometimes I think I see my own worries in other people. I think perhaps we share a pain. This means we can share more. It is a good thing!"

Wairere can see that, but also, it's a lot.

Aliana and Walty are getting louder and louder. There has been an exchange of stickers that wasn't entirely voluntary, and now it is clear they are both on the verge of tears. Sera rises to tend them, and Wairere sees her opportunity.

"I'm sorry. I like your . . . tea. I just have to go, but tell Mum I'll be back soon, please?"

Sera looks alarmed, but her hands are full separating the two children who are now actively trying to steal each other's stickers.

Wairere swings her backpack onto her back and stands. She takes a step, cocking her head to the side in a pleading way. "I'm really sorry. Thank you for the tea and the biscuit."

"Please, tell me where you are going so I can tell Keri?"

Wai likes the way Sera places the emphasis at the end of Keri's name, tilting it up in a strangely joyful way. "It's, um, I'm just going to the swamp, you know, the estuary . . . for . . . um, for a school project I have to do. I'll be back before dark!"

"I would like you to stay here, but I understand," Sera says. "I hope I didn't scare you away."

The smoke and tight breath return to Wai then, as she shakes her head and tells Sera it's okay. She feels so tired, but she can see something else in Sera's eyes: aroha, she might call it, because love or compassion aren't quite the words, but she knows it's something like that. This woman has been broken and put together again by her own love, she understands, even though there are still missing pieces.

And then she is out the door.

It is the smoke she runs from, the feeling of panic, the feeling of having nowhere to go and no good air to breathe. She knows where no fire could follow, where the air is as fresh as a forest, where she can forget the oppressiveness of other people's lives suffocating her own. Wairere goes to swamp because she can see the full colors of life there: the teeming minutiae, microbes and fungi, nematode worms and copepods, midges and mudfish, consuming each other, recycling nutrients, always engaged in a kaleidoscopic and continual dance, springing into life, decaying into death. And somehow zooming in on all of that allows her to zoom out from everything that worries her—making her fears distant and insignificant.

One time she saw a white-faced heron out on the water, a thick eel freshly caught in its beak. The eel squirmed and wriggled until it found the heron's neck, then coiled its body around the bird while the heron tried to swallow the eel and keep hold of it simultaneously. They were locked in battle like that for twenty minutes: the heron swallowing as much of the eel as possible, then regurgitating it when it wouldn't stay down; the eel never letting go of the outside world, holding fast to the body of its predator. Wairere felt the wonder of it, this drama playing itself out right in the middle of suburbia, houses all around her but no other humans to be seen. It was glorious, and she was all alone. Maybe that was why it was glorious.

Eventually, the heron began to triumph. The eel went down more and more each time until the bird managed to close its beak over its sleek, dark opponent. Wairere had been rooting for the eel, but the bird was strong and graceful, and deserved the prize after their battle. Neck bulging, the bird swam to a post, knocked a smaller heron off, and perched there, content in the sun. That heron would be sleeping it off for hours, days maybe, confident in its status and capacity to survive. Wairere left the scene, filled with the bird's contentment. If an eel had to go, she thought, good for it to go to a bird rather than a human. She had this other feeling too: that they came out for her, the beasts of the swamp, that they let her see things they revealed to no one else.

It's a world down there, for sure. If she concentrates, Wairere can almost *be* that water, wading in among the zooplankton and algae, not so much swimming as floating with intention. It's all color with them, once you get that close, whole worlds opening up into universes once you get inside them. She goes into their world, sees it as they do, and there is no human language for that. What she sees is the immensity of it—the immensity of the space between even the most infinitesimal atoms. As if the smallest things we can possibly imagine mirror the greatest: galaxies in a speck. Yeah, it's a head rush. Spacey, as her mother used to say.

Spacey's the right word for it, she supposes, in a good way. Not like the headfuck of dealing with all the other stuff she picks up daily, and now these new things close to home. She hasn't been able to name what she's faced with, not directly, out loud, or even to herself, but if she's ever going to, the swamp is the place to do it, out where she can think, where she feels safe. So, what is it? Sera and her family bring sadness, a tiredness like she's never known, but nothing harmful. A whisper of fire, thirst. It was overwhelming at first, but it's alright, she thinks, because of all they bring with them, because of what she saw in Sera's eyes. No, it's the other neighbor, Mrs. B's son, that worries her, and the feeling her mum brought home after her night out. Could those two things be connected? She hasn't come across anything like either before, not close. It feels malignant somehow, a poison. Something that can kill, or get into the bloodstream and contaminate.

A strange thought, but even as it comes, she's sure of it. That's why it's so terrifying: it's not just him, it's *them*. There's more than one. But also: they're not at all close; they don't even feel real. She sees a TV in her mind's eye, a vaudeville act on a caricature stage, an old black and white reel of a performer in blackface. She has learned, over the years, not to discount these images that flash into her head at times of stress, despite the fact she wishes they wouldn't, and it's never exactly clear what they mean. Which goes against what Nan said that time, after she got used to her strange grandchild, after she figured it out:

"You're gifted, kid. Matakite."

Wairere shuddered. "Don't tell Mum. She'll make a fuss."

Her nan was sitting to her right, and leaned into her, knocking her sideways a bit. "She will have noticed something. Sorry, my moko, but it's pretty noticeable."

Wairere slouched, shrinking into herself as much as she could. "What does it even mean?"

"I don't know. I'm not the one who's matakite, eh?" Nan cackled, the most comforting sound in the world. "That's for you to figure out. Don't sweat it too much though, bub. It is what it is. Lots of your tūpuna had it. Not me, or your mother, but in the whakapapa, it's common as."

"Easy for you to say."

"Yes, it is easy for me to say, actually." Nan lifted her nose in the air.

"Yeah, I know . . ."

"I may not be matakite, but . . ."

". . . you know everything else."

"It's a lot of work being this wise and all-knowing." Nan got down then, off the sea wall they were perched on, and ambled along, collecting sticks and shells. Walks with Nan always went like this: a slow perusing of the tide, collecting bits and pieces as they went.

"Don't fight it. I can't speak from experience, but I'm pretty sure that'll make it harder to live with."

"I can't get rid of it, can I?"

"Nope. I don't think so. You could try, but I don't think suppressing that kind of thing works. It just comes out anyway, in some warped way."

"I can't cut it out."

"Don't be silly." Nan sniffed and stretched, looking out at the island. "Best to make friends with it."

They walked along until they got to the estuary. A couple of oystercatchers running in front of them, sounding the alarm. Each day the water shaped the beach differently in this spot—today it was shallow, but the coming rain would carve out deep trenches.

"I'll be here, you know, a place to land when you need to get back to solid ground. We don't have anyone left who can teach you about the sight, but I'll be there for you to come back to if you ever feel lost."

Except she wasn't. She was gone a couple of years later, when Wairere was twelve, and now she didn't have her solid ground person to come back to. Just Keri and all her worries, and Walty, a baby. All of them missing the woman who was big enough in their lives to exert her own gravitational pull.

Wairere has to stop a moment, and take stock, because it feels like something is building, and how is she gonna manage it all? Why does it even feel like it is hers to manage? She looks around her and feels the comfort of the harakeke, and tussock, and tī kōuka, just young replantings, but still, it's enough to hold her, since Nan can't. Maybe this is her place to come back to, maybe this will hold her steady enough to deal with what she is seeing.

A man bringing others with him, but only shadows, and something more, something very bad. And then her own family—her mother turning herself in knots to pay the bills, and satisfy the welfare and benefit ghouls. Trying to do everything as if she were an octopus with eight arms or a goddess with a hundred. That's what makes it so hard to be close to her. Wairere hardly ever lets herself feel the unfairness of that, but she feels it now, because she needs someone to stand in the bog with her.

Bog can be blacker, and more treacherous, than regular swamp. It can pull you down, suffocate, infect. Wairere knows she has to find a way to keep light enough to walk through it, like the white-faced heron or the spoonbill, who filter the good stuff from the bad. The way she feels about people, the way she feels about her abilities—and the world—that has to stop, at least for a while. She has to find a way to be *in* the world the way she is, instead of trying to escape it. There's something about the coming together of all these people—she doesn't know what it is, but she knows she has to be awake for it. It's hard for her to really be in the world, it's painful, but that's nothing compared to what she can see coming. If she isn't present, and solid, she won't be able to protect her family when the time comes. The time of what, she can't be sure, but she feels it as plainly as she feels the bite of the wind in her ears, as surely as she hears the harakeke seeds rattling in their stems. It's coming.

Seventeen

SYMPHONY

By the time Keri pulls into the driveway, it's after five already. There's a man running up ahead of her, and he turns up Mrs. B's driveway. She's distracted, so she doesn't notice anything unusual at first, but there's something familiar in his gait, and then she realizes she's never seen a man at Mrs. B's before. The man is opening the garage door, and as she passes, they lock eyes. She watches as his face falls into the same expression as her own, mouth slightly ajar, eyes widening just enough to register shock. It's him, she thinks, the guy from the bar—Conor. She quickly looks away, pretending not to see, pretending not to care, but as she edges her way into the driveway at the far end, she can't help but take a few surreptitious glances in his direction.

She can hear the kids are starting to get scrappy from outside. "I'm so sorry!" she says as soon as Sera opens the door.

"Thank you so much!" Nothing will really make her feel better for the way the afternoon has gone, but at least she is here now. "You must let me do the same for you sometime."

Sera smiles. "Of course. Please don't worry. It is not your fault, and it was nice for us to have someone here." But she has barely said the words when both children begin to wail, a sound that gains momentum and pitch the longer it goes on.

"I'll tell you about it next time I see you!" Keri starts collecting Walty's things. "Did Wairere turn up?"

"Yes. She said to tell you she was going for a walk to the swamp. Homework, or something. She won't be too late."

"Oh. Right. Yes, that sounds like her. Thank you so much!" Keri backs out, repeating her thanks and her catch-up-soons, but Walty drops to his knees, his arms stretched forward, fingers grasping. He's building up a head of steam, his face reddening. Finally, he throws himself full length to the floor and kicks his legs. "Stupid-bum-dog!" he bellows.

Keri doesn't know whether to laugh or be embarrassed by Walty's inventive insult. "Walty—that's not very nice—can you ask for what you want?"

But Walty is beyond words. He simply continues kicking his legs and grasping toward his friend. Simultaneously, the two women click. Aliana still wears the dinosaur helmet.

"It's okay," Sera says. "Ali, Walty needs his helmet. I bet he'll let you play with it another day." Aliana considers the women and the furious boy, blinks slowly, and reaches up to remove the helmet. She passes it to Walty, who starts gulping down his sobs with the prized possession safely back in his hands. Keri, relieved they have found such a swift resolution to the impasse, smiles again at Sera, gives a little wave, and pulls Walty with her gently, gathering their things before a new crisis can erupt.

Wai returns before six, quiet. Walty is at the table scooping mashed potato into his mouth with gusto. They could afford a small block of cheese this week, and Keri has sprinkled some in for flavor and protein, resulting in a very contented four-year-old. Wai is not so content. Keri wonders if, just this once, she can help without it turning into a thing. It's like playing a game of Fish or Poker—is it this, or this? Will she be sent fishing? Will she have to pay for calling a high-stakes game when she should have folded?

But she's never shied away from a challenge, so she asks.

Wairere sighs. "I'm just tired. There's a lot going on."

"Tell me about it." What a day. "What's happening with you?"

"I don't know. Everything."

"You might need to be more specific, Wai." She knows she's pushing it now. The vagueness is usually a warning to stay away.

Wai looks at her, looks like she's about to say something, then just shakes her head and runs down the hall. Were those tears in her eyes? What the hell? She checks on Walty, he's content with his mash, so she follows.

"Wai? What's going on?"

"Just leave me alone." She's on her bed, head down so Keri can't see her face, though she can hear the tremor in Wairere's voice.

"You know I can't. Not when you're like this."

"Do you ever think maybe you should though?" She's angry now, that much is clear, and when she looks up, fixing Keri with a glare, Keri is almost thrown back by the viciousness of it.

"There's no need for that, Wai. I'm not your enemy. I don't know what's up, but you know you can come and tell me when you're ready."

Wairere says nothing, just glares, and Keri feels defeated by the enormity of her anger. Just hang in there, she thinks. It's all she can do.

"I'm here, bub," she says, and then she backs away, returning to Walty and the mess of potato needing cleanup on his face and hands.

It's absolutely infuriating. She thought she was going to come home and talk to her mother—she'd daydreamed about it on the way home—how she'd lay everything out. What a relief it would be. And she wouldn't be alone in her worries anymore. But then she'd arrived home to the usual stuff, and she had all her usual reactions—it's so oppressive in the house sometimes, she just wanted to get away. Keri does it because she cares, Wairere understands that, but her questions are so irritating, and Wairere's reactions seem to come from somewhere else, not her conscious mind at all, and everything dissolves into a haze of negative emotions, Keri on the other side of the room looking sad and worried. If her mother could just leave her alone long enough, Wai might get to the point where she can tell her what's going on. So now, instead of talking to her like she should be, Wai is just sitting on her bed, fuming. And she's even pissed off with herself: she knows now is not the time to go solo, but she's already pushed away the only person she can really tell.

She waits until it's late to come out. Keri has already put Walty to bed, and has returned to the kitchen to do her coursework. She always gets the books out after Walty's asleep. Wairere's hungry, but she had decided to stay away from the kitchen and living room for the rest of the night. Annoying how her resolve seemed to dissipate as her hunger grew.

"There's a plate in the fridge," Keri says. "I made tofu green Thai curry."

She thought she smelled something good. She sets to heating it and takes a seat at the furthest end of the table from where her mother sits surrounded by books. Once she starts eating her hunger grows. The food warms her and she eats too fast. What was she even so mad about?

"You'll get indigestion," Keri starts, but then stops herself before she says anything more.

They are quiet for a while, the only sound chewing and tapping, an occasional page turning. Wairere puts down her spoon.

"Mum," she says, but doesn't say anything else.

Keri half closes the lid of her laptop, as if she has been waiting for this cue. "Yes, bub. I'm here."

"You know how Nan said I was matakite, and I said I wasn't, and then you guys had a fight about it?"

"Yep. It was a stupid thing to fight about. I fought with your nan about so many stupid things."

"Yeah, well. I just don't like to talk about it." Wairere looks around the kitchen, aware that Keri follows her gaze: the worn blue paint on the cupboards, the tired grout around the sink, the netting curtains they tie back into knots to let the light and air in. So ordinary. But the world is not as ordinary as it appears sometimes. Does her mother know this? Like her grandmother did? It seems as if the unspoken and the unseen have been keeping them apart for a long time. "It's there, Mum, all the time. Nan was right, I think."

"I knew there was something." Keri is hesitant, as if she doesn't know quite what to say. "I don't even know why I fought with her about it. Not like I disagreed. It was just how she always had to know things first, you know, always held that up, as if I didn't know my own daughter."

"Yeah, well, I didn't want to tell you."

"Clearly." Her mother is staring at her, that intense look she gets when she's worried. "I just want to make the world easy and simple and safe for you. Why didn't you tell me?"

"Because of this. Because of the way you look right now. I don't want to be this way. It's everywhere, all the time. I don't like to be around people because of it." It feels dangerous, to say the things she has kept to herself for so long.

"No. I can imagine." Keri almost laughs. "This all explains a heck of a lot, but today of all days?"

"I just needed to tell you. Because things are . . . weird around here. More than usual. I don't know what to do about any of it. I thought I should say something."

"Well, I'm glad you told me. I'm relieved. I didn't know what was wrong. But what's weird? Is it in our house? Things are weird here?" Her mother looks anxious again, weighed down by all the things that could be piled up at their door.

"Maybe. Not in *our* house. Around us. The neighbors."

"You don't like Sera and Aliana?"

"Yeah, no, I like them a lot. But they bring . . . some hard things."

"Yes, they do. They've been through some stuff."

"But that's not it. There's another one."

Keri's face shifts, the anxiety twists a bit, into something different. Guilt? "At Mrs. B's?"

"She says he's her son."

"Oh. No."

"There's something around him, but I don't know what it is."

"Do you want me to go—"

"No. I just wanted to tell you. Please don't tell anyone else." Her face closes. Whatever was there a moment ago is gone, replaced by a more capable mask: responsibility, competence.

"Of course, I won't. Are you okay, bub?"

Wairere goes to her then, bends and wraps her arms around her shoulders. It has been so long since Wairere has done this, neither of them quite knows what to do, but she holds on tight. Hesitantly, Keri stands and places her arms around her daughter. Wairere collapses in a bit, and holds tight. There it is, that feeling she's been missing: solid and warm in a way that belongs only to mothers.

Eventually, Wairere makes a noise, a little struggle.

"No! I've got you now and I'm not letting you go!" Keri locks her arms, and when Wairere tries to free herself, follows her movements, so that they end up swinging back and forth, a lop-sided dance.

"Muuuum!" Wairere cries, but they're both laughing.

"You have to tell me these things, sweetheart. Maybe I can help. I need to know you kids are safe."

"I don't know for sure, but I think it's bigger than us. I don't think the danger is immediate, with us here."

Her statement sits between them. There is danger then.

"How do you know?"

"Most of the time, it's just a feeling, like instinct but stronger." Her mother always had good instincts. "Like if intuition was a physical sensation. Sometimes I get images, but not as often. I think we're okay, Mum, for now. But that might not last."

"Tell me if anything changes. And I'll keep an eye out for anything odd around here."

"Okay."

"Love you, Wai. It's so nice to talk."

"Ew! Don't get used to it!" Keri makes a face, but she knows her mother will be pleased that her sense of humor is back.

Later, when she's too distracted and tired to study, Keri finally shifts her full attention to the day and its strange conjunction of events. How could she have missed it? She's so grateful that Wai is finally talking to her, but it's frightening too. She just has to stay with her, stay solid, not melt into a puddle like she wants. And to see Conor at Mrs. B's for the first time, even though he must have been there for weeks? The universe has a way of piling up the shit until you've got no choice but to start shoveling. Could it be that Wairere simply sensed what had happened between Keri and Conor, or is it that there is more to know about him? Whatever it is, she's unnerved. What if he's a predator, a perve, some kind of creep, living close to her and her children? She didn't get that vibe, although she definitely did get *a* vibe—perhaps that's the reason she pulled away after all. When she thinks about it, there was an awkwardness about him she should have paid attention to earlier. Not that he was shy, but that he'd had a weird bravado, as if he was imitating a confidence he hadn't earned. She had been too tired to maintain her usual vigilance, and he hadn't seemed dangerous, not really. His mother spewed bog-standard prejudice, maybe her son has some version of the same thing.

She doesn't know which version of ickiness she wishes for, but she does know she would prefer it to stay away from her and her family, whatever is going on.

Somehow, the earlier events of the day have shaded everything that happened afterward too. She's infected by the desperation of the Pākehā man in the high-vis vest—a desperation she is sometimes only steps away from herself. Something broke for him that morning, and in a single moment everything he was trying to keep together had fallen apart. She'll never forget the sight of those kids lined up by the van after the police got them out, looking down at their feet, because when they looked up all they could see was their father being handcuffed and the prying eyes of strangers. And then she had to stay and speak to the damn cops, and it seems ironic that she should be called on to witness a thing that for her looked quite different than the official story would ever say. If asked who the victims and perpetrators of the scene were, she is sure her interpretation would differ from the Work and Development staff by quite some margin. For her, the actions of the Pākehā man in the high-vis vest were the final notes of the final movement of a symphony in which any one person is only a string, a reed, a drum stick, a bow, the wood, or brass, and the one thing she is sure of is that neither she nor the Pākehā man in the high-vis vest would ever be the baton dancing in the hand of the conductor, though they would always be subject to its direction.

Nothing in the world has felt settled since her mother died. They'd done so well, getting away from Walty's father when they did. Coming home. And it did feel like home, immediately, even after twelve years in Sydney. It had meant a lot that her mother came back with her. The rest of the whānau were still over there, having become accustomed to Australian wages and the cost of living. She got it, but once she returned, she felt like it was a mistake, all the time they'd spent in that other country. It was good, at last, to be back, even if Koro Walt was no longer around to offer them a place to rest. And for a while, since neither she nor her mother were distracted by the men in their lives, they could actually talk, for the first time since, well, maybe ever.

And then her mother's diabetes caught up with her diet, and her heart gave out. She was too young for it to be over so quickly. And Keri was alone with the kids, trying to figure out how to be everything to them, trying to figure out how to reconnect with a cultural heritage they'd all grown distant from while they were away.

But most of all, she mourned the years her mother would have had with her children. If they weren't going to have a father around, a nan was a good substitute if not a better option altogether. Wai had been approaching the teenage years fast, and Keri knew from her own experience that the last person she'd want to be around was her. Her mother could have been there while Keri dealt with other problems. There's always someone to fight, it seems, if not the kids' fathers, then Income Support, or the school, or whoever needed money from her that week.

She's doing her best to keep something else intact too, something she recognized in herself after her babies were born because she saw it in them. A precious thing that remains soft and vulnerable and slightly otherworldly, despite it all. That's what she fights for. The thing that Wairere finally told her about, thank goodness. She feels overwhelmed by affection for her angry, confused, magical daughter—it must have taken some guts for her to speak aloud of things the world is bent on believing don't exist.

She's managed to protect them, so far, anyway. As much as she can. She keeps them away from harm, even if it means she lives a different kind of isolation. She's always known whatever she's protecting is particularly alive in Wairere, that her daughter is wired into the all of everything in a more intense way than anyone else Keri has ever known. But she hadn't given it a name, even after her mother brought it up, she'd refused to call it a particular thing, thinking that would force particular qualities, and force a reckoning of some kind. Well, here it is, from Wairere's own mouth. She finds naming it doesn't worry her as much as she thought it would. Maybe it can be lots of things. Maybe it means a particular thing to Wai. Maybe matakite is the only name they have for something that is beyond explanation. It's a name that connects them to others—a long line of them, beginning with their tūpuna Kui Wairere, who could see what Te Ao Hurihuri would bring.

So why is she so unsettled, then, if the idea of matakite doesn't frighten her? She's seen worse, experienced worse in her own home, than what that stranger can bring into their lives. But even as she thinks this, she feels a tiny stone of doubt, as if it is nestled between one toe and another in her shoe, rubbing insistently whenever she tries to make her way in any direction. An annoyance that must be dealt with, sooner or later. She may not have the sight, but her intuition is rarely wrong, and right now it's telling her to pay attention.

Keri is surprised when Sera makes an impromptu visit the following afternoon, after Aliana's nap, with an invitation.

"Ali will be three years old next week. It will be our first gathering of friends here."

"That's exciting! What can I bring? How can I help?"

"No, nothing. We are hosting. We will provide."

"A present for Ali, at least?"

"Of course, as you wish, but please don't go to any great expense. It is an excuse to celebrate everything we are grateful for."

"We're the lucky ones, I reckon. Despite the great bike helmet debacle of yesterday, Walty has been asking when he gets to see Ali again all morning."

"Debacle?"

"Mmm—disaster, I suppose?"

"Ah, yes. Very distressing."

They both watch the children for a moment as they sip their tea. It's dress-ups again. Walty is wearing Wairere's old fairy tutu, and Aliana is dressed in a homemade version. They're excavating the toy basket, Walty telling an elaborate yet incomprehensible story about fairies and pirates.

"I'm sorry about yesterday," Keri says again.

"You! You are not allowed to keep apologizing for something that wasn't your fault and does not require apologies!"

"I know, but I feel so bad, as if I was taking advantage of you."

"Keri, if we are going to be friends then I will take advantage of you too. You will pay me back eventually, I am sure of it."

"You're right. I know this. Sorry." Walty's father called her many names, but the things that have stayed with her longest are the simplest: she was useless, she was ungrateful, she was arrogant. The logical part of her brain tells her these are untrue, but they cut her the deepest, and she's spent a lot of time since performing an advance guard, ensuring no one can ever accuse her of similar offenses again.

"You are no longer allowed to say sorry." Sera says it with such confidence, then laughs. "I'm the same though: always fretting, always feeling apologetic for imposing on others." Keri relaxes a little—this is permission to be imperfect, this friendship. Everything is such a mess, and she doesn't have her mother or her grandfather and she doesn't know what's coming, but she has this.

"Please, tell me about what happened yesterday," Sera says.

So Keri tells her about it, and Sera tells Keri about the morning of the shooting at the Processing Center, and the two women sit for a while, stunned at how similar their stories are, even though they happened worlds apart.

"We're all just being processed, aren't we?" Keri says eventually.

"And somehow we are all in exile, too. Don't you think?" They watch the children. It is a long time since either of them have felt the confidence of belonging, fully, to a place. And yet they have the beginnings of community here, and that feels like something more than existing, something more than occupation. Behind the voices of their children, they both hear the quiet rumble that begins then, sounding at first like wind, or a car, but increasing in volume until they recognize it as individual drops on the roof, and then the chorus of a full downpour.

Eighteen

HATCHET

Sera passes the neighbors' on foot most days, out for walks with Aliana, down to the beach or the park, sometimes with Adam, but mostly just the two of them, getting some air. She loves going to the water, but she doesn't see any evidence that all the streets she walks were once water. What no one can see, walking around the neighborhood, is how little it resembles what it once was, how this tidy suburbia was once rich with swamp plants and eel, kōkopu, mudfish and matuku. Dried and drained, what Sera sees is cultivated green, devoid of the many eyes which might have once watched her passing.

The previous day, she thought she'd found a solution: just keep busy. Attending to the immediate needs of the children, the entire afternoon had left her without a moment to dwell on anything else. And she liked it, that feeling of being busy and needed. She felt as if her presence was helpful and of consequence, especially when Wairere turned up, though she is sorry the girl left so quickly. Yes, these things are important: friends, community, something to do. Although she is also relieved her "something to do" these days doesn't include securing water or sanitation or safety. There are worse things than existential angst, worse even than psychological pain. She knows the time will surely come when she is busy again, when she must work out in the world—she can feel it under her skin, deep within her muscles and bones. This time of quiet and contemplation won't last forever, and can she make the most of it? If the scariest thing in her world is to settle, in herself, in this new place, can she meet that challenge? Perhaps keeping busy is not a solution to everything.

But the other thing about being at home so much is how big small things become. Sera sees Mrs. B when she passes more often than she likes. Mrs. B is often in the garden, or out with her dog, or coming back from somewhere in the car. Sera avoids eye contact, turns away, or pretends to be busy with Aliana. Sometimes Mrs. B says hello, and Sera nods curtly, moving as if she's in a rush to be somewhere. Lately she has seen a younger man too, a son she supposes, much younger than Mrs. B, but a little older than Sera. He ignores her just as she ignores him, which is a relief—one less awkward interaction to navigate. But Mrs. B is a problem that must be solved eventually, as old white ladies with opinions often are. Well, it was more than opinion, the things she said to Sera, and all the cake in the world cannot take away the sour taste that has remained in her mouth ever since.

It isn't the worst or most racist thing that has happened to her, by any measure, but it was the way the words had been presented to her as advice, as something she was too ignorant to already be aware of, as some kind of revelation about who she is and what she should expect in this country. She has so many hopes for Aotearoa, yet it had only taken a few days in her new home before her right to have a home at all was called into question. She can't stand it. This woman—how dare she threaten everything they have in so few careless words. She knows, as deeply as she knows the sound of her daughter's voice, how precarious their position is. How the fractional probability of them even making it here in the first place was one in many hundreds of thousands if not millions. She still feels that in her heartbeat at night: how easily it could have been someone else who had received their luck and passage to New Zealand. And maybe someone else needed it, or deserved it, more than them. She feels it in the background of everything that happens here, as if there is another Sera who still lives in their old home, watching with Adam as their daughter struggles to breathe.

She doesn't want to have anything to do with the woman, but she knows she has to reconcile this. She wants peace in her home, and outside her home. She wants to live without fear, and she must live without shame. It is the only way, for Aliana. She cannot believe she is letting this old woman dictate her feelings. She has lived through so much worse.

"Maybe if she gets to know us, and we get to know her, we can find some common ground?" Adam suggests over breakfast. He is always the pragmatic one. He is in some way right, she knows, but Sera hates this. What has that woman done to deserve their friendship? It's as if Mrs. B has come to represent all the people who have ever said something ignorant to them, or looked at them a certain way, or crossed the street to avoid them. And behind the words and looks, all the systems and structures that gave people like Mrs. B the confidence to say such things, to feel as if their view of the world is normal, that their way of thinking is the standard by which everyone else should be judged. Most of all, Sera is tired, she's so tired the ache of it feels like it'd be a relief if the flesh melted from her bones right where she stands.

She breathes deeply in through her nose, and sighs her agitation and resignation out.

Adam spreads his hands wide, a habitual and strangely religious movement. He is the tolerant one, the compassionate. "I know. I know. But, my heart, even though it is tiresome, is it not better to keep our enemies closer than even our friends, as they say?"

"I don't know. I don't want the enemy too close."

"Maybe we can invite her to Ali's birthday?"

"What? No. Why would we?"

"She is right there, next door. She will see and hear us anyway, and she made that cake."

"Lucky it wasn't poisonous."

"Yes, yes, but you still ate it!" Adam smiles at her mischievously. Indeed, she did have some after keeping her distance for a day. It *was* cake, and there was a lot of it. An entirely practical decision.

She sniffs. "But why are you so insistent that she be at the party?"

"Ah, I'm so sorry, Sese. I bumped into her on my way to my way to work, and she wanted to know all about it. She caught me off guard."

"We'd only just decided—"

"I know. I was excited about work and I didn't even think about it, it just slipped out. I wanted to celebrate all that is happening. Then she started talking about her own children and their birthday parties. I think she will feel sad if she's not invited. Maybe she will even feel resentful."

"Oh, Adam." The disappointment sinks into her gut, and transforms into anger at her husband. "How could you? This was supposed to be a celebration!"

"It is a celebration. I will invite her to come later, and when she arrives, I'll take care of her. It's my fault."

"Yes, it is." She's still angry at him, but he's doing his best, as he always does. It can be infuriating, in fact, because she just wants to vent her anger, but she can't vent it at him. "I will do my best to ignore her."

"But, my heart, it might even be an opportunity to . . . bury, what do they call it, the hatchback?"

And then she's laughing too hard to be angry anymore, at least at Adam. "No, oh no, Adam—a hatchback is a type of car!"

"What do I mean then?"

"I don't know, and why would you bury it?"

"It's a hatch-something, and it must be buried!" He takes the opportunity to grab her, delighted that she's laughing.

“I wish I could bury Mrs. B altogether.”

“Shhh. I’m sure she will hear you through these walls. And you know you can charm her, she is already charmed by Aliana. Maybe she will discover how wrong her prejudices are.”

“But Adam, why is it our job to teach her?”

Wairere is leaving for school when she sees Sera across the lawn that separates their homes. Sera’s door is open and she is barefoot, using a small jug to water the herb garden she has planted by the house. Sera sees her and straightens, waves. Wairere waves back. She wants to go over and say hello, but she hesitates. What would they talk about anyway? She’s meant to meet Felicity in ten minutes, but she also doesn’t want Sera to think she did something wrong the day before. Whatever Sera has been through is hard, and Wairere is uncomfortable sensing it, especially uninvited, but there’s a difference between this and the everyday shit she encounters most of the time. The majority of people are wrapped up in things they have the power to change. They might not think this, they might feel powerless or sad, full of rage or anxiety or desire, but what goes on inside them is more their choice than they care to admit. Sera and her family have no choice. Nothing can make their homeland inhabitable again, not easily, at least. Not quickly. Not without a lot of people looking in that direction and deciding to do almost everything differently.

Wairere has been standing so long that Sera calls good morning to her. Her silent watching is awkward, so she takes a few steps across the lawn and returns the greeting. Sera looks happy to see her.

"I'm sorry I left yesterday," Wairere says, "I just needed to get some things done."

"I understand. But we must finish our tea and our talk soon."

"Yeah. I like your garden."

"It is just a beginning. I only have rosemary, basil, and mint so far. I will keep adding more when I can."

"It must be nice, gardening in bare feet."

"It's such a Kiwi habit, going barefoot. I am adjusting, but I like it too."

Wairere always feels better when her feet connect with bare earth. "Same. I wonder why it feels so good?"

"We like to dig our toes into the sand at the beach too."

"Yeah, it's all alive under there, isn't it? It's like all that life gets into us. Like plugging in a charger."

Sera gazes at her now, a long, contemplative stare, not unfriendly, but curious, surprised. Wairere has said too much. She would like, just once, for someone to know what she's talking about. For it not to be this strange thing that belongs only to her.

"I mean, that's what it's like for me."

Sera's face breaks into a wide smile. "Yes. A charger. I shall think of it this way whenever I feel wrong for taking my shoes off to feel the ground underneath."

Wairere realizes nothing is wrong here, in the space between the two of them, even if she is being weird. But she has to go, and so she tells Sera that school, and Felicity, won't wait.

"Come by anytime," Sera says, passing her a sprig of rosemary to smell as she goes.

The difference between meeting Wairere outside the house and seeing Mrs. B almost every day is stark. The last thing Sera wants is to interact with the old woman, but when she leaves home the next day, there she is, in the garden, chattering away to Zadie until she sees Aliana in the pushchair, Sera coming up behind. Zadie runs to them and Aliana squeals excitedly, a sound that is sure to attract Mrs. B like a magnet. As she approaches, Sera knows she won't be able to maintain the wall of silence she has thus far kept like a forcefield between them.

"You can pat her," Mrs. B calls. "She won't bite!"

Zadie jumps around the stroller until she finds purchase on Aliana's knee, causing more squealing and a kind of dance between the two: Aliana swinging between wanting to touch the dog and shrinking back in fear.

"It's okay, Ali," Sera says quietly. "She won't bite. Mrs. B says she is friendly."

Aliana looks at the old lady then, curiously, while Zadie finds a way to position her head directly beneath the girl's hand. This causes Aliana to beam, and focus intently on the dog. Sensing imminent triumph, Zadie jumps up and lands on Aliana's knee, turning in a circle for balance. She then find's the child's face and proceeds to lick it ecstatically, causing peals of giggles.

Mrs. B is directly in front of them now, and Sera is forced to make eye contact and nod.

"Hello!" Mrs. B is in a great mood. "I'm so sorry about Zadie. She has a good nature, thank god, but she isn't well trained."

Sera is surprised there's no animosity in the old woman's voice, even the hidden kind that she seems particularly good at.

"God, it's a beautiful day, isn't it? Off for a walk, are you?"

Clearly, they are walking. Why do people here ask such obvious questions? Sera nods, offers a tentative smile.

"Zadie needs a walk soon. I should do that too."

Sera is gripped by a sudden fear that Mrs. B will want to join them.

"Good boy. Good boy!" squeals Aliana. It's unusual for her to speak around strangers, around anyone these days, especially in English. Maybe Walty has been a good influence.

"She's a girl, is Zadie. Aliana, is it?" Mrs. B looks at Sera for confirmation. She nods again. Mrs. B bends closer to the girl and the dog. "Aliana, Zadie is a girl, but you're right, she is a very good girl."

Aliana blinks, looking from Mrs. B to Zadie and back. Mrs. B straightens.

"Good girl, Zadie. Good girl, Zadie!" Aliana says.

"Coming out of herself, isn't she?" Mrs. B says, nodding at the pair approvingly. "Zadie will be devoted to that one now. She loves children."

"Yes. Aliana loves animals." The old woman is being nice today, and Adam is keen to see them on good terms. Sera will try.

"Maybe we can walk together sometime. Not today—I've got to get this laundry done before we're free to go. Got to take advantage of the weather."

Indeed. Sera should have done this too. "I wish I had thought of that," she volunteers. "I'll wait until Ali is sleeping."

"Ali, that sounds cute. *Ali Baba and the Forty Thieves*, just like the story, eh? 'Open sesame!'" Mrs. B chuckles, her eyes twinkling.

She's oblivious, Sera thinks. It's such a strange association, but Mrs. B seems pleased with herself for making it, as if she's found a good story to link them with. Wrong culture entirely, but such details don't seem to matter to Mrs. B. Sera is struck by the contrast to her encounter with Wairere, who was so substantial, as if looking into her eyes made Sera more real. What an odd thing to think, but that's it: she felt as if Wairere's presence gave her own more substance. With Mrs. B, she doesn't know if she is seen at all, she doesn't know what Mrs. B is capable of seeing, how they could possibly connect. Her smile is strained this time.

"Your husband, Adam? He said there's a birthday party soon. How nice for you all."

"Yes." This is the moment to say something, and despite herself, Sera feels the urge to do the polite thing. "We will have a few people over, just a small thing."

"Well, don't mind me, I just wanted to say don't worry about coming onto my side of the garden if you're outside. If the children need more room to run and play, let them use the whole space. Walty is used to it anyway. He'd be over here more if his mother let him. I assume Walty will be one of your guests? I noticed you've had him a couple of times."

So, Mrs. B is jealous. But this is a nice offer, all the same. "Yes, Walty. He's a funny boy. Thank you, Mrs. B."

"Janet."

"Thank you, Janet. It'll mostly be the little ones we have met since we've been here, so that will be nice. We'll call you over when it's time for cake, if you wish?"

"Well. Can't say no to cake. But I won't impose for too long. Not with lots of little ones running around."

"Just a few—Walty, plus the other children Aliana's age from the refugee center."

Mrs. B's expression shifts before she can freeze it in an unconvincingly polite smile. Sera looks away, and sees that Zadie has wandered off and Aliana has begun to twist in her stroller. "I better be going, Mrs. B. See you next week."

Sera starts off again, hearing only Mrs. B's correction behind her—"Janet!"

The truth is, Janet hasn't even had lunch yet, so after the laundry is done, she makes a pile of cheese toasties—two and a half for Conor, one and a half for her. It's nice to have someone to go halves with these days, though she's surprised how easily they've fallen into old habits—she does all the cooking and the cleaning, he offers her money when he has it, which is regularly these days. She doesn't know where he gets it though, that's in the back of her mind all the time. But then her suspicions are always smoothed over because there are a few things that are not like old habits: he's consistently respectful, polite enough to listen to her over dinner, and does the heavy lifting when she asks him. Never used to be that way when he was younger. Even though this is nice, as is the regular board money, she doesn't really trust it. All he does is sit in that room on those computers, and work out. The working out is new, and she feels a kind of relief that she doesn't have to worry about his physical health as well as his mind. Surely it can't be good for him to spend all that time alone, on those screens? A man his age should have a family.

Sometimes she is so deeply sad that her son doesn't have a girlfriend, or a wife, and children. Did they do something wrong, apart from the obvious, or was he always going to be this way, alone, the faulty toy in the toy box? At least if he was a womanizer she'd know that he was dealing with normal male appetites in a normal male way—wouldn't approve exactly, but at least he'd be, dare she say it, doing the manly thing. As is, she's afraid that his sex life exists entirely on those screens. It disgusts her to even think about her son's sex life, but his lifestyle begs the question. It's not really normal, is it? For a man in his thirties to live with his mother and not have anyone his own age. She wouldn't necessarily want him to be gay either, not that there's anything wrong with that, she just wouldn't want that life for her son. But maybe it would be better than this. Maybe not.

In a shady corner of her memory, there are other possible reasons for Conor's isolation. She doesn't think about them if she can help it, and she's found this is a perfectly adequate way of dealing with things that were unpleasant in the past. What she has always assumed is that other people deal with things like this the same way. Her children particularly. She's quite fine now, with all that over and done with years ago, and so she imagines they must be too, although that's not the way people deal with stuff these days, is it? She's watched enough *Oprah* and *Dr. Phil* to know that domestic abuses should be brought to light, that people should see therapists and that healing can only happen when you talk about it, but when she tried to bring it up with Conor and Rebecca she was filled with such an intense feeling of despair, she thought it best for everyone not to mention it again. When they showed little interest in talking to her, she stepped back. She'd done her part and, anyway, she didn't want them to feel the way she did if they talked about it.

And when she did allow herself to think about it, no more than once or twice a year—at Christmas sometimes because Christmases had always been bad, and whenever she ran into someone from back then—she found that, with a bit of effort, it no longer mattered. Richard pushed her around a bit, yeah, but it was never really *violent*. He didn't draw blood, not once, and the few bruises were minor, nothing to look at. They did get to the point where they hated each other, but how unusual was that? Marriage. It's what happens. She refuses to feel guilty for the way it was. Though the things that stay with her, that echo just a little too loudly when she's feeling worried about the kids, or lonely, or just a bit empty inside, are the words he used: useless, slovenly, lazy, ugly, stupid. He didn't swear at her, but the way he said *woman* could make her want to die. And the eyes. That glare that told her all she needed to know about how valued she was in the world.

So she doesn't think about it. Not if she can help it.

At least Rebecca is happy, or she thinks Rebecca's happy anyway. She's got all the things a woman should have: husband, children, a home of her own. She won't have anything to do with Janet, and that is another sadness, but life is filled with shadows as well as light, is it not? She would like to be involved in her grandsons' lives. It's not exactly Christian, is it, leaving your mother out, despite that being the label they've given themselves. More like a cult, she suspects. After Rebecca met David she quietly faded out of Janet's life. But Janet thinks she'll be let back in at some point. If there's one thing she's learned in this life, it's patience.

As she heads down the hall, she returns to thinking about Conor, and his life in that room, a room she's currently entering with his cheese toasties, having knocked once and pushed the door open. Usually it's locked, but the handle turned readily in her hand, a nice change to see he's not barricaded in there like he usually is. She's preoccupied by her own thoughts, so she doesn't think, in that moment, about how long it's been since she's actually entered the room without Conor standing there, holding the door slightly ajar, his body blocking the space.

Afterward, she'll remember it's been months. At the time, it's the smell that hits her first—fetid air with a touch of something metallic, body odor and stale breath. "For god's sake, open a window, Conor!" she says before she registers what she's looking at—three large screens set up side by side, columns of writing and pictures on the left, like the social media images she's seen on the news; a newsfeed on the right, with headlines running along the bottom of the screen and a commentator in the top-right corner, and a computer game in the middle, men in combat gear walking through a run-down village, shooting and slicing anyone they come across, blood-splattered body parts exploding across the screen. The soldiers look American, like in the movies, the victims Asian, some of them cowering and running before being gunned down. Conor wears headphones and a headset into which he speaks, describing what he's doing as he methodically eradicates everything in front of his soldier. He's oblivious to Janet's entrance for more than a minute, but slowly he registers a change in the stasis of the room, some shift in airflow, the presence of another life. Janet sees it in the way his posture stiffens. He turns slowly, not stopping the game play, his eyes not leaving the screen, just turning in his chair. Then he looks quickly and reaches up to mute his microphone and move one earphone aside.

"Mum, you can't be in here." He turns back to the screen, not stopping the game. "I'm working."

"The door was unlocked. This isn't work, Conor."

"Yeah it is—I'll explain it later, but please don't ever come in here again. It was meant to be locked."

"Why?" She looks hard at the screens, takes in what she can, feels the drop in her gut. Something about this isn't right. She knows it.

"It's fine, Mum. Please go. I'll see you at dinner."

"Toasted sandwich." She reaches forward to place it—somewhere. Every surface is covered with equipment. Maybe computer equipment, but she sees other bits and pieces, and tools. Weird. What's he doing with those?

"GET OUT. I told you to get out!" Janet isn't ready for it when it comes. Conor swings around, glaring. She knows that look, and it paralyzes her. It's been a long time. She feels her body shrink into something small and timid. She's a snail at the bottom of a jar, and it's being filled with water.

"I said get out, you busybody old *woman*. This is NONE of your business."

Janet flinches, and diverts her gaze. She sees two odd socks and a T-shirt on the floor near the bed; she sees the carpet needs a vacuum, she sees her own feet.

She leaves, closes the door, goes into the kitchen to make a cup of tea. Zadie rises from her basket and trots over, sitting on Janet's foot and leaning against her leg. Janet reaches down to pet the dog. She just needs a cup of tea. He didn't mean it. She shouldn't have gone in. He's a young man with his own life. This is what happens when people don't have their own homes. Just a bit scratchy, that's all.

But she can still see the computers, the bloody battle, the racial slurs and sexual threats that leapt out from the screen in the few seconds she looked at it. She drinks her cup of tea and makes another, and eats half a packet of Tim Tams even though there is a pain just above her belly and she isn't hungry. She can still see the shape of her son and hear the sound of his voice before he knew she was there: a stranger to her, his shoulders a dark silhouette before a world she didn't recognize.

Nineteen

RED PILL

What does it even mean, their way of life? What are they even protecting? When he hasn't spoken to Johnny for a while, and especially since he's been home, Conor gets a bit fuzzy about that part. He knows he wants freedom, and he doesn't want to be told what to do, and he thinks all this stuff that's popular these days—snowflakey, communist nonsense, intersectional man-haters, Māoris and border jumpers and liberal cucks dictating what can be said, who's allowed to say it and how—all of that feels like it's imposing on his freedom to be who he is. But who is he? He really didn't know until he met Johnny, and now Johnny is encouraging him to find out more, especially while he's home. There might be pictures, records, information about his ancestry. And he should take a DNA test. It's important to establish just where he comes from, so that he can stand on solid ground when it comes time to claim their place. Know thyself, Johnny tells him, it's a powerful thing to do.

So that's how he finds himself out in the garden with his mother, despite what happened the other day when she came into his room. He knows she'll like him asking about where they came from, originally, and it's his way of saying sorry—taking an interest in things, helping her in the garden. Her unit is by the road, so she has charge of the front lawn as well as her side—not that she minds, she's happy about that. She gets him to do the lawns while she prunes the shrubs. It's an easy job, especially with the lightweight electric mower. He doesn't mind so much, not like he used to. Time away from the computer and the physical work is good for his body—he almost wishes there was more.

Janet takes her time warming up to him and his inquiries. Fair enough. He kind of deserves it. But he is protecting her, really. She has no idea what she's walking into. Wouldn't do for her to know more about his life. Eventually, once the lawns are mowed and he's hauling hedge trimmings to the compost heap, she starts to open up. Slowly, and in a roundabout fashion, she tells him what little she knows about the men and women in her line. She doesn't seem to particularly enjoy talking about them—they were bitter women, she says, the ones she knows about, and the men, rough as guts. Not much to romanticize in those stories, but he can see she's chuffed he wants to know.

"They got themselves here, though, didn't they? Under pretty harsh conditions," Conor says when Janet pauses.

"I suppose so. You'd think it would've made them happy, to be in a better place."

"It would have been hard, wouldn't it? Fighting off natives, taming the land. Not much joy, but I bet they wanted that for their kids."

"I don't know which generation is supposed to be happy then, son. Are you?"

"I wasn't before. Ever. But I have been feeling better lately."

"I can see that. Good. I'm happy if my kids are happy."

"Do you know how my sister is?"

Long-lost Rebecca.

"I haven't heard."

"Any more kids?"

"How would I know, Conor? You think I have magic powers?"

"Course not, Mum. I thought she might be talking to you again."

"No. I don't expect it. Unless she gives up that husband and the religion."

"Still going strong, then."

"Do you know what she told me? She said she had nothing more to say to me. I didn't give you kids any foundation, she said, no god and no church."

"And a drunk dad who liked to beat his wife, did she say that too?" Surely that was the real reason for her distance.

"Oh c'mon, Conor, it wasn't that bad."

"It was bad enough." Bad enough to turn Rebecca religious.

"Well, I've told you kids I'd go back and change it if I could, but what's done is done."

"Yeah, I know, Mum. It wasn't your fault the old man was an arsehole."

"Do you think she thinks it was *my* fault? She said she wants her kids to have values, as if we didn't have any. And she wants them to be protected from all the evils of the world as long as they can be."

There is some truth in it, but Becks is being a brat. No one is taking away her precious "values." Time to grow up and make up. Their father can't hurt them anymore, and she should honor her mother if she's so religious.

"She'll come around, eventually. She'll see that you did your best." He doesn't believe it as he says it, but he's trying to be the dutiful son. Janet's eyes are distant now, the lines at the corner of her mouth tight.

"Hey, so, speaking of things we don't like talking about—where did Dad's people come from?"

She tells him Ireland and England, though there's a sprinkling of Danish and/or German, it's a bit unclear. Good, hardy, brilliantly white stock. He laughs. They might not be white supremacists, but Johnny's group sure do like their white to be pure—this will go down well.

It's late afternoon as they pack up, Conor picking up the final scattered branches with the wheelbarrow, Janet gathering the tools. Conor is pleased with himself—it isn't too bad spending time with his mum—he feels virtuous, and he has the information he's been assigned to get. As he puts away the wheelbarrow and closes the garage, he suddenly loses his smug glow. Last time he was in the garage he'd just been for a run, and heard a car coming up the drive behind him. When he'd turned to look, he'd locked eyes with the driver of the car, and couldn't believe who he saw. Could it really have been the woman from the bar, Keri? He had watched her pull into the far driveway, then get out and rush to the middle house, knocking at the door. It certainly looked like her—the way she moved, her figure.

He shakes his head at the memory and hustles inside, suddenly eager to put his mind at rest.

"Mum?" he calls. There is no response, so he calls again, louder.

"What? Why are you yelling my house down? I was just in the loo." His mother stops when she sees him. "What's so urgent?"

"Yeah, uh, nah. Hey, who lives in the third house down the driveway? You know everyone, right?"

"That's Keri—you know, mother of the girl who walks Zadie sometimes, Wairere. Why?"

"Ah, yeah. I thought it was someone I know."

"Well, you probably do know her. She used to live here before her family moved to Aussie."

He nods. At least his mother hasn't clicked. "Yeah, you're right. I probably know everyone around our age." The truth is, he doesn't know anyone anymore. Can barely name a single kid he went to school with, and certainly isn't in contact with any of them.

"Anyway, just so you know, this isn't gonna get you off the hook with me."

"Aw, Mum. I said I was sorry."

"I've got one more thing you can do for me, then we can call it even."

He spends the rest of the day in his room, like every other day, checking the accounts they're watching, maintaining the aliases, making an appearance in chat rooms and monitoring what activists and researchers are saying about "extremist" groups like theirs via social and mainstream media. The itch to run the loudmouths into the ground is always hard to ignore, but he usually manages it by reminding himself that they're in it for the real thing: something much greater and more permanent than a little online baiting. He must stay disciplined. And he has responsibilities, one of which is to make sure their own secret communications are encrypted and as untraceable as possible through various VPNs. In between all of that, he streams his scheduled games on Twitch, earns a little money. Not as much as he anticipated—he'll have to spend more time on the boring but more reliable online data-gathering work. Personal information is money, and he's good at getting information.

The thought of Keri so close by stays with him—the awkward grind of embarrassment at their false start mixed with a little surge of excitement. He doesn't want them to, but his thoughts keep circling back around. The way her body felt against his, how her mouth opened, so willingly, to accept his. Despite himself, he keeps replaying the scenes for any remnant sensations, until he feels her, almost as if she's in the room with him.

Later, he joins his mother for dinner—she usually makes them trays to eat in front of the telly—good, stodgy, old-fashioned fare that he enjoys for the nostalgia as much as the taste: corned beef, mashed potato, lamb chops, mince with mixed vegetables. He lets the routine dull his senses, thoughts of Keri drown under the weight of so much stodge, and mind-numbing TV. They used to watch the 6 p.m. news together every night, until he couldn't stand it anymore and asked if they could switch to anything else. After a long debate, during which Conor had to go into detail about how mainstream news is run by a corporate government that uses media to manipulate and control them, his mother relented, but he could tell she didn't really believe him.

"I'll just watch it in my own time," she said, patting his hand. "We don't get much time together, so we might as well watch something we both enjoy."

He rolled his eyes. "Okay, Mum. But if you're going to watch it, just remember you shouldn't believe everything you see."

"Of course. I'll remember that. So, what shall we watch instead?"

That's how they ended up addicted to *Married at First Sight*.

"You could be in this, son," Janet says. "You couldn't be in most of these shows. But you might find someone lovely on this one." Which is weird, but he says sure, okay. At least the old girl is happy.

After dinner, and the semifinal of *Married at First Sight*, Conor heads back to his room. This is when his real work begins, and tonight he has a call with Johnny scheduled.

"So, I think it's time to take the next step."

Conor has been waiting for this. It's after midnight, same time that Johnny always calls, always from an unidentifiable number. Johnny changes his phone constantly, and doesn't write down numbers or keep them on his phone. He's just good at remembering them, maybe something to do with his really high IQ. Johnny could have been a doctor, a lawyer, anything he chose really, if he had stayed at university. It's just one of the things he gave up because he couldn't stand the lies and he didn't want to toe the line. He lives by the principles he preaches, no question about that. That's the way to do it really: live the example. Conor is trying to do that. He's shown his loyalty, done what he's been asked, consistently, for months. He knows better than to ask too many questions, and Johnny has told him that when it's time, he'll learn everything he needs to know. It looks like that time might be now.

"You've grown into the movement and I see you as one of our strongest foot soldiers, but you understand my caution?"

"Of course. There's a lot at stake. It makes sense to test me."

"Look, Conor, I like you, but I've had to hold some things close to my chest. You've given me a few signs that you might not be ready."

Conor is dismayed. Surely not? "I don't know . . . I'm doing everything you've asked of me."

"Yeah, I know you are. It's more, you're just quiet sometimes, you know? And I don't know if you get it, what we're really talking about here, and if you'll be reliable when the time comes. What we're talking about ain't for the fainthearted."

Conor is quiet, even though he knows he shouldn't be at this moment. Truth is, he doesn't know how to react. Sometimes he has to think about what Johnny tells him and shows him.

Sometimes he has to work out a way to think about it in his own mind. It can take a minute to find his own logic in terms of the work they're doing. But he believes in Johnny. That's what he knows. He feels like he belongs more than he ever has in his life, and that feeling comes from Johnny. He would do anything.

"Look, Johnny, I know I'm quiet. It's just the way I am, eh? But you tell me to do something, brother, and I'm there. Because even if I don't understand something fully, I believe in you, and I believe in the cause. I can see how fucked up everything is, and I know if we don't shake it up, people like us are just going to keep being excluded, when our ancestors ran the whole world. We're losing everything, and they would be ashamed of us, because soon people like us won't even exist anymore. Everything has been turned on its head."

"And what are we going to tell our kids about that?"

"Yeah—what do we tell our kids?"

"Our culture is dying."

"Exactly! We are becoming the minority—we have no freedom to speak, no freedom to make the choices we want to make, for ourselves and our families. You should fucken see it, Johnny. Our neighbors are refugees from god knows where, ethnic heathens for sure. And the other neighbors are Māoris. Even in my own driveway, I'm a minority. The only white man."

"So, you see how it is."

"I see it. I really see it, man."

"You willing to hurt people? To kill if necessary? To risk your own safety?"

Conor pauses then, he can't help it. But the fervor is still with him.

"If we are brothers, and you ask this of me, I will do it." Deep down, he doesn't know. Not about whether he is capable—he's pretty clear that he could carry out violence if he had to—but whether he *should* do it. He pretty much figures it's wrong on some level, even for a cause you really believe in. But he would wear it. He would live and die by the sword if he had to, because that's how much the Brotherhood means to him. He won't lose Johnny and the rest of them because of his own cowardice, that's for sure, or for any high morals that have never been any use to him before.

"You're a good man, Conor. I'm going to tell you what's what, and that means we're bonded, okay? That means you're in, all the way in. You are choosing to take the red pill right now, tonight. I know you thought you were doing that before, but red-pilling isn't instant like the movies, eh? Tonight, I want to offer you freedom. You have been a slave, all your life, just like everyone else, born into bondage, kept in a gilded cage. Imagine that I am reaching my hand out to you and offering you a way out. Do you accept?"

Conor swallows. He sees Johnny's hand, and he imagines taking it. "Yes." It comes out as a whisper, and he clears his throat so he can say it louder. "Yes."

"I know you have reservations when I say there might be violence." How does he always know what Conor is thinking? "So I'm gonna be straight with you. I have reservations too. But if anyone gets hurt, that's collateral. There are necessary sacrifices that must be made if we are going to break ourselves and everyone else out of our bondage. How do you think they keep us down? Through fear. We're so scared of breaking the rules and hurting someone, we stay in the prison they've built for us. And they know we can't disrupt things without the possibility of hurting people. So we stay passive, we stay under control. Only by freeing ourselves of guilt for the pain of others can we be free to act."

It makes sense. Conor lets himself imagine what it would be like to act without worrying about other people. It does feel more free. It feels like liberation. But also, he already knows, hate can take you a long way. Does he hate their enemies? Yes. The thing he has learned is, the freedom to hate is a thrill. The freedom to use all those words the world says are wrong to use? There's a power in it. And the power says fuck you. The power says he is the master of his own destiny, and he can say anything he wants to say. And when the words come spilling out in a tirade of cursing, he is really *cursing*, you know? Like in the old days—he's flinging them all into hell. Why? Because he can. Because it's his birthright. Because he comes from superior stock. This is what he's learned. The hate has become delicious, intoxicating, addictive. And he feasts.

He only has to do what he chooses to do, for the movement. The greater good. They're not asleep like the others; they know what's really going on, and with that knowledge comes responsibility. "You're right," he says to Johnny. "I agree, one hundred percent."

"Conor. I'm going to tell you something in full trust. I am

placing my life in your hands now. What you choose to do with this information will determine all of our futures, and our future relationship with each other."

"Okay. I'm here. I'm ready."

"We are an independent cell. Our objective, like all independent cells in other countries, is to disrupt if not destroy the system, to bring the government and all other authorities into disrepute, causing widespread distrust and chaos. That is all. The second part of the plan is to instigate new rules and power structures in the vacuum left by the destruction of the status quo, but that won't happen until the first part of the plan has been successfully executed. We are the frontline—nothing else can happen until we do our job. The movement is relying on us, and can't begin without us."

"How will we do it?"

"I've taken the risk of initiating and training a number of you, and sending you to different parts of the country. We are an exclusive and small group. Our independence and isolation protects us. We will soon cease to communicate with each other. That's important. You will then all become your own cell."

Conor feels dismayed, the sense of loss already palpable.

"Is that . . . permanent? Cutting off contact?"

"It's a security measure, leading up to our action, and then for some time afterward. But once we feel free and clear, we can be in contact again, through encrypted channels."

"Of course. What is . . . what are we leading up to?"

"Each cell is charged with devising a strategy of disruption that must be three things: unexpected, shocking, and destructive in a way that will destabilize people. It can be random; it doesn't even have to target certain groups. They believe in the law to keep them safe, right? The authority of the police and courts and government? What if none of that can keep them safe? Spreading confusion and fear is the point. Chaos is a vacuum we can exploit."

"Okay. This is it."

"Can you feel it in your blood, Conor?"

He can feel it alright. Adrenaline pumping in his veins. But also in his bowels. All he can manage is an affirmative grunt. He hopes it sounds triumphant.

"To keep all of us safe, I've planned separate actions for each of you. But we must act on the same day of the same month—eighth of August. That means there will be a series of explosive events all at once, and the authorities as well as the masses will learn very quickly that everything is beyond their control."

"We'll just watch the others from afar."

"Like everyone else. And where possible, these events will be executed in very public places—the more multicultural, the better. Bonus points for a disruption of something that is the antithesis to our Identitarian values."

Conor exhales slowly, audibly.

"This is where you get to show you're a real man who can do what it takes, not hide behind your computer bitching out feminists and gender freaks. Anyone can do that, even a pimply kid with no friends. You've proven that's not who you are, but this is the final test."

"Yeah." He's still quiet, despite wanting to reassure Johnny.

"Are you with me?"

Conor thinks about his life before Johnny and all of this, and his life after. He's had more purpose and more energy in the last year than the rest of his life combined. A lot of the time he feels something he might describe as happiness. There's got to be something in that. And even if he does have doubts, he knows he's not going anywhere. He can almost hear his mother's voice: *If Johnny jumped off a cliff, would you?* Well, yes, Mother, yes I would. I absolutely would. He chuckles.

"I'm in, Johnny. With you all the way, and then some."

"And then some!" Johnny laughs with him then, both of them sounding a little manic, a little delirious, perhaps even joyful at the possibility of a world of their own making.

Twenty

RĀ WHĀNAU

The rain continues for three days, but on the fourth day a stunning sun dries the ground so quickly the mud turns hard as brick. The women in each house are relieved: Sera because the party is the day after tomorrow, Keri because Walty can at last go outside again, and Janet because her memories of the last "one-in-a-thousand-year flood" are still vivid, and every time it rains too heavily she feels the anxiety tense every muscle in her body until her neck seizes up.

Keri is welcoming when Sera asks if Aliana can spend the day playing with Walty so that she can shop and start on her party decorations and food. It will take her most of the day on the bus to get to each of the three different stores she needs to get the best deals. Much easier without a tired toddler in tow.

Keri seems delighted to return the favor at last, but Sera still needs many reassurances to leave Aliana behind.

"Go, go—she'll be fine. You know she loves Walty and I'll ply her with food and stories when she needs a rest. Eventually even Walty naps—not every day now, but I bet he'll love the opportunity to be indulged alongside Ali. And if all else fails, TV!"

"Yes, you're right. She will be fine."

"Of course she'll be fine. Not sure about you, though. You look like you've eaten kānga pirau for the first time."

"Kānga pirau?"

"Rotten corn. Not for the fainthearted, but a delicacy if that's what you're into."

"Rotten?"

"Fermented, really. All the rage these days, fermented kai."

"Do you eat it?"

"No! No no no. No. But your face."

"I feel a bit sick. I know I should be brave, but I've never left her for a whole day."

Life has become so easy, so routine. Sometimes Sera almost forgets how far they have traveled and under what conditions. Then she'll find a simple task in front of her, and it feels like she is crossing into a foreign country again, looking into the indifferent faces of armed border patrol, or indifferent flames consuming everything in their path. She doesn't think about those things, she just feels them in her body—a constriction in her chest, a sudden inability to breathe that forces her to take great gulps of air. A dry, dry mouth and thirst that can't be quenched with water. She can't explain any of this, but when she panics, it still helps to take stock. A refugee counselor had told her to do just that: notice the ground under your feet, notice the world around you, what you feel on your skin, what you smell, what you hear, and what you see. Sera can get herself unstuck doing this, but sometimes she gets stuck in the exercise instead, transforming it into compulsive counting, arranging, rearranging. That's usually when she's at home. Now, at Keri's, it helps. She feels the seat under her buttocks, the scratchy fabric of the ancient couch against the back of her legs, her bag under her hands and fingers. She feels the urge to go through its contents and check her money and ID and bus card and bank card, but she did that moments before entering Keri's house, so she continues registering everything she perceives instead: the breeze from the open window on her right cheek, the odor of porridge and milk and something sweet from breakfast, the faint buzz of a fly that dives close to her and away again repeatedly.

Keri is in full flight telling the story of the first time she left Wairere—how it felt like physical pain, how she could barely eat—before she repeats that it's important to get some space. Sera is present enough to nod her head, and when Keri is done, she is able to say she feels better, even though she thinks it might be the exercise rather than the story that has eased her anxiety. She doesn't yet know how to tell Keri about the anxiety, or even the right words to talk about it in English, but she does think of one thing to say:

"I know we are safe now, but often I still seem to react as if we are not."

Keri nods. "It takes a long time, once you're out of danger, doesn't it? I still feel that way about Walty's dad sometimes. He's a long way away now, but if I think about it too much I can get myself in a real state. You know, I get the shakes."

Sera nods. They don't always have the right words, and they don't have the same experiences, but there is enough familiarity between them now for some things to be left unsaid, and for her to feel ease around the friendship, a knowing that she can go away and come back again, and all will be the same. It is a long time since she's had a real friend, other than Adam.

Keri has been thinking the same thing, maybe not in this moment but as the weeks have passed. When did she last have a friend she could drop in on unannounced, drink tea and gossip with? The friends from the pub are girls she's known since high school, and kept seeing on and off throughout the years because they were her crew then and she'd thought they would be for life. But she's been feeling for some time that she doesn't fit anymore, in that scene or in that group, and the interaction with Conor seemed to confirm that, even though she was the one who encouraged him. When she's around them, she acts like someone she's not; they, and she, keep things on the surface. With Sera it's almost impossible to keep anything on the surface. Every time one of them tells the other a piece of their story, it's impossible not to acknowledge the gravity of their pasts, the vortex of elements swirling below every decision. She's done this before and she's wary of it: fallen hard and fast in love with a man or a friend or a concept. But the fierce loyalty growing for Sera and her family feels right: her new friend has as much at stake as Keri.

Neither of them realized how much they needed this friendship before. And now, if it were to disappear, it'd be like demolishing a room in each of their houses, their lives left open to harsh weather and whatever evils can climb in through the gaps in the wall.

The party is at 10 a.m. on a Saturday, and since most of the guests are toddlers or the families of toddlers, they arrive promptly so as to enjoy as much fun as possible before the inevitable midday meltdowns and naps. Most of them have been up since 6:15 a.m., or 5:45 a.m., or horrendously for one parent, 5:02 a.m., and it already feels like the day is half done. They start inside with balloons and streamers, chippies, drinks, and musical chairs, followed by a full game of pass the parcel, in which every single child magically gets a prize. Keri and Wairere are the games masters, while Sera and Adam organize the food and hospitality for the other parents. Many are unfamiliar with the games, or know slightly different versions of them. Most have never been to a birthday party in New Zealand before.

"You will show us how it is done!" Sera had declared the day before as Keri helped her prep food. Keri had already advised what party foods should be on an authentic Kiwi child's birthday list, modified by cultural preferences, of course.

At eleven, they head outside for the piñata, a game of statues played to the *Moana* soundtrack, which devolves into everyone just dancing, and the food. Adam has set up tables outside and people lay out blankets and deck chairs to sit in the sun. They talk of good weather and community events and childhood development, comparing notes on ages and stages, food preferences and the quirks of growing vocabularies. Few of them come from the same place, so they speak English and avoid any mention of the people and places they've left behind, in case they stumble accidentally into the quicksand of grief that can appear at the center of such conversations, always at a different and unpredictable spot for each person. They are careful with each other this way, instead focusing on the availability of certain foods or the cost of clothes, the best places to find bargains, and New Zealand slang. So much is new and needs deciphering.

While Wairere occupies the children outside, Keri hides treasure inside, under couch cushions and beds, behind table legs, in the corners of shelves, then Wairere leads a snake of children into the house, holding hands on the hunt. Wairere loves the simplicity of little kids' birthday parties, which produce the kind of noise that masks the stuff that usually causes her to shy away from people. If she wanted to tune in, she supposes she could do it, but since that isn't in her best interests, she is able to exist in a bubble of children's chatter, all the adult noise pushed to the edges of her consciousness. Aliana and Walty and the other children watch her with devotion as she carefully explains the rules of each game and allocates blindfolds and pins and sticks and prizes, holding chubby hands and leading the dance, or timing the music just so. Sticky faces lean close to her planting kisses, random children climb over her in small packs, even the odd outburst of wailing doesn't bother her. She might describe herself as something close to happy.

Janet comes outside around midday, crosses the lawn, and joins the party of adults, toting an assortment of Kiwi biscuits: homemade Anzacs, Afghans, sprinkles, and peanut brownies. She also brings something else no one anticipated: Conor, looking uncomfortable in jeans and a blue T-shirt that are both a little too smooth not to have been ironed.

"Kia ora!" Adam exclaims, after the crowd has taken a moment to peer at them and away again, adjusting themselves to these new arrivals. They have already settled into an easy comfort with each other, even those who didn't know one another before this day, and they now have to make some space in the group, mentally and emotionally, for the neighbors. No one says it, but more than a couple notice that these are the first white people to arrive, and whether they consider this for long or not, the reorientation is more pronounced than for previous arrivals. They're used to this, so used to it most of them don't even register the switch, but each of them feels it as a kind of loss, the undoing of a particular type of ease that was present a moment before their arrival.

"Kia ora, e hoa!" Adam exclaims again. He is learning a little te reo at work, as much as he can fit around the medical emergencies he attends. It will help when he assists Māori patients, but it also helps him attend to living in this new place, and to his preschool daughter who will one day speak this language. He speaks three languages, but she has only two so far, and he so wants for her to have more than him in every way, and to belong to this place properly. He can't imagine belonging to a country without speaking its language.

Adam does the gracious host rounds, introducing Janet and Conor to each of the families. Janet and Conor are the only childless people present, although technically Conor is Janet's child, and Janet makes a joke about this to ease the new arrival nerves. Everyone laughs and bows a little or shakes hands as they are introduced.

Conor is rattled by the exchange of manners. He feels like a traitor to the cause. He knows Johnny would tell him to consider this an intelligence-gathering exercise, sussing out the "enemy," perhaps even a way of keeping his cover, like a spy, but Conor is no good at acting the part. He feels disgust rising up in him, associating with these people, these leeches on his country, but his mother has been so quiet since he yelled at her and he feels guilty about it. He hasn't seen her like that for years, shrunken and sad. She's usually such a bossy woman. He hates that too, but not as much as the pathetic thing he's encountered every mealtime over the last week. She'd talk about this party, how not being invited reminded her of the grandchildren she didn't see, but then, at last they'd asked her to pop in. And how she didn't want to walk in there alone, like she didn't have her own family to be proud of, like she wasn't good enough to go to the whole party. Oh, for fuck's sake, Mum, he'd said, don't do this to me. And she'd said, it's not always about you, Conor, even though I might have given you that impression, and she'd left the table. The cold war continued for three days until he couldn't stand her moping anymore and told her he would come, just for a bit, so she wouldn't have to walk in alone, and she'd perked up and hugged him and started baking a ridiculous array of cookies.

There's something else that got him there, too. Something that he's even less likely to admit out loud. He's curious about Keri. He's hardly seen her since that first time—even as neighbors their paths rarely cross. He keeps odd hours, and her life revolves around school and preschoolers. Admittedly, he's not too keen on coming face to face with her alone, but he figures in a crowd like this he'll be able to observe her from afar. The night they got together seems distant now, but still, in some kind of fantasy scenario, he would have liked it to have gone further.

But he sees neither Keri nor the birthday girl's mother, or even the children he expected to have to avoid, so he eats some chips as they're passed around and offers an imitation of a smile as he's introduced. There's a lull, during which Janet explains loudly what the names and recipes for the cookies are. The Afghans cause some confusion, for not just the Afghan family in the group but everyone else, and the peanut brownies are whisked away so that peanut allergens don't cause trouble by occupying anyone's airways. Conor finds a spare seat and moves it a little distance from the others, planting it in what he hopes is an inconspicuous corner. He pulls out his phone and is suddenly intensely engaged with what he sees there, clearly too busy for small talk.

Eventually, the children begin to spill out of the house and find their parents to show them their prizes. Keri tells Wairere to take a break—it's cake time now. Sera lights the candles, and Keri leads her outside, holding the door open as Sera exits, holding the cake aloft. They both start singing, tentatively at first. They start with the Māori—rā whānau ki a koe—then move to similar words in Sera's own language, which Adam is able to join while he runs alongside, filming proceedings, while Keri tries to shade the burning candles from any breeze. By the time they reach the table, the others join them in singing "Happy Birthday." Aliana, who has been riding a newish trike up and down the footpath, stops and stands, eyes wide, while Walty pulls at her hand and tells her it's cake, over and over. The other children move toward the table, hypnotized, and Aliana finally allows herself to be pulled forward so that she stands in front of the cake, decorated with rainbows and her name and some kind of messy approximation of words that might have once said happy birthday in one of the three languages, but now melts together in a sparkly ooze.

"Blow, sweetheart!" Adam coaxes when the singing and cheering ends, and so she does, as does Walty, a little shower of spit landing on the cake between them. Two candles are extinguished, while the other burns on defiantly, and when Ali fails to blow it out on subsequent tries, Sera bends to blow with her, and another cheer goes up as the flame fizzles into a smoky coil.

Keri holds a knife upright, away from little hands and heads, ready for someone to do the honors, but as she waits for the cake area to clear, she looks up and meets Conor's gaze. A sickening lurch laced with a dusting of thrill kicks her in the gut. Fuck no. What is he doing here? Keri can't get past the question, nausea rising into her throat, but she manages to quickly avert her gaze so that she isn't eyeballing him directly.

"Cut the cake for us, Keri? Please." Sera is all smiles, her eyes bright. It's the most animated and excited Keri has seen her, and she is happy for her friend. This celebration is obviously doing her good. Sera told her they've never been able to have a proper birthday party for Aliana before. Imagine. Keri feels her life is constrained in so many ways almost every day, but she's always been able to celebrate her children's births, and feed them, and put a roof over their heads. Just.

The thought is a good distraction. She's able to focus completely on the task in front of her, small hands reaching for cake, mothers and fathers coming in to help or get their own serving. Eventually Adam begins ferrying slices to the outer circle, and Sera and Keri watch as he takes the last pieces to Janet and Conor. Sera frowns, briefly, then returns to helping Aliana with her cake, her face lit up with delight as she watches her daughter. Walty has never needed help with cake in his life, so Keri is left suddenly without a job. She looks around, hoping for a task or a person to speak to, but everyone is otherwise occupied, and the next thing she sees is Conor approaching her.

"Hi," he says, and he suddenly looks very red.

"Hi," she says. She reaches for something else to say, but there's nothing.

"This is weird."

Weird, yes, that's something she can speak to. "Yup, very weird."

"I didn't know, I swear."

"No. Of course not. Me either."

"Anyway, I thought I should say hi."

"Sure, yes. But, we don't have to, you know . . ."

"No. We don't. But if you wanted to—if you ever want someone to talk to."

She looks at him then, seriously, full in the face. "No. I just . . . I told you that night . . . bit of a mistake on my part, and I wouldn't . . . not around home . . . I would never . . . around my kids."

"Of course. I'm not asking for anything either. Of course."

They are quiet for a while.

"I didn't come to be a creep, eh? Mum asked me especially. Didn't want to come alone. Anyway, I'm here."

"Thank you."

"Except now I'm going over there."

Keri laughs. "Okay."

He shrugs his shoulders and thrusts his hands into his pockets. "Okay. Bye."

And there it is. Wairere comes out to sit on the front step to sing "Happy Birthday" with the others, and sees the stranger, who she quickly realizes is Janet's son. She has trouble bringing him into focus, trouble making out his features. If she were asked to describe him, she'd say he looks like every other nondescript Pākehā guy she's ever seen. Nothing to distinguish him. But even as she thinks this, something else is encroaching on her awareness—something she notices at the same time she becomes aware of her mother's body language shifting. Keri lifts the knife and her face braces with tension, all the muscles in her arm tightening at the same time. She sees her mother look, recognizes what she is looking at, and feels a sinking feeling that isn't supersensory perception, just simple dismay. The same way she feels when she has a stomach bug and she can feel a vomit coming. An unavoidable unpleasant sensation building in her gut.

When Keri finishes giving out the cake, Conor moves toward her. Wairere can see his intent, her mother's defensiveness, the script they both act out to get what they want from each other. For Conor, it's to make a positive impression, to impress Keri with his gentleness, his safeness, his ability to be someone she might actually look at. So that's it. Part of it anyway. He likes her? For Keri, it's to get away as quickly as possible without angering him, without making herself a target, to deliver a firm message while also avoiding any damage to his ego. She sees her mother's fear that if she makes a wrong move he might take it out on her, or worse, her children. She sees, shockingly, that this isn't the first time her mother has had a version of this conversation with Conor. How she leans to one side, her hand tapping her thigh. How he plants his feet toward her, his shoulders forward as if she has some magnetic pull. The way Keri looks everywhere but into his eyes. There is familiarity locked into the air between them.

How could her mother have been so blind, so stupid? Wairere has only just found a way to talk to her, and now there's this? And Keri had left Wairere alone with her worries instead of sharing what she already knows. Wairere had trusted her mother with her most private worries and Keri had not reciprocated. She feels like she might cry, but instead she rises and leaves swiftly, returning to her house before anyone can notice she's gone. She is alone again.

Conor looks for his mother, but she has managed to ingratiate herself with a group of parents and is now leading them on a tour of her roses. She's in her element, and she might even manage to keep her opinions to herself long enough for these people to like her, though Conor is sure he'll hear what she really thinks over dinner. The awkward conversation with Keri is already turning to sick in his gut. Why did he do that? What did he think it was going to achieve? It was like he lost his mind for a moment, watching Keri, the way her smile lit up her eyes as she watched her friends, the flicker of something more going on beneath. He had this sudden compulsion to be the recipient of a smile like that, and this sudden impulse to be near her. He hadn't paused long enough to think it through; he'd just found himself in front of her, suddenly, with nothing to say.

Anyway, it would have been weird not to say hello. At least it's out in the open now. But also, he's stuck at this party, probably too early to leave. He'll wait another fifteen minutes, catch his mother's eye, and go. He sidles up to the food table and starts picking at the offerings. Johnny is right, of course—the imagined Johnny in his head, anyway—this is the perfect opportunity to eavesdrop. This peaceful little gathering is exactly the kind of thing they want to prevent: all of these people, foreigners—worse, refugees—acting like they belong here. Acting like this is their place now, like they can go about their business freely. The objective is to make them feel uncomfortable, make them aware that they will never belong in this place. Go back to where they came from. In fact, he doesn't care where they go. And fuck Keri. There's probably some little white chick tradwife who would eat all that up and more, whatever he served up, that's what he should aim for. Some girl who loves the movement as much as he does.

It bolsters him, thinking about the rewards that will be his once he gets this thing done: loyalty, status, admiration, and the right kind of woman. He just has to stay on the right path. But it's also different looking around this party; it's all been abstract until now. He doesn't like these people, in fact, he feels kind of repulsed at the sight of them, but the flesh and blood that disgusts him also makes him want to back up, fast. It's like hurting an animal: not a big deal in your head, but pretty bloody full-on when you're faced with it. He had to deal with the rats in his mother's compost only last month; she'd brought some of those sticky traps that catch them but don't kill instantly, and there they were, screaming into the night in horror. So he'd taken a spade to their heads: three of them eventually. Didn't get any easier despite his distaste for the filthy, diseased creatures.

He watches as a father helps his son ride one of the bikes, his business shirt tucked into business pants with a belt. The kind of thing his father would have worn to work, not to a kid's party on the weekend. As if his father would ever have gone to a kid's party. The women are talking about which universities they have to choose from in New Zealand. Not the kind of thing he expected to hear, their kids aren't even at school yet. Another father is trying to juggle, and Adam is taking photos, which Conor sidesteps—he doesn't want to be in those. And then the women's talk turns to the Culture Fest coming up at the high school, how Keri invited them to get involved if they were keen—bring food from their different countries, maybe their cultural songs or dances. But then someone falls off a bike and it sets off a chain reaction: everyone crying and whining, wide open mouths filled with half-chewed cake or Cheezels. The women stop talking to attend to their children. Conor looks away. It's the cue he's been waiting for to leave.

It has to be big enough to make an impact, Johnny said. Cause fear, instability, distrust. Break down the bonds. People might get hurt, but that was the price for change. Real change takes guts and sacrifice. Sometimes, when people get stuck, there's only one way to put them out of their misery.

Twenty-One

DIVERSITY

By the time Wairere leaves the party, all the fun she had earlier in the day has been wiped out by the shock of her mother's encounter with Conor. She's aware that there's more going on, and maybe she should be vigilant about it, maybe she should notice what Conor is up to on top of sleazing around Keri, but she's suddenly too overwhelmed by it all. Felicity is meant to come over to study in the afternoon, as if she could do that right now. They'll have to change plans. She texts her friend, *I'll come over to yours instead. With party food. Gotta get away from this place.* Felicity is thrilled. *Lollies? Chippies? YAS.*

Good thing some of the food had been prepped at their place. She grabs a few things, and prepares to leave the back way, better to avoid everyone still gathered out front. Still, she's not looking forward to going past Mrs. B's house. She slides her arm through her tote bag, slips on her shoes, and sets out. It's only a few dozen steps to get past the neighbors, no more than a minute or two before she'll be off the property. As she passes Mrs. B's back windows, she can't help but look. There's a gap in the curtains shrouding one window, through which a ghostly computer screen light can be seen. And she knows—that's where he lives. She looks away, immediately hot and cold at the same time, and shudders. Keeps moving. She's just about off the property when Wairere hears Mrs. B's back door open. Don't look, Wai, she tells herself. Don't look. But he's right there, she can feel it. It only takes a small turn of the head, her eyes flicking up. Conor, stepping out and starting down the steps. He doesn't seem so nondescript now. There's something about him, slick and suffocating. She's frozen, staring.

Conor goes to the bins by the back steps and starts rifling through the recycling, pulling out bottles. Wairere can't seem to move and she still can't think. She just stares. Conor looks up then, right at her.

She doesn't know whether it is happening on the inside of him or the outside, or just in her imagination, but she watches Conor's form flicker before settling: he's a ten-year-old kid yelling, a teenager hunting a possum, a bitter old man losing his teeth, a toddler in a onesie. He's a small, furred creature, trembling. Finally, he's a fully grown man full of rage. He's both nothing unusual and something terrible. Worse, he has the ability to maim. Perhaps even the *intention*. Her mother is the least of it, she sees that now.

The moment has stretched on too long. "What are you looking at?" Conor shouts.

Wairere is scared, but she lifts her chin, eyeballing him. She doesn't know what to say. She wants to cast a powerful spell to protect her family. "Stay away!" She yells, but what else to say? "Stay away from my mum!"

What the hell? That isn't even what she wanted to say. She's so embarrassed that's what came out when she had the opportunity to say something. The truth is, it's so much more than that, but she can't figure out exactly what it is. There's something terrible she can't name—something acidic, noxious, cloying—hanging around him. Nothing in the world, nothing she knows of, comes close to this sensation, like it's glued to her insides, trying to take her air. Like a disease. And with things that spread and replicate themselves, you have to deal with the primary carrier, don't you? Patient zero, as they say in zombie movies. And if you don't have proximity to patient zero, then whichever carrier has brought the sickness into your community.

Janet holds certain values as sacred, among them that one should learn to live with one's neighbors, be polite and hospitable, follow the laws of the land, both written and unwritten, and that the majority vote rules. Above this, that she should speak her mind now that she has the freedom to speak it. All those years with a domineering man weren't for nothing. And somewhere beneath, somewhere she is barely aware of, hidden inside the values she keeps proud in her chest, is a subconscious constructed by a certain upbringing, a certain cultural sphere, a certain way of seeing the world shaped by generations and generations of white communities being pushed out into a world that wasn't theirs, convinced of the primacy of their way of life. So Janet doesn't see any contradiction between her doubt and disdain for her former refugee neighbors and their former refugee friends, and her extension of friendship. It's altruistic, really. Charitable. You have to give a little to get anything, and while she'd rather have Kiwis as neighbors, now that they are here she may as well be friendly. Might even rub off on them, and that has to be a good thing.

Janet enjoys the party, what's left of it. She enjoys sharing her culture, which at first revolves around her biscuits. She doesn't particularly want to know about their cultures, but she hears about them anyway because it's all they ever talk about. That makes her feel like a bit of an outsider, but she's damned if she's going to be made to feel alien in her own country, so she tells them about all the things she can think of that define what New Zealand is to her. *Country Calendar*—that was one—sheepdog trials and sheepshearing, A&P shows and gumboots and jandals, pavlovas and *Footrot Flats*. A lot of it doesn't seem to make much sense to them, but they light up when she names the haka and rugby and the mud pools and geysers in Rotorua, the volcanoes of the central plateau and Auckland, the Southern Alps and Queenstown, and all the pretty places. Even with the flood cycle, and a few too many summer fires in native forests each year, they still have so much more to enjoy than most places. A few faces drop when she mentions this, a few gazes politely shift away, then someone starts talking about fantails and pūkekos and then it's birds, birds, birds, and Janet has to agree, birds are pretty important to the Kiwi way of life. She asks if they plan to go visit some of the tourist spots, and most of them want to but won't be able to afford it for a while—they're still settling in, even though some of them have been here for a few years now.

Well, they're lucky, she tells them, most New Zealanders can't afford to travel at all anymore, but they've hit the jackpot—they got to travel the world and settle here. She hopes they know what a privilege that is. Janet doesn't see the look Sera gives Adam, the way he touches her elbow—a gesture that says *Just give it a minute* and *I'm sorry,* both at once. Janet is also unaware of what the others realize as they listen—that she is simply playing the same old narratives over in her head and saying them out loud to anyone she speaks to. Where Janet and her new friends do converge is in understanding that she really believes that what she's saying is somehow right, that she believes she's doing a good thing.

Then things get fractious with the little ones and everyone starts packing up for the day and going home for naps. Janet thanks Sera and Adam and gets on her way. She tells them to keep the Tupperware until all the biscuits are gone. And she makes sure little Aliana gets her gift—a whole bag of building blocks and stuffed toys from the thrift store where she volunteers. The week before, she tells them, she spent the whole afternoon, in between customers, choosing the best ones.

"Well, thank fuck that's done," Conor says when Janet walks in. He's at the table, downing a beer, flicking through his phone.

"That's not necessary," Janet says. "They might not be like us, but they're okay."

Conor scoffs. "You don't even like them, Mum. You're always going on about how they're skiving off the State, taking homes and income that should belong to New Zealanders. I've heard you complaining about their spicy food and the way they keep to themselves ever since I can remember. Remember you and Dad when those islanders moved in next door back at the old place? All we heard about for months was how much noise they made, how there were cars full of them parking on the lawn and the verge."

"That's true enough, but it was a different time."

"Mum. Come on. You've said almost the same thing about these ones. They're quieter, but why don't they speak like us and dress like us, and what are they up to, keeping to themselves."

Janet purses her lips, then opens her mouth as if to say something, and closes it again.

"It's okay. You don't have to be PC with me. I agree with you. Frankly, I wish the lot of them would fuck off back to where they came from. Make more space for us. No Kiwi should be homeless when foreigners have a place to live."

"I've always said that—you're right. I still believe that. But these ones have been okay so far. Even Sera is warming up, and I thought she was a bit thick at first."

"Nah, just playing you, Mum. You never know what the plan is, eh? But eventually I know they're gonna push us out of neighborhoods like this."

"Oh, I don't know. They seem pretty harmless. I don't mind them so much."

"Making friends, are we?" Conor's tone is sickly sweet, mocking.

Janet turns away. "I'm tired," she says. "I'm going to go watch some telly."

Conor watches her leave. It's irritating how he can see her falling for it and she can't see it for herself. He can't wait to get out of here. He heads to the fridge for another beer and takes it to his room.

Conor hasn't heard from Johnny for a week and he knows he won't hear from him again until long after it's done. He begins each day with the plan but is overcome by the heavy feeling that sits in his chest and keeps him from getting up and getting on with things. On day seven, the day before the party, he realized he's gutted. He misses his friend and he misses the group. The contentedness of the past year is gone. He had been happy, for a bit. Now that it's over, he feels much worse than the regular daily grind of discontent he used to feel. Now he knows what he's missing. He knows what it is to have friends he would kill for. He knows what it's like to have purpose. And he's angry. Really fucking angry. What kind of world is it where a man can't live the life he chooses, keep the friends he chooses, and be free to go about his business? Why is the life they want to lead—the Brotherhood—so curtailed by all the rules and regulations of the State? He's the one who's dispossessed, not the Horis and the border jumpers and the boat people, not the faggots and the trannies, not the whiny fucking women. The world is theirs—all the rules bent in their direction, because they're always complaining, always making the loudest noise, always somewhere they shouldn't be. And people like him—the ones who brought progress and created modern society—they have to shut up and stay on the fringes. Where would this country be without them? Still undeveloped—bush and bog and short, brutish lives.

Someone like Keri should be grateful to have someone like him. What's she got to be so stuck-up about—she's just a single mum on the benefit. But the way she looked at him at the party. If only she could see, they were closer than she thought. All he wanted was a cultural renaissance for white people, just like the Māoris had had. He couldn't see how it wasn't exactly the same thing. But someone like her, he knew what she'd say: it's not the same. Special treatment for the Māoris, as usual.

He thinks back to the Othala retreat. Their whole lives could be like that. He doesn't remember ever feeling that way before, truly part of a family, and the only way to get back to that is to see this through. They need to make their way of seeing the world, their way of life, a viable option again. Like it was for the Vikings and the Celts and all the other white races, the ones who made their way here millennia ago. That history has been rewritten and hidden, but they'd be able to bring it out again and stand proud—they just need to loosen the stranglehold that the snowflakes and communists have on society. If Keri could just come down off her high horse and *see* that, they might have something. Strictly speaking, it isn't encouraged, but he's heard about Māoris who are on their side. And he's read plenty about breeding the natives out of existence—Keri is evidence of that herself. The further down the bloodlines you go, the whiter the result. In some countries, it has even been official policy.

And he would treat her good, that's what she couldn't see. Better than the fathers of her kids, from what she told him the night they met. But it was over even before it had begun.

Johnny is right—destabilize everything, and offer a different way out. Chaos begets new life. Even the environment seems to know this—all that hippie talk of environmental collapse is useful to the Brotherhood's cause.

Remembering the Othala retreat moves him to take real action. He's already collected the chemicals, buying a couple at a time from different places so as not to rouse suspicion. He's been collecting glass bottles, which is harder than he anticipated since everything comes in plastic or cans these days, but he thinks he nearly has enough. Twenty? Twenty-five? Enough to make a scene and freak people out. He wants a mixture of common labels, not alcohol, so he also bought a bunch that won't rouse suspicion. He just needs to assemble them and work out how to time the release of water, acting like a fuse that will set the chemicals into action.

On the one hand, he hopes the bottle bomb idea isn't too pathetic compared to what the other guys are doing. On the other, he's relieved to have been given something easy to make at home that doesn't entail buying weapons or more heavy-duty ingredients. He just has to make sure he's doing enough to have the desired effect. From what he's read, these things can kill people, but he couldn't find any actual reports of that. More likely to sever a finger or damage an eye at most, cause superficial wounds and chemical burns. He can live with that. The main thing is to create fear. In fact, he can amplify the fear by placing the bottles in random places at the Culture Fest: on the corner of people's stalls, or in the crowd. Just place it down and walk away. They'll go off in people's faces when they least expect it. A scene on stage would cause the most widespread mayhem. Stage is the goal. He just hasn't figured out how to get all the parts together and get the bottles in place without exposing himself or severing his own fingers.

He'd seen the posters for Culture Fest—a night to kick off the school's Diversity Week—at the shops, and had considered making it his target, but it wasn't until the birthday party that he realized how perfect the scene would be—all those people getting together to celebrate and instead receiving an entirely different message. There's still a part of him that thinks he should feel bad about that, but he can't locate any hesitation about it anymore. It's what needs to be done. All he feels is a determination to do it. The alternative is unthinkable. The alternative is to feel isolated forever, and to say goodbye to the possibility of seeing Johnny and the boys again. He can't let them down. They're gonna make the world a better place.

Twenty-Two

WAIPUKE

The rain comes down, light at first, then a heavy drum on the corrugated iron of each roof, loud enough to wake the inhabitants. Keri opens her eyes in the half-light of early dawn, disturbed by the noise, the insistence of it, drowning out the possibility of any other sound. She feels the twist in her gut: Are the kids okay? Will she hear if they are not? Hopefully they won't wake. She knows in that same gut that they're fine, but she also knows she'll have to check now, that she won't be able to rest again until she sees for herself, so she climbs out of her bed and creeps softly—she doesn't know why since no one would hear her over this noise—to the door of their room. Twin beds—Wai curled under her covers, fetal again in her sleep, the only time Keri sees her vulnerable these days, and feels that tug in her chest, just beneath her sternum. Walty, sprawled, as abandoned to the whims of the world in sleep as he is any other time. The boy fills her with sweet joy and dread at what the world might do to him.

Janet lies in her bed and listens, and thinks, and listens, from 3 a.m. to 6 a.m. The rain, by turns thunderous and regular, but always insistent. There's something unsettling about the unrelenting steadiness of it, as if it requires something of them, as if it needs her to notice something. In the semi-dark, she hasn't risen out of the nighttime logic that gives the rain a personality, a temper, or the strange idea that she knows what it's angry about. The boy, what he said about the neighbors last week, what she saw on his screens. She's always known the line between common sense and taking it too far, always thought it was clear to him. She has her opinions, but they're pretty normal. She's never been a racist. Never. She didn't believe in the Springbok tour. She agreed with Martin Luther King, but the blacks had it much worse than the Māoris, everyone knows that. She had Māori friends at school and they agreed with her—everyone got on in those days. And now, they don't. Now, her son has taken to ugly ways of talking, ugly ways of thinking. Something to do with all that time he spends on the internet, she thinks. The thoughts swirl around and around in the dark, dancing with the rain, until she gets up to make a cup of tea.

Conor isn't asleep when the rain starts; he's too amped about the plans, running them over and over in his mind, thinking through all the scenarios: the supplies, the timing, the weather. The forecast is a worry, but it's supposed to clear tomorrow, so it shouldn't change anything. He's filled with doubt about his ability to pull it off at the same time as he's filled with determination to follow through.

If one unit fails, there are others that will work. That's the beauty of this thing: it's too big for any one of them, and he's an important part of the plan. He'll be a goddamn hero if he succeeds. That's the thing he rides the hardest when he starts getting freaked out: no matter what, he has lifelong membership to a very elite, very private club. It doesn't matter how others see him. They probably won't even know how powerful he is, and if he does get caught, if they do find out, well, notoriety won't be a bad thing—at least he won't be a nothing like he was destined to be before.

By 2 a.m. he's still not close to sleep, so he moves on to porn for some stress relief—at least it'll relieve the tension in his body, if not his mind. When the rain begins to come down so heavy he has to turn the sound on his headphones right up, he worries about his mother coming in—old habit from when he was a teenager, he supposes, and brushes off any further thought—the sweet distraction of the bodies on screen like a tranquilizer.

There are some things Sera finds comforting, despite how annoying they seem to be for other people. One is her husband's snoring—not that it doesn't wake her up, but when it does, which isn't often, she finds the sound peaceful, reassuring. That someone can sleep so deeply, that he can experience such peace? It seems a miracle, and fills her with a fondness for him similar to the fondness with which she beholds Aliana's sleep: the two of them like characters from a fairy tale in which a slumber spell has been cast on the princess and her whole family. That must make Sera an outsider: the evil fairy, bestowing only barbed gifts on her kin. She is still in exile, while those two sleep the sleep of the blessed and innocent, the returned. Something about Adam's disposition, and Aliana's youth, mean they can sink their toes into the soil here more easily.

But it was always that way with Adam, and it used to be that way with her. Whatever alarming situation they found themselves rocked by, she would find a way to plant herself, steady; without that, she might have simply whirred away into the ether, a bug buzzing too fast and too close to the sun. Perhaps the rawness of her nerves since they settled is a result of how much she suppressed before. Maybe she just has to work through it. There was so much she chose not to feel while it was happening. So while she envies Adam's peace, it reassures her, like the rain that now comes thundering so loud upon their roof it drowns out her husband's snoring. She has always loved rain, never understood why others complain about it. Her people come from dry mountain territory originally, where heat alternates with snow and ice, brief respite brought only by the spring and autumn rains. By the time Sera was born, most of her people lived in the cities below the mountains, and seasons were no longer reliable, but the genetic memory of rain stayed with them, any downpour bringing with it new growth except, that is, after the worst of droughts, when the parched ground was too hard to soak in the waters, and everything turned to mud instead.

Despite being woken first by her husband and then by a rain louder than any she's heard since they arrived in Aotearoa, it's not surprising that Sera is lulled back to sleep by all the noise, as if the sound can drown out the world she has known, as if the curtain of water falling all around their houses can douse the lifetime of heat and fire she has seen, her skin cooled by the wet air that filters through the window frames.

The neighbors wake, one by one, after their broken sleep. Janet has been listening to the news since her cup of tea at 6 a.m., while doing the crossword, and baking scones and a pie to keep them going for the day so she doesn't have to go shopping. She pets Zadie, who has curled up in her basket after breakfast, having deemed a world so wet unworthy of her attention. Every half-hour the news bulletin runs alarming speculation about what this latest bout of bad weather will bring—they don't think it's going to be too bad, but they've said that before. If their estimations are off, this could become the third one-in-a-thousand-year weather event in five years, especially if there's too much water falling per hour for the sewage systems or the dams to hold. They know by now that old patterns have been obliterated, so it's difficult to gauge. Something will have to give, the experts tell the breakfast hosts in grave tones, it's just what and when. Residents are advised to stock up and stay at home and ensure they've done what they can to mitigate the likelihood of flood, all at the same time. They'll be alerted if evacuations are needed, but that shouldn't be for a few days yet. Not at all if they're lucky.

Janet periodically goes to the window to look. There's a constant flow of water down the street, which is mostly flat, but dips a bit lower at one end. The drains are holding up so far. The ocean is eight blocks away, which Janet thought sufficient, but the estuary and the streams are closer. She's always envied those flash houses that got their own communal water feature in the shape of a man-made pond, but she's glad she doesn't live there right now.

She's worried, yes, and she'll get Conor to go out and check the guttering and the drains, and maybe even organize sandbags for the doorways once he gets up, but she also feels a small thrill underneath it all. Excitement isn't what you're supposed to feel when there's a disaster brewing. Excitement is what makes her feel a warm glow as she potters around her kitchen, the lights all on even though it's 8 a.m. and the world should be light outside. It's so gray, and so dark, and what she thinks of then is that time it rained at Christmas when she was nine years old, how she and her cousins closed all the doors to the bedrooms, so that the hallway was almost completely dark, and played hide and seek, bullrush, Chinese whispers, the delicious freedom of the absence of adults, the way the darkness allowed them to go right to the edge of what was allowed in the light. She feels the danger, out there, but she also feels more alive, like that kid in the dark hallway, young and hopeful about all the things she didn't yet know.

Conor has barely slept, so when he wakes with a jolt around 8:30 a.m., he tries to coax himself back to sleep, resetting his alarm for 11 a.m. He'll need the rest, for tonight. His instructions are that his action should occur late in the day, between 5:30 and 6:30 p.m. There's to be a ripple effect, a continuous stream of incidents to build confusion and fear, and he's proud that his action is to be near the end of the day. That must mean something. The build to a climax.

Sleep doesn't come to him again. He feels like he's never been so wide awake, even as he lies there with his eyes closed. The rain is heavy and loud on the roof, but it's not like this sleepy suburban village is ever going to be anything other than mundane, solid, reliable. That's what makes the strategy of targeting this place so genius. It's a place where people go for dependability, a place for old people and young families, a place that doesn't think about the big picture the way Johnny and him and the boys do. A place that needs shaking up. He's not going to let a little rain get in the way of that. He wishes he could flick Johnny a text. He wishes he could get one last check-in, one last thumbs-up, but he's on his own. He needs to get used to that.

There's no mistaking it. Wairere knows as soon as she wakes, and the knowing is like the cool steel edge of a knife: cruel and sure. It's no surprise to her that the moment is approaching. It seems like she's been waiting for it since he came, but the inevitability is still crushing. What is the point of having the sight if you can't act on what you see?

"School's off!" Keri calls from the door, unusually perky. "Dunno about Culture Fest yet. Suppose we'll find out later."

"K, Mum." Wairere burrows deeper into the bed. "Close the door!" She hears Walty thumping past before the door swings shut. That boy only ever goes at top speed.

She's left alone with the sound of rain, a thrum that peaks in waves, soothing in its intensity, blocking out everything other than its own thunder. She imagines standing in the downpour, the way it would feel on her skin, thousands of tiny fists pummeling her, through her hair, her clothes, onto her face, her arms, her feet, each drop joining others and forming rivulets behind her ears, down her neck, under her clothes, into her shoes. She's flowing with the water then, following the streams that urgently, urgently, seek their way back to the mother: the river, the ocean, the swamp. Down the paths, the gutters, seeping into the lawns and out again through the pipes, in the gaps between tar-sealed road gravel, rushing, rushing. Inside her the voice of every drop, calling: Swamp Mother, take us, make us clean again! She is hurtling with them to their only desire, down into the many waterways that will take them, eventually, back to river and sea and sky.

Swamp Mother. Take us.

Suddenly, she knows why she is drawn there. Swamp is the place of cleansing—her microbes, bacteria and fungi, her peat, her tussocks, reeds and tall harakeke, the clever kūwāwā and purei plants. Her rich mud and hungry invertebrates, her sludge and sediments. Wairere needs Swamp Mother to make everything clear. She needs Swamp Mother because swamp takes all the dirt and grime of the world into her generous body, and returns her children to the world refreshed; she replenishes every life form that needs water and air—every body that walks the earth, two- or four- or eight-legged, every creature that flies above it, every plant and tree and patch of ground, every frog and fish.

She rises and gets dressed. Quietly leaves her room. She can hear Keri and Walty in the kitchen, the regular sounds of a morning, the TV in the background. No one will notice. She slips out the door.

Over breakfast, Adam mentions it'll probably be a long day. He's due at work anyway, but any time there's a weather event, things ramp up. Or so he's heard. There hasn't been anything major since he started, but his workmates told him that when it happens, at least a few times each year, they're often needed long past their regular finishing times. He told Sera that when he talked about where they came from, the constant and relentless "weather events" that made their entire city and much of their country unlivable, the other staff were at least a little relieved by the comparison. Locally, they've only had to permanently evacuate particular pockets of Ōtaki Beach so far. Most people are still able to live normal lives, most of the time. At least for a while. Up north, there are whole towns in the process of being moved: parts of Gisborne, Northland, Waihi, and down south into Marlborough and Westport. The rest of their neighborhood is on the list, of course. All coastal places are.

"I'll try to be back at lunchtime to check in," he says. "The outlook is okay. I hope the rest of the day will be manageable too."

"Of course it will. You will be fine. We will be fine!" Sera looks out the window. The lights are on inside. It's so dark today, but Sera can't feel negative about a rainy day, no matter how heavy.

Adam searches her face. She can tell he's pleased to see her positive, lighthearted. Maybe they've turned a corner at last. He picks up his things, and bends to kiss Aliana. She squirms away, and doesn't stop squirming. Time to get down from the table. He lifts her up, throws her in the air, and she squeals. He puts her down and she runs to her small table and chairs where the blocks are set up. She looks happier too. They have so much to be grateful for.

Sera has taken some leftovers out of the fridge, and wraps them for Adam's lunch.

"Be safe," she says, passing him the parcel. It's their customary saying, through all the years when they didn't know if whoever was leaving the house would return.

"I'll be back soon," he says. Then he kisses her, and is gone.

The school is by a waterway, half stream, half drain. There are eels in it, and a path alongside, and it makes for a good walk. Keri takes Walty there sometimes with his bike or scooter to let off some steam. They lean over the bridge hoping to spot the eels, and throw sticks in to watch them float downstream. She doesn't suppose the waterway is natural—it's too uniform, too straight, and too conveniently placed out of the way of the houses on either side. And in recent years, it floods during most heavy downfalls. In the worst weather, the school has to close when the sports fields and netball courts are underwater—something about old sewage pipes running under it all. The school needs to get all the plumbing done, but can't afford it until the next budget round, and summer, when the kids will be away.

It'll be nice to have Wai home. Maybe she can look after Walty while Keri gets the groceries. Keri needs to go today, flood or no flood. And she has no clue what is happening about Culture Fest too. Surely the organizers will have to cancel, but they might not announce until later in the day. Should she buy the flour and oil for the frybread Wai wanted her to make or not? She can't afford to buy it for no reason. She starts making calculations—how long can she wait for the event to be canceled before she does the shopping, whether she should just pull out anyway, how much she can afford to piss off Wai. The girl has been even more sullen lately, and she'd thought they'd made a breakthrough. She'd tried to talk to her a couple of times, but there are a few forces more frightening than an angry teenage girl, and she thought it best to wait it out, not poke the bear.

There's never a crossover period between when the food runs out and when the money comes in—in fact, every week there's one day, sometimes two, when she has to get very inventive. Pancakes are the fun dinner they get when all she has left is flour and sugar, oil and one egg. If she doesn't have any canned or frozen fruit or yogurt, she makes a sugar syrup to go with it. It's all empty calories, and she tries hard to have something more hearty to go with it, but they have pancakes for dinner most weeks. Walty is eating a leftover pancake now, running back and forth from the kitchen to the living room. Mrs. B gave them a good store of real fruit jam a month ago, so he has a bit of that. Sugary, but at least there's real fruit in it. That's gotta count? He seems well occupied, so she checks her account, tapping the four-digit PIN without giving it any thought.

The number that comes up is not the number she expects. $2.46? There must be something wrong. Her benefit would have come in yesterday. It's usually always on time, and every week she knows exactly how much will be there, down to the last cent. She has to.

The panic in her gut already knows. The panic in her gut tells her that what she sees is true. Something has gone wrong, some decision has been made, some glitch in the human chain that their lives are bound by. Because it's happened before, she knows it will take them at least a day or two to fix it, even if it's not her fault. If they deem it to be her fault, she could be stood down for much longer. It doesn't seem to concern them that she has mouths to feed.

She rings the 0800 number, and tries not to lose her mind while Dave Dobbyn's "Welcome Home" and two other mid-2000s-era Kiwi classics rotate on repeat. She should try and do something else while she's waiting—it could be ages—but she feels a kind of stress paralysis that keeps her glued to the chair, willing someone to answer. She doodles a shopping list in between taking stock of her last interactions with Work and Development, and her most recent spending. When she clicks into her account transactions, she sees that she did receive a payment, but it was half her usual, and her rent auto payment immediately used it up. If she only got 50 percent of her regular payment, that can only mean one thing: she is being penalized for something. She knows she did everything right this month: her work preparation obligations, her part-time work obligations, her child welfare obligations. She remembers every excruciating detail, stripping her of time and dignity, right down to her last visit to their office. Even more memorable than usual because of the situation with the Pākehā man in the high-vis vest and his kids. So she knows she got all her sign-offs and put all her paperwork in.

After forty-two minutes, she's connected with a live person, Cheryl. She has already plugged in her numbers, explained her situation to a machine, answered a string of automated questions, and been told the conversation will be recorded. Even so, Cheryl asks her the purpose of her call, so she explains her situation again.

"Right. I can see here that you haven't met your work eligibility assessment obligations so your benefit has been reduced by 50 percent for four weeks."

"What?! But that's not right. I put all my paperwork in—I've done everything this month. I can even tell you exactly what happened on the day I went in." Keri can't control the panic in her voice. She describes the dramatic scenes she witnessed in the office that day. “I was a police witness. There’s EVIDENCE I was there!”

“All I can see is that there is no evidence on your file that your obligations have been fulfilled. You also have other paperwork pertaining to part-time work and child welfare obligations outstanding.”

“But I put all of that in. And why wasn’t I notified that my benefit would be cut? I have kids to feed and no food in the house.”

“A letter was sent on Monday.”

“A letter in the post? That’s insane. Mail takes over a week to get anywhere! You have my email. You have my phone number. Who uses post?”

“Is there anything else I can help you with?”

“No—you don’t get it. I mean, yes. This is all wrong. I fulfilled my obligations. This is a mistakc.”

“If there has been a mistake, we can start a review process. This usually takes three to five days.”

“I don’t have three to five days. I have two hungry children.”

“Emergency loans can be obtained, but you will need to visit your local office to apply for assistance. Would you like me to make you an appointment?”

“Yes. I need an appointment immediately. The weather’s packing in, and I have to get food before it’s impossible to go out.”

“Just let me see what’s available.” In the pause, Keri feels like she might cry. She wishes her mother were there. She’s so tired, and she’s hungry too.

"It looks like I can get you in to see Meredith at 4:15 p.m. Shall I confirm?"

"Is there anything earlier?"

"I'm afraid not."

"I'll take it."

The woman says goodbye after giving her a list of things she must bring to the appointment and asking if there's anything else she needs today. Keri's feelings solidify into anger. Yes, there's something else she wants. So many other things she wants. But it would suffice to be able to punch Cheryl right in her smug face. It's not Cheryl's fault—after all, she's just a pimple in the gaping orifice of her workplace—but would it ever be satisfying to slap someone.

The pure impotent rage of not knowing where your kids' next meal is coming from. She thinks again about that day in the office, the way the Pākehā man in the high-vis vest completely lost it. The way she'd left the office and run after him, a rash decision, dangerous even. It was stupid, but she understood now better than ever why she'd followed him. She'd definitely left her paperwork on the desk for the case manager. It had all been completed correctly. It should have been filed. Should have. But had anyone filed anything after that?

There is little gratification in knowing. She still has to get through the day. Even if they grant her a loan until they fix their own mistakes, the money won't land immediately. She has to come up with a plan B.

"Wairere?" she calls down the hall. "Wai? I've got to go out in a bit. A problem with my benefit." She pushes open her daughter's door. "Will you watch Walty?"

But Wairere isn't there. She isn't in the bathroom, or anywhere else in the house. Keri doesn't know where she's gone. She walks around the house three times, searching and calling, looks in the garage and out the windows. On the windowsill, she finds Wairere's phone, and her stomach drops. Walty joins her, shrugging his shoulders and splaying his palms in an exaggerated gesture of confusion. "Where's Waiwai?" he asks, looking up at his mother. She doesn't know. Her daughter is missing.

Twenty-Three

HIDE

Even wearing her jacket, Wairere is soaked almost immediately, but it doesn't matter. The water pooling and falling in rivulets finds its way under her clothing and behind her ears and inside her socks. By thc time she reaches the swamp, she feels like she has become water, just like in her vision. She heads down the boardwalk, among the reeds and tall harakeke, the sodden tī kōuka offering little shelter. The wooden planks beneath her feet soon give way to dirt and gravel tracks, where water accumulates in deep puddles. The distinction between off-track swamp and underfoot path is beginning to weaken: soon everything will be under water, just as there is no distinct horizon any longer, only rain and mist blurring the boundary between earth and sky in every direction.

Wairere allows herself to be taken by the rhythm of the rain deeper and deeper into the swamp. She knows there's only so far she can go before she starts coming out of it again. She doesn't know where she will stop, but she trusts she will know what to do and when.

There are particular moments in a life when a person decides who they are. Every other moment is proof of those decisions, but occasionally we cross a boundary, or make a conscious choice between one fate and another. This happens to Keri on the morning she finds herself without money and without food and without her daughter. She has been fighting so hard for so long by herself. Ever since her mother died, and before that Koro Walt, all those years in another life in another country that wasn't her home, with men who didn't know how to see her, or even the children she bore with them. She has been alone so long. Exiled first by way of her location, second by way of her fear—it has taken her a long time to come home, and she's not there yet.

She thinks about who she can reach out to, all the people she knows close by, old friends and vague relations. She can't imagine going to any of them with her story. She knows they will offer help if she asks, but she also knows something will break inside her if she has to ask. She is ashamed. Her job is to look after her kids—to feed them and keep them safe—and today she has failed at both. But something is already breaking inside of her. Wai is too precious—too fierce and too soft and too much for this world. She cannot let anything happen to her girl.

And yet she must ask for help from someone. She needs help with Walty so she can go look for Wairere, and she might need help with food until she can secure an emergency loan. Even if she can get to the foodbank before their noon cutoff, she's already had her allocation of food parcels for the month, and she might not be able to convince them to give her another. Besides, she has no time to go there now. She needs to find her daughter first. The faster she can begin searching, the better.

Of course she hasn't known Sera long enough to land this on her. She knows Sera will be kind, but is she ready to show her what she's hiding, her vulnerability, the fact she can't even think of anyone else she could go to? And to ask for food like a beggar? Yet Sera is the one person she can think of who has come out of exile, like her, and who has known shame and hunger, and who has had to turn worlds over to save her daughter. They come from places so far apart that sometimes they have trouble understanding each other's words, even when they are speaking the same language. Yet Sera is the only person she feels able to open up to.

It's easier to think all of this than to actually explain to her friend what is happening. Over a quick cup of tea, while the children settle, Keri forces the words from her own mouth—each staggered revelation an exposure, each problem a weight pressing down heavier on her shoulders. She can't keep the high note of panic from her voice, and she can't hold back the rush of words.

"I just don't know where she would have gone in this downpour. I've left the lights on and the house unlocked in case she comes back." Keri feels the tears coming, and she knows she can't hold them back, but oh god she wishes she could. She places her hands over her face. "I'm so sorry, Sera, I didn't mean to lay all this on you. I—I don't know what to do." The tears pour down her face, as if she's turned on a tap. "I'm so sorry."

Sera grips her friend's shoulder, and leaves the room. She comes back with a box of tissues. Keri wipes her eyes and blows her nose, but the tears keep flowing.

"You must go and look for her. And you must eat. Walty will stay here with us. We have enough food for all of us for now. But you must find Wairere first."

The calmness in Sera's voice stills Keri.

"I am not very good at many things," Sera says. "I am nervous all the time since we arrived. I don't sleep. I am anxious. I count cups—"

"Cups?"

"Bowls, spoons, plates. I count everything we own. Then I count again. Sometimes I have to count it all five times before I can rest. I am a mess."

Keri can't help laughing, right in her friend's face. Snot and tears everywhere.

Sera looks concerned, and then she smiles, narrowing her eyes quizzically.

"Please ignore me—I'm an idiot," Keri says. "I shouldn't laugh. It's so ridiculous! Everything. It's all so hard." At least her tears are drying.

"Yes. It is all so hard. That is right. For me it is hard when nothing is happening. When life is supposed to go on as normal. What is normal? But when the world is falling apart, I am very good. When I was pregnant and we were on the verge of homelessness? I was a lake of calm. Running away from our burning city? I slept well. You will go and find your daughter and speak to your welfare agency. I will stay here and look after the children and organize the food for all of us. We have enough to last. And if we need more, we will find a way."

"Are you sure? I'm so embarrassed about all of this."

"No, you must not be embarrassed. I have told you my most embarrassing secret. We receive the welfare too. Tomorrow, if Adam no longer has a job, we may come to you for food. Now, go! But take a bread roll with you."

Sera goes to her cupboard and fridge, pulling out a cheese roll and an apple, looks at Keri, then turns back for one more of each.

"Wairere will be hungry when you find her," she says, holding out a lunch bag containing the food. Before Keri can take it, she rushes down the hall again and returns with a blanket. "Just in case."

Keri is so relieved. She hugs her friend and takes the gifts, yells goodbye to Walty, who extravagantly blows her a kiss from the other side of the room. As usual, he refuses to leave Aliana's side.

Keri heads out into the squall. It's so gray, and the wind is so intense, the rain comes at her sideways. Surely Wai wouldn't have gone to the swamp in this? She'll try Felicity's, and the school first, and then she'll go to the place her daughter usually goes when she's trying to work something out. She just hopes Wai hasn't gone toward water.

Culture Fest will be inside, and there ain't no flood yet, despite what Janet says when Conor finally makes an appearance in the kitchen. She bombards him with the news reports, weather predictions, and her checklist of what they need to do to prepare, not that she's left much to chance. She already has a giant wheelie bin filled with emergency supplies. He indulges her, curious about what she's heard on the radio. Today is the day, but he hasn't heard anything yet. Maybe the rest are like him, waiting until their allotted time to make an impact.

Janet switches from radio to TV at midday, to see any footage of storm damage. Apparently it's the West Coast that's hit worst, but only between Taranaki and Wellington. The storm passed over the South Island before it gained any strength, and the rest of the country won't see it until tomorrow. The usual images of waves dwarfing roads, houses with roofing iron flapping in the wind, and overflowing waterways flicker on screen in quick succession. They switch to a reporter holding a small, shivering dog and talking about the local animal shelter, which has been flooded out overnight and is now looking for foster homes for all the pets, when a yellow and red banner starts moving across the screen announcing breaking news of explosions in three different towns across the country. Janet takes Zadie into her lap.

Conor, who is standing in the doorway, as if he's just catching the news in passing, feels his heart beating faster and louder in his chest. He tries not to let his expression change.

A female news anchor, looking slightly flustered, suddenly appears on screen. *Now to bring you breaking news—we're receiving multiple reports of explosions in different parts of the country . . .* The reporter's tone is low, serious, quiet. *Police are fresh on the scene in Ōtepoti-Dunedin, Warkworth and Tāmaki Makaurau—Jordan, what can you tell us?* The image switches to a young male reporter wearing a high-vis rain jacket. *Rosalie, police haven't made a statement yet, and it's unclear whether these incidents are related. However, they all occurred around the same time and in crowded places: a mall, a cafe, and a gym. We also don't know what explosives were used. As you can see from the ambulances behind me, there have been some injuries, but we have no reports of death. We do know that the immediate areas of the explosions have been secured, and police are in the process of evacuating homes and workplaces nearby.* Rosalie's head is to the side—her brow furrowed in dramatic concern. *Thank you, Jordan.* Her gaze subtly shifts. *We expect police to make a statement in approximately ten minutes. We'll keep you updated . . .* Janet pats Zadie furiously, her eyes glassy and wide. Conor wants to see the updates, but he doesn't want to be too obvious.

He goes into the kitchen, makes them both a cup of tea, sits in the armchair beside Janet, and passes her a cup. She looks at him, surprise clear on her face. He never joins her during the day, and doesn't often make her a cup of tea.

"You looked like you needed it, Mum."

"Oh, it's shocking. Makes me feel sick. Not supposed to happen in New Zealand, is it? Especially when it seems random like that. Bloody mad bastards."

He looks at her, and shrugs.

"What—you don't think they're mad bastards?"

"Dunno. Depends why they're doing it."

"What d'ya mean, 'depends why they're doing it'? There's no reason to do it, son. The world's gone to hell."

"Maybe that's why they're doing it."

"Eh?"

"Because the world's gone to hell."

"You don't even know who's doing it. Could be terrorists!"

"No, I don't. That's true."

Janet stares at him. He shouldn't have said anything.

"Look, Mum. It's coming back on." He lifts the remote, and clicks.

There's a hide in the center of the swamp, between Paraparaumu Beach and Waikanae Beach, for birdwatching. It's mainly dry in there, surprisingly little graffiti, insects, or bad smells. Wai has forgotten it's there until she stumbles upon it. She can barely see more than a meter or two ahead, the rain so heavy a dense mist steams up her path. By the time she steps into the hide, the water is up to her ankles, even at the highest point of the track, but she isn't concerned. The swamp might rise up, but it will not hurt her. She may as well be a matuku or a kōkopu or pīngao, for she is as much a part of the swamp as all of them.

She sits on the little bench seat in the hide and watches the sky, all water. Occasionally she stands and paces, looks out as far as her human eyes will allow and sees very little, hears only the thunder of countless drops, smells damp and bracken and mud. It doesn't matter. She has other senses now that are stronger—nothing matters except the slow in and out of her breath, which matches the infinite in and out breath of Swamp Mother. How could she not have known before? It's so obvious to her now. When she closes her eyes, Swamp Mother's vision takes her own in all directions: to the East and West, arms stretching far out to a horizon that wraps around the earth; above and below, fingers stretching up into a universe that extends beyond imagining, and down into the earth's beating-heart core and out again forever in the opposite direction. She can pivot on the spot and feel her self stretching in any direction infinitely, feel the connection with every thing, through every drop of water, every connecting pipe, every thirsty mouth, every drop of atmosphere, every atom.

To be held in this. To be held by the infinite. She doesn't notice the water rising. How can she? She is the water. The water rising is the rising of her own breath.

Adam doesn't return at lunchtime, and there is no message or phone call from him, but this is expected. Sometimes things get so busy he can't stop until his shift is over, sometimes well beyond his shift. Sera knows he will come when he can. They had so many years of this before Aliana was born that Sera learned not to worry, though it is true her body will hold a small band of tension along her spine until her husband's return, no matter how well she knows the routine.

Keri returns, soaking wet and frantic, after 1 p.m., alone. She tells Sera how she searched for her daughter, how high the water is, how it's getting higher. The swamp was the last place she went, and the water was up to her knees. Wairere couldn't be in there. Keri heads next door to clean herself up. When she returns, she calls the police. They don't have officers spare at this time, she is told, and her daughter hasn't been missing for very long, but they will send someone before the day ends.

"I can't believe it," Keri says, over and over again. "I just can't believe it."

Sera nods. She has nothing more to offer her friend. This is the worst of their nightmares.

"She will come back, won't she, Sera?"

Sera wants to say yes, she will, but she doesn't know how to lie about this. It's too important. "I hope so, Keri. I'm so sorry."

Keri nods. "The police said they can't come yet because of the bomb threats. Have you heard about this?"

By way of an answer, Sera turns on the small transistor radio they keep in the kitchen. It's not the latest technology, but it carries with it the nostalgia of their past lives—a radio can be a useful thing when there's no reliable internet.

Do we know anything about the origins of the threats yet, Eric? an announcer asks.

No. The police aren't releasing any further information at this time, but the number of threats is rising. Last report, there were thirty-five. I've just had a message that twenty-three further threats have been made public. Schools are either locking down or sending children home immediately.

Do we know which schools are affected?

Yes, I'm able to give a full list of schools, as follows . . .

Sera and Keri say nothing as the schools are listed. All schools nationwide are closing for the day, even the ones unaffected by flooding, just in case. Culture Fest is most certainly off, but this is the least of Sera and Keri's concerns now. They both recognize the feelings, the sensations that flood their bodies—too familiar from the last time they found themselves under threat. Even though the threats aren't directed specifically toward them, they each know deep inside their bones that, in some way, the fear is.

By 2 p.m., there have been over eighty bomb threats against schools and other community centers, marae, mosques, and health units. Police have their hands full helping to lock down each area, while also dealing with a number of unexplained explosions, and two gunmen, who issue threats but don't manage to fire their weapons before they are apprehended. The bomb threats are horrifying, and violent, but some of them sound like jokes, the work of children, or amateurs, so says the terrorism expert they have on the news.

Janet is glued to the telly, and hasn't let go of Zadie since midday. Even Conor has remained interested, not slouched off to his room like he usually does after lunch, although he constantly watches his phone at the same time. Normally, she wouldn't stand for that, but she's too distracted to say anything about it.

"This is all so strange and awful. It's so upsetting."

Conor stares at the television. Janet can't read his expression, and he doesn't say much.

"Isn't it, Conor?"

"Eh?"

"Upsetting. This is not who we are, eh."

"Who?"

"Us. New Zealanders. The Prime Minister's press conference is coming up soon. I've never liked her, but I'm sure she'll have strong words for whoever is behind this. I hope she does."

"I should get going, Mum. I'll see you later."

"Where are you off to?"

"Just got some work to do. I have some errands to run in town."

The rain hasn't let up. The afternoon's programming has become a constant stream of news and weather. Janet doesn't know what to be more worried about.

"I can't imagine anything going ahead today. They're telling us to avoid unnecessary travel."

Conor frowns. Hesitates. "Yeah, but they always say that, eh? Is it alright if I borrow the car in that case? It'll be safer."

"If you must, but turn around at the first sign of flooding, okay?"

Conor nods assent, and gives the TV one last, long stare. "Maybe they have their reasons, whoever is doing this," he says. "Maybe they're trying to get our attention."

"That terrorism expert was saying it has the hallmarks of

an extremist thing. I don't know what they call it—right wing, neoconservative, and what have you. The university professor with green hair was talking about white supremacists. Can't think they have anything useful to say if they have to say it with threats and explosions."

"That's the thing. Maybe no one is listening and they're trying to warn us. Maybe the way you're feeling right now is the way we should feel all the time—because of what's going on in the world." Conor pauses, looking a little flustered, as if he hasn't meant to speak so passionately. "Don't mind me, Mum. I'm just frustrated. People wouldn't have to use threats and explosions if they were allowed to speak freely."

Janet looks closely at her son. What is he even talking about? His face is all angles—his baby fat gone—his words all have hard edges too. "Are you trying to give them excuses, son?"

They both return to staring at the TV screen, not willing to look each other in the eye. Images of a tall man with long blond hair come on screen, his face obscured, tucked into the neck of his shirt. It's one of the gunmen, allegedly, being taken into custody in Christchurch. Then a black and white symbol comes up on screen: a rune, the reporter says, an emblem linked to the events of the day—if anyone sees it anywhere, they should be very cautious, and call for help.

"Conor, isn't that the same symbol that's on your arm?" The question comes out before she can think about it. Should she be worried? Scared, even? The idea is ridiculous. But nothing is going to stop her saying what she needs to say in her own house. "That's not who we are, Conor."

"That's who I am." Really? Has he really said it?

"What are you talking about? I didn't teach you this."

"What did you teach me? To cower to my old man? To work in shit jobs for the bare minimum? Anyway, you're the one who'd prefer to have white neighbors."

Janet looks down. What is happening? "Not white, just Kiwis," she says quietly.

"Face it, Mum, you mean white."

"That's not what I . . . I never said that . . ."

"But what do you believe, Mum? About those ones next door, and Keri and her lot. You're always acting superior to them."

"I do not, thank you very much! Anyway, it's not about me, it's about you and this thing . . ." She's disgusted. Her own son.

"Well, you don't need to worry about it, Mum. I think there might be valid reasons for taking extreme action in the times we live in. But I haven't done anything. I'll see you later." He turns to leave.

"Conor?" He turns back and holds her gaze, his eyes hard, all the anger from his youth still there behind his pupils. She feels the recognition in her body first: the familiarity of those eyes and that anger. But this time she also feels sad. This is who he is. Things haven't changed that much, then. She wanted so much to believe that his life was better now, but deep down she's known. It has been there since he returned. Most of the time they go on as if everything is fine, but every so often, like now, when the world twists in its sickly fashion, when the blinkers fall away, she can see, plainly, that something is terribly wrong. What would she want him to know, if she could give him anything? What can she reach for in this moment? Zadie shifts on her lap, looking from her face to her son's, catching the tension in their bodies.

"Conor, listen." She looks out the window, seeing nothing but gray, then forces her gaze back to her son's impassive face. "People are basically decent, you know."

Twenty-Four

SLAP

Water will come and you think it will be soft. You think it will be smooth and find its way around your things: your houses and cars and furniture, your gardens and windows and hope. You think it might carry away some sticks and birds and rubbish from the drains, but it won't touch your crockery and photos and family heirloom kete, your beds or your cupboards of food. But water can be the foot of an elephant, the horns of a moose, a herd of buffalo running from a lion, water can be the kauri tree falling in the forest, a two-ton truck, a whole stadium filled with 50,000 people, screaming. Water can be the boulder, the cliff face, the whole mountain, the cold surface of the moon, a planet hurtling through space, the terrible gravity of a black hole, the crushing, centrifugal force, water can be a whole galaxy of stars, the density of them, their dazzling power. Water is life, and water can be death.

Wairere slips between dimensions, her heartbeat following the rhythm of the water drumming down from the sky in waves. Sometimes she is just a girl with cold skin, her jeans and socks clinging clammily, her pores saturated. For a long time she stares at the gap between the hems of her jeans and her shoes where the skin is visible, stares at the wet hairs she missed when shaving, the veneer of her skin, so solid yet so permeable. She pokes at her leg, imagining how the skin would split if she did the same with a knife, the way her blood would mix with the water below, which rises pleasingly. She sits hugging her knees on the bench, then occasionally kneels up to look out. Nothing changes except the water level.

Most of the time, though, she leaves that physical body behind and joins the swamp, slipping all the way through its different parts: the bog, the estuary, the seepages and flushes, the lagoon. She works her way down the swales and into the runoff, through the stormwater drains and out into the neighborhood. By the end of the day she knows it all, every secret underground pathway that water can infiltrate, all the mires, earthly and human, all the places and ways to get stuck, the quicksands and the brokenness, the way water seeps through. By the end of the day, she has mastered how to flow with the water, how to run where it runs, how to attend Swamp Mother's wishes, how to gather strength enough to realize her own.

She finds she knows what to do. How could she not have seen it before? She sees what Conor is, how small he is, how small they all are really, how they only mean something in relation to each other. She sees how the things he thinks he wants only make him smaller, that if he keeps going that way he will become as small as a molecule of the suffocating toxic algae that kills off rivers and fish, invertebrates and pet dogs—a poison to anything that touches it. Maybe he is already that.

But she is with swamp now, and swamp is in flood. And no matter how toxic it gets, river sludge can be washed away. She is no longer scared of Conor and people like him. She is no longer scared of what she is. She thinks of her nan, and knows that somehow the old lady is still with her. They all are. For a long time, she felt like she and her mum and Walty were all alone in the world, but they never have been. She feels so many others now, thrumming around her. They are ready to ride the floodwaters with her. It's like Nan always told her—the right teachers are already here, and swamp is the place of gathering for them all.

Conor can't fucking believe it. Everything is happening, and he's already feeling exposed, but for what? His big moment has already been canceled? Johnny is already in custody? It's all fizzling out before it even began. He needs to get out there anyway, find a way to distribute his bottle bombs somewhere they'll make an impact. Culture Fest was the perfect event to send a message. Now? He just needs to go somewhere public and well populated.

And what the fuck? Johnny didn't tell him half of what was

going on. He thought there were only a few of them—he thought the group he met was it. Now it sounds like there were cells all over the country that Johnny must have known about or set up, before they were busted apart into separate cells. He should be grateful—Johnny would have been protecting them all, keeping their identities as secret as possible—but what he feels instead is something like jealousy. In Conor's head, they were a small, selective group. Elite. Close. Now he doesn't know what they are. He and Johnny weren't as close as he thought. He wasn't trusted with the big picture, he knows that. He'll keep the faith with Johnny, but he's pissed off it didn't go the other way. Nah. He's disappointed that he wasn't more important to the whole operation. He's got to earn his place even more now. Better get out there and make a big bang while he can, even though some of the buzz has gone out of it.

Genius, though, the scale of it. Johnny's ability to muster. Or there could be someone above Johnny, pulling all the strings. He knows now that he's just a small part of it, but he supposes there would be no "it" without plebs like him. Revolutions can't happen without the many.

He carries his boxes to his mother's car. The chemical mix is in each bottle, ready to react to the release of the few drops of water he'll funnel into each one before tightening the caps. It's volatile—a bit of premature moisture can set the whole thing off—so he has to be careful. Once he triggers the mechanism for the water to be released, the buildup of pressure will cause a small explosion, spraying glass shards and caustic chemicals everywhere. He manually opens the garage door and peers out;

the rain is so heavy he can barely see past the driveway. He thinks of Keri then, imagines her cozy, inside with her children: the boy and that strange kid, the girl who yelled at him. Yeah, he can deal with the idea of hurting strangers, even people he knows, as long as it's no one he likes. He's so fricken soft sometimes.

Keri leaves her appointment at five. It was routine, at least. They believed her, given the circumstances of her previous visit, and implemented an immediate reinstatement of her full benefit, which means she only has to wait two days to receive it. Then they gave her food coupons. Embarrassing, but better than nothing. The appointment was distracting, especially since she couldn't tell them, under any circumstances, that she has lost her child. She had to pretend everything was all good, and to do that, she had to believe it was all good, just for a moment.

As soon as she leaves, she's frantic again. It's dark already, the streets so waterlogged she's unsure about driving some of them, the water flying up in thick, blinding spray as she enters the wide puddles. Occasionally she can feel the wheels slipping under her, a momentary loss of control. She slows and reroutes to avoid the streets that already resemble small rivers, but she's desperate to go faster. As far as she knows, her girl is out in this. Her Wai. And the police still haven't come to investigate, the whole country caught up in what the media have inadvisably started to call the toddler terrorist attack, because it seems to be made up primarily of noise and disturbance, but no real harm.

Commentators are warning that the distraction might be to draw attention away from something else, something bigger, so police have been extra vigilant, but so far there have only been a series of frightening yet impotent explosions, a ridiculous number of bomb threats, and a couple of crazy-looking dudes with guns. Keri would laugh at the stupidity if she wasn't so frightened for her girl. And another thought has been pushing insistently at her all day, but she hasn't been willing to go there. She couldn't entertain the thought, because if she did, it might mean all of this is her fault—but now she can't hold it back any longer—she has to consider all possibilities. Wai tried to tell her—Wai had been so worried about Conor—she'd known something was wrong, and Keri hadn't been willing to contemplate just how wrong it could be. What if Wai's disappearance has something to do with him?

She will need to go to Janet's to confront Conor herself, just to be sure. And then, when she's sure it's not him, please gods let it not be him, her next step is to keep after the police until they do something. She could threaten to gather a group of searchers to head out into the rain and flooding. Emergency services won't like that, so they'll have to act. Either way, she's going to go looking herself as soon as she organizes some resources. She'll need to bring in as many mates as she can—everyone through school, in the neighborhood, even old Janet . . . so much for Keri's shame. None of that matters unless she finds her daughter.

She pulls into the driveway and immediately sees Janet's garage open, the lights on. Conor's in there, loading boxes into the boot of Janet's prim and tidy hybrid. He turns to look her way as her headlights sweep up the driveway, and squints into the rain. She gets the feeling his stance is a warning. She feels the coldness of that stare, something off kilter about the way tension holds his body. Everything about this day has been a nightmare, but it is this moment that causes a sickening lurch in her belly. Oh no, she thinks, is it what she suspects? But just as swiftly as the thought comes to her, she knows that's not it. The picture isn't right. She's missing something.

Then she sees it, again—the geometrical shape tattooed on his arm—just a flash of it half covered by his sleeve. She'd thought it was cool the first time she saw it. A rune, he'd said, meaning ancestry or homeland. She could appreciate that, she'd thought at the time. Now she understands it means something else. She'd seen it as she sat by Sera on the couch that afternoon, after they switched to television news. That madman, the shooter who didn't manage to shoot anyone, thank all the atua. The reporter said it was something to do with his group. And he'd been going on about a homeland and freedom for white people, as if white people weren't already the beginning and end of every power structure in the country, as if white culture wasn't already embedded in every system and institution.

She frowns. What the hell is he up to? She isn't in the mood to tolerate any bullshit from this dickhead. Her girl is out there, her fridge is empty, and she's tired of working so hard to keep all their heads above water. Every day, the relentless grind to keep them alive and healthy, and maybe even happy? She has worked and loved too hard to let arseholes like this take away her sense of safety and joy. For so long, she's been scared of everything that could happen to them, but if Conor turns out to be who she thinks he is, she'll get out of her car right now and slap the silliness out of him.

But Keri doesn't need to get out of her car. At least not yet. And she doesn't need to lift a hand against Conor. Because something else takes her attention then, something that will reach him before she does.

Twenty-Five

TAHUTAHU

As the sky darkens, Wairere finds that she can still see. The water rises until she's submerged, but she doesn't feel wet or cold, nor can she feel the boundary between her and the swamp anymore. It's peaceful there, and she wishes she could stay like that, buzzing and flowing with life, reaching and tasting every place. She tells Swamp Mother all that she knows and all that she fears and everything she doesn't understand. Swamp Mother will know what to do with it, all the things she carries. She feels tremendous relief in the unburdening, but the message that comes back is that it's time to go back to her other life. It's time to go back and deal with the things that are in front of her, now that she knows how. All she has to do is step out into the flow.

So she does. Water has been flooding through the hide all afternoon, and as soon as she steps out, the old wooden hut begins to splinter, shuddering sideways and collapsing. Wai is surrounded by a swirl of old timber, so she reaches for a wide plank and pulls her upper body onto it, her feet kicking behind. And the water carries her. It moves with her body the way a horse moves with its rider, responding to the direction of her intent. And as they travel, they lift time with them, so that the swamp becomes what it has always been, at every moment—primordial twitching ooze, prehistoric reptilian bird lands, ancient food storehouse—pātaka for the ancestors who rise out of the softening ground and join Wairere on her journey. They travel through and around the houses, pulling back any boards or nails that are loose, freeing any errant plumbing, rejoining with long dormant underground springs; then they come upon Kenakena Pā, the sports fields already several feet under water, making it easier to see what and who is there behind the watery veil of night: the men and women of the Pā rising from their fires, stowing their belongings, and climbing into their waka. Te Ahi, with her red hair tied into a topknot, still young and with only one baby on her back; Tautohe, ready with his new musket strapped to his shoulders, though everyone knows it's his mere that you have to watch out for; Wiremu, already old but still formidable with his words, ready to do battle with that white boy if he's called on, though he knows his mokos, grandchildren, will deal with it, the rest of them are just coming along to support. Dozens of waka are spread out far on each side of Wairere, following her lead. At the old cemetery, the first white settlers come up out of their sleepy tavern, they haven't been woken for ages, and what's this now? A bit of a to-do with the natives, enough to wake them?

They'd tried to get along with the locals, that was the only way to do it, the only way to get by in this world. You had to respect those who were here first, learn their ways if you wanted to do well in trade. But they've been left alone for a good six score and ten, so they're cross, and they let it be known, the indignity of being lifted up in their nightclothes, no time to even don a hat. They make sure to berate their descendants as they pass, the ones who built the road that is now crumbling under the weight of so much water, the ones who built a bridge in the sacred places, a bridge that will collapse in the coming days, cutting the area off from any northern travel, the ones who pushed the railway through only to abandon it when people needed it most. And when they're done bringing up the dead, all told, there's a lot of them, looking bewildered, but determined to make things right. They'd thought they were making the world better, but were they? They'd heard bad things, or dreamt them, which is the same thing. A white ghost has got to take his chances, since his descendants rarely pay attention to his existence, likewise a white ghostess. This one now, Olivia, doing her best impression of a ghoul to scare some sense into a sleeping descendant who spends his time harassing the council about any expensive environmental initiatives they undertake. *The trees, Andrew!* she screeches. *Those were trees we planted for you and your children and the birds. I did always love the birds here.* And then she produces a number of native species from her mouth before her husband, Whitlow, drags her out of her great-great-great-great grandson's petrified, sweating head.

They flow toward 12A, B, and C Pine Street, all of them, they hurl, they surf, they paddle, they swim, they float, they rage, they propel, they breaststroke, they butterfly, they pull each other along, rafts of them behind and around Wairere. It is she who compels them; it is Wairere within whom they concentrate their energies. She knows they're all there, but it no longer feels like immense pressure. She is swamp, and therefore nothing feels too much anymore. It just is, even the bog, the filth, the hate, the sludge, the evil, the mires of the world—all of it has its place. The key, Swamp Mother reminds her as they travel, is balance. Everything weighed against everything else. Oh, you don't think I have a place for everything? You think I'm messy just because I'm a swamp? Have you not noticed my perfection? Take out a microscope.

But Wairere doesn't need a microscope, she's seen down into things, seen the perfection.

The waterfowl, led by kōtuku ngutupapa, float and glide; the worms and snails surf the current; an īnanga swallows a dragonfly nymph as it hurls along with its mates; tuna coil around each other, vying for a primary spot to watch the action. Wairere finally reaches her destination. She sees her mother's car first, and lifts it, shunts her mother away to where she is safe. Sends the force of water over the lawn, toward the houses, and into Janet's open garage, where Conor stands dumbfounded, watching a tide that has appeared out of nowhere roll toward him, engulfing him in seconds. Wairere flicks her wrist so that her hand sweeps toward Janet's car, and the water jumbles the bottles out of the boot so that they spin in whirlpools before hurling toward Conor, clattering against each other so hard that water gets in and mixes with the chemicals, causing a loud crack that makes everyone, even the dead, stop in their tracks.

What Keri sees is a rolling wall of water coming toward them off the street. That's not supposed to happen. That's not something she has a reference point for, except in footage from the islands, or Japan, or Italy, after too much rain in too little time, or after an earthquake. So she sits, stunned, in the car, watching the water come in, not computing the danger it poses to her. Not computing anything, to be fair, because rolling along with the water, holding on to a plank of wood, is her daughter, and even though the water roils fierce and fast, making a thunderous sound, ploughing everything in its way, Wairere seems serene and unwavering, her face and shoulders held aloft without any struggle that Keri can see.

And then Wairere looks right at her, and lifts her finger almost imperceptibly, and the water lifts Keri's car and moves her away from the garage where Conor still stands, a blanket of water speeding toward him. Keri is set down, steady, still watching, as the water fills Janet's garage, lifts the items from Conor's box and throws them toward him, all this happening faster than the seconds it takes for her to comprehend the movement, so that by the time she understands what that loud crack is, by the time she sees the glass explode, slicing Conor's face and hands, by the time she comprehends that the way he screams and holds his face and arms is not because of the glass but because of something else, that his contortions fit the movements of someone burning, even though he is not on fire, by that time, she has already left her car without having thought about the consequences.

Keri reaches the garage at the same time as Janet, who is at the top of the stairs from the house to the internal garage door. Janet steps down and retreats once she sees how high the water is. Along with the water, she sees her son, making an awful guttural screaming sound and holding his face, bottles floating around him.

"Conor?" Janet yells. "What the hell?" But she can't be heard. And then she sees Keri wading toward the garage, and Wairere in the water—what are they doing here? Water everywhere. Flooding, just as she'd warned everyone.

"Janet, get back!" yells Keri. "It's dangerous!"

Well, of course it's dangerous, she can see that for herself, but why is Conor making that awful noise, and is that blood? And then there's another loud crack, and she sees the glass flying into Conor's arms, something else hissing and causing his skin to drip off in chunks. Conor starts moaning, an awful pained sound much worse than the screaming. Janet can only stop herself from going to him by gripping hard onto the fear that if the same happens to her she won't be able to help him.

"Keri? What's this? I don't think Conor can hear me. What do we do?"

Keri has stopped at the garage door, the water rising past her waist, still rising, but slowed now in its force; Wairere is now where the entrance to the driveway used to be, still held as if in a trance, watching. The water will keep coming, Keri thinks, and a teenage girl, no matter how powerful, should not be left to manage everything. She turns to her daughter, and calls to her, voice as calm and serious as stone.

"Kāti, Wairere. That's enough. Pull back now."

Wairere meets her gaze, surveys the garage, and the energy leaves her immediately, so that she is just a girl soaking wet in the rain, up to her chest in floodwater. For a moment, Keri thinks she can see shadows moving around Wairere, hear voices murmuring, even singing, but it must be the rain, the surging water, those damn fizzing bottles.

"Will it go down now, Wai? Are you okay?"

Wai blinks slowly, and stands, unseeing. "Mama?" she calls, as if confused. The water, almost as fast as it came, starts to recede. Conor still moans.

"Go to Sera's, Wai. Walty is there. Look after your brother for me." The relief at seeing her daughter is tempered by the strangeness of her arrival. She can't think about it now. Only that she is safe. "And Wai?" Her daughter turns. "Tell Sera we need Adam. Urgently!"

Wai nods, and her eyes flick toward the man in pain and his mother behind him. A shudder runs through her. Did she cause that? All she knows is that she needed to take the swamp to him, that swamp had the power to deal with everything she couldn't. She feels cold for the first time that day, so cold she can barely breathe, so she puts the thought away and moves to obey her mother. Walty needs her.

"Don't go near him, Janet," Keri calls out. "Conor? Can you hear me? We're going to get you some help. But first you've got to move away from those bottles." He's whimpering now. The water is down around her knees. "Come out of the garage."

He's still holding his face, but he starts moving toward the door, and nearly collides with another bottle.

"Watch out! Don't go near those bottles! You're going to have to uncover your eyes."

"What have you done, Conor? What have you been doing?" Janet is panicked. She doesn't want to believe what she already suspects is true. "Are you really part of this? Are you *insane*? This is not who we are!"

"Let's just get him safe, Janet," Keri says. Maybe this *is* who you are, she doesn't say.

She watches Conor bring his hands down. His face isn't too bad. A few lacerations, but his eyes are streaming tears, and there are sickly patches around his jaw and on his arms where something has melted the skin.

Conor moves toward Keri, the sound of her voice, too shocked and embarrassed and pained to do anything but obey her directions. He's so fucking stupid. Such a fucking loser. But the freak way that water rushed in and shook up the bottles—how could he have known? He was being so careful. And now he just looks like a fucking idiot. In that moment, it feels like his shame and the caustic burns that sear his skin are the same thing, and that he deserves every sickly, disfiguring moment. He can't help the sound he's still making, a pathetic moan.

"Conor," Keri says when he reaches her. "I think we need to wash it. That's right, eh? You always get water onto burns, but whatever was in those bottles, I think it's still melting your skin."

He tries to focus on what she's saying, but the pain blocks everything else out.

"Janet! Bring lots of water. In a bucket. And detergent. And rubber gloves! Or garden gloves?"

"Water? There's water everywhere!"

"It has to be clean, Janet. We don't know what this water carries. It could have been through the sewer. And it's receding fast anyway. Quickly!"

Janet looks at her son, anxious to help. But she doesn't know what to do, and Keri's clear instructions seem as good a direction as any. She heads back into the house.

Conor is near Keri now. She's scared to touch him in case she hurts him, and in case he has caustic chemicals on his clothes, but she pulls her jacket sleeves over her hands and grabs hold of his sweater in a patch that looks clear.

"Just follow me, Conor. I'm taking you to the front doorsteps. Janet is bringing soap and water." She needs to check this is the right thing to do, but she can't bring her phone out in the pounding rain. She's thankful, though. Without the drenching they're getting, she doesn't know what kind of state Conor would be in.

Conor is just holding on. It's like he's in a burning room, and there is a part of him set back from everything that can hear and see and think, but it's getting smaller and more charred as the fire sucks all of the oxygen out. Keri promises cleansing. She promises something cool.

Under the eaves by the front door, Keri pulls out her phone, but she has no data. She calls Sera. "Do you know anything about chemical burns, Sera?" she asks. "Or just first aid in general?"

"What is happening? Wai told me you needed Adam, but she couldn't say much more."

"Might be easier for you to see. Can you come out on your step?"

"I think so. Just for a minute."

Sera comes out immediately, and Keri waves. They look to each other across the sodden divide between the houses, Conor whimpering between them. The world is a strange, aching place, and easily as full of pain as it is of anything good, but both of them are grateful, in that moment, for the woman at the other end of the line.

"We need to know what to do for chemical burns, and lacerations, though they don't seem too deep." Keri tells her friend.

"Water, just water, lots of it. But I will look it up. I'll send you whatever I find."

"Okay. Thanks, Sera."

"Adam will be home soon. He'll be able to help. Come in from the rain as soon as you can."

Sera goes back inside. Then Janet is on the front step again, complaining about hauling the bucket, finding the gloves. The woman doesn't know when to stop. Finally, she takes stock of the situation.

"Oh, Conor," Janet says. It's the closest she's been to him.

Keri is relieved Sera texts screenshots from a first-aid site almost immediately: twenty minutes of washing, it says, no soap. Remove his clothes and put him in the shower. She'll let Janet do that, but she'll help get him there.

"Get his clothes off," Keri says. "You need to put him in

the shower for twenty minutes, flush whatever is causing the burns."

"But the bucket . . ."

"We'll throw it over him now. Then get him to the shower. Pass me the gloves? We should get these clothes off straight away."

Still on the front step, they start stripping Conor of his clothes. He acquiesces limply.

"Thank you, Kerry," Janet says as they get Conor into the bathroom. Keri waits outside while Janet puts him in the tepid shower in his underwear. She should leave. She wants to get to her children. But there's something she needs to say.

"Janet?" she calls, tapping on the door. "A word before I leave? If he's okay . . ."

Janet comes out of the bathroom, closing the door three-quarters of the way behind her.

"Adam will be here soon with the ambulance. I need to go home to the kids. Look, I think someone needs to call the police." Keri speaks quietly enough so that Conor won't hear.

Janet looks at her for a long moment, emotions moving across her features. Her eyes search past Keri to the window, the world outside, the thunderous rain, then back to her neighbor's face. Finally, she says yes.

Twenty-Six

SWAMP MOTHER

And now this story will find a place to land, though this is not the end, for there is no end to stories.

The mother makes the phone call while her son is attended by the son of a different land. Adam, named for the Christian and Jewish and Muslim first man, who comes from a place where those three faiths have their roots intertwined deep in the soil but behave as if they have nothing in common. His people have been wandering for a long time. The other son, Conor, hates him for the wandering, as if no man should step over the made-up lines that divide one country from the rest, as if no man should travel ocean and sky pathways. As if they have nothing in common. He hates Adam for the foreign sound of his voice, for the color of his skin. Adam attends to him anyway, and that shames Conor, because he needs the help. Somewhere, very deep in the dark recesses of his psyche, a slight fissure opens, and light begins to filter in.

The mother tells the police what she thinks her son has done. What she knows, even if she doesn't think she can believe it. Adam leaves and the police come and she watches as they take away her patched-up son, and she thinks about all the things that could have led to this, struggling against the urge to patch up her own wounds with stories that will make her feel better. There can be no denying that something has gone very, very wrong. She cannot find comfort, even in the softness of her dog's fur. Her unease means she must take out and examine all the days of her life with her son, and all the days prior. She finds herself wanting. It is unwritten whether this wanting will take her in one direction or the other. Whether she will be able to sustain the unease long enough to become something more than she is, or whether her discomfort will cause her to weave elaborate narratives as a protective shield.

But let it be known, she is my daughter as much as anyone. My waterways stretch into the lives even of those who will never see me. My edges are nebulous, generous, engulfing. I have no borders.

When Wai enters her neighbor's home, Sera sees what she has seen many times before: someone made mute by what they have seen at the center of a flood, a firestorm, a terrorist attack. Sera knows instinctively what to do. It's never much use to try and make sense of a situation until much later. She helps the girl into a hot bath, then bundles her up and sends her to bed, and Walty decides to climb in with his sister to keep her warm, then refuses to leave her. After they both fall into a deep and soundless sleep, Sera is left alone to wonder about what she has seen, in Wai's eyes, and outside.

Adam will come home after he attends to Conor. Keri will be back shortly too. Ali has fallen asleep on the couch, as if Wai's arrival has brought a sleepy enchantment into their home. All the most important people in her life are accounted for. She doesn't need to count anything, for now. She feels held in this place, protected by some invisible force, even though she won't hear until much later how the arrival of Wai and her wall of water flushed out the terrorist in their midst.

Keri comes back first, and tells Sera everything. Then Adam arrives, exhausted by the long shift. The water is rising and receding outside, he tells them. It might be worse tomorrow, it might be better. They should prepare to evacuate if necessary. Sera expects the familiar fatigue, the breaking apart feeling she's had lately whenever she thinks back to those days of running and running from the fires. The many evacuations they lived through have left a scooped-out shape in her gut and heart and she doesn't know if there is anything left to keep her going through another run. She thought she'd reached the end of her reserves, but she doesn't feel it on this dark, rainy evening. She feels only warmth as the adults gather around the table to eat heartily and feed the children, who wake blearily to the wetness of the world.

Before they are finished, she opens the door to Janet, who

brings with her a pie to set down on their table. She doesn't ask to eat with them, but they insist.

Bringing the waters back in is like taking a deep breath, which I do once the skies clear. I leave mud and dead things in my wake, enough to stink up the place so they'll have to spend days cleaning and remembering the way water can return any time it decides to. They sometimes tell stories of righteous floods, as if it is male gods that have dominion over such things, but no, the decision to swamp them is mine. They should know better than to forget this by now.

Wai returns to me when the sun is strong and enough days have passed for her to be strong too. She is clearer than ever before, free of the darkness that she carried with her. It will come again. That is the way of things. But it's good to feel her walk so lightly for a while.

There she is. See her now? She brings the little ones, Walty and Ali, and the dog, Zadie. And who's that? The mother Janet, coming up behind them, keeping her sharp eye on the babies. The other mothers not far away, talking and working, as mothers do. Here they are, everyone who belongs to my swampy waters, no matter how far they and their ancestors have traveled. There is work to do, to belong here, there are stories to hear. It's a good thing they're coming now; it's a good thing they're ready.

Author's Note

This book pays tribute to the power and majesty of swamp; but the truth is, maybe water can't "return any time it decides to." According to the Waitangi Tribunal 2200 #A197 Porirua Ki Manawatū Inland Waterways Historical Report, from 172,335 hectares of historical bog, fen, marshland, seepage, and swamp, only 1958 hectares remain (465). That is a loss of 170,376 hectares, or 99 percent, of wetlands, which mirrors the pattern elsewhere in Aotearoa. The outcome is a devastating loss of habitat, flora, and fauna. Traditional food sources have become extinct. Within my lifetime, waterways that were once abundant with native species like tuna (eel) and īnanga (whitebait) have become too polluted to sustain life. Floods and other environmental disasters are exacerbated by our destruction of wetlands.

While there is incredible environmental and historical work being done throughout Aotearoa in different areas, the most extensive and invaluable sources of information about repo, whenua, moana, and awa (wetlands, lands, and waterways) are the research reports commissioned by the Waitangi Tribunal and the resultant Inquiry Reports, which include rich testimony from local whānau and hapū (traditional owners of the sites). These reports are repositories of our memories of, and relationships with, our wetlands.

Sera's recollection of the environmental devastation that made her family refugees is based on the actual Northern Hemisphere summer of 2022. I made up her family circumstances and the Refugee Processing Center, but almost all the heatwave descriptions are drawn from real reports of the heatwaves in Europe and China that year.

I would like to acknowledge the fifty-one victims of the Christchurch terror attacks, their families, and friends. I would like to acknowledge all who stand with them, and all anti-fascist and anti-racist activists throughout Aotearoa and the world. I started thinking about this book five years before it was completed, before the events in Christchurch, when New Zealand seemed to be a different place. The things that have happened since then are beyond anything we could have anticipated; and yet some of them, like extremist racism and terrorism, had already been recognized and experienced in our communities.

I have deep faith in the power of stories to change us. This is only a modest offering that makes no claim to understand any of it, but as a friend once said, the gift of fiction is interiority, and that is all I have hoped for in writing this. The mistakes and inadequacies of this work are my own, but any power it has is due to the collective power of aroha emanating from those who stand against all forms of prejudice, extremism, and hate.

I haven't attempted to emulate the most extreme elements of far-right radicalization, disinformation, online hate, or real-world violence. Those things have no place in any world, imagined or lived, and are beyond the bounds of any usefulness to a narrative like this. But there are certain elements of radicalization and far-right extremism that are known patterns to recruitment and action, and I have made use of those where appropriate. For a better understanding of how such things work in the real world, I recommend:

Julia Ebner, *Going Dark: The Secret Social Lives of Extremists*
Talia Lavin, *Culture Warlords: My Journey into the Dark Web of White Supremacy*
Byron Clark, *Fear: New Zealand's Hostile Underworld of Extremists*
Arcia Tecun, Lana Lopesi, and Anisha Sankar (eds.), *Toward a Grammar of Race in Aotearoa New Zealand*

For a better understanding of the lived experience of contemporary refugees, I drew from the following books:

Dina Nayeri, *The Ungrateful Refugee: What Immigrants Never Tell You*
Behrouz Boochani, *No Friend But the Mountains: Writing from Manus Prison* and *Freedom, Only Freedom: The Prison Writings of Behrouz Boochani*
Kao Kalia Yang, *Somewhere in the Unknown World: A Collective Refugee Memoir*

Author's Note

The Ministry of Public Assistance Work and Development Office is entirely my own invention and differs from contemporary social service providers in a number of ways, though elements of it are derived from memory and anecdotal accounts of similar welfare operations.

Acknowledgments

NGĀ MIHI AROHA

Ko te mihi tuatahi ki te repo, te moana me te whenua o te rohe o Kāpiti. I am thankful for the fourteen years we spent living in and walking the shores, swamps, and streets of the Kāpiti area. This book would not exist without the beauty and manaakitanga of that place. He mihi tuarua ki tōku whānau: Lawrence Patchett, taku hoa rangatira, who always understood the power of swamp and trekked through their stories before I even looked in their direction. Thank you for your patience and humility and for always reading everything. Kōtuku Titihuia—there's lots of you in Wairere. Thank you for teaching us to see, and for all the bird and beast and plant magic. Aquila Merewitikau—our worldly toa. Thank you for the evergreen *stupid-bum-dog*, here immortalized in your honor. Please come home for good one day. Thanks always to extended whānau for giving us so many homes to come back to. He mihi arohanui ki te whānau Skipper a Waikawa—the last few years of mahi on our land, me te mahi o Te Whakaruruhau, have been transformative and more important than I even have words for.

Acknowledgments

E te rangatira, Moana Jackson, thank you for your care and guidance, and for your permission to dedicate this work to you. I wish you could have read the book and told me how to make it better. Katarina (Ani) Gray-Sharp, your courage and deep knowledge are a profound privilege to witness. I'm lucky to know you. Thank you for your reading and wisdom and especially our friendship. Arohanui ki a koe, e taku hoa.

Massive Mihi to my other first readers, for your time, advice, friendship, and company in this world of despair and terrible human characters. Your solidarity gives me hope: Mahdis Azarmandi, Tīhema Baker, Behrouz Boochani, Byron C. Clark, and Deidre Dahlberg. One of the gifts of this book has been the opportunity to spend time with people who are smarter or more experienced than me in relation to these kaupapa. Ngā mihi hoki ki a Ingrid Horrocks, Nic Low, and Dougal McNeill for all of the above, useful conversations about writing and publishing, and just shooting the shit, all of which have become increasingly important to living through this time.

Olive Nuttall—I've learned so much from you. Thank you for giving me your thoughts about calling people bad words in fiction. May you always be held by good words. Thank you to my writing group for the reminders that all that matters is the work and friendship: Sarah Jane Barnett, Alison Glenny, Lynn Jenner, Bill Nelson, Rachel O'Neill, Lawrence Patchett, and John Summers. And to my students—you teach me so much! I thought about you a lot while I was writing this. Thank you for your trust and faith.

And thanks to Dad, without whom Janet would not exist, and

for once telling me, when I'd almost lost my faith in everyone, that "people are basically decent, you know." You were such an unexpected source of this truth.

I have been surprised and delighted by the path this book has taken already in the hands of my agent, Charlotte Seymour, and my publishers, HarperVia (United States) and Footnote Press (United Kingdom). It is incredibly exciting to work with inclusive publishers who are dedicated to highlighting international voices, promoting marginalized stories, and countering dominant narratives. Thank you so much to Daphney Guillaume of HarperVia for ushering this book into the world for US readers. Massive thanks to Serena Arthur of Footnote Press for bringing it to UK readers. Additional thanks to Ghjulia Romiti for saying yes to *The Mires* early in the process. I am so lucky this book found its way into all of your hands!

I owe particular thanks to Creative New Zealand and the University of Canterbury for the Ursula Bethell Writers Residency 2022, Te Herenga Waka Victoria University of Wellington, the International Institute of Modern Letters for financial support and time to write this book, and the Michael King Writers Center for a two-week writing residency in 2020 where Swamp Mother first emerged. Without financial support and the gift of time, nothing could have been written.

Massive aroha, all ways. It takes more than one person to make a book. and I'm grateful for all my communities and places: extended family, friends, and colleagues. Mauri ora.

About the Author

TINA MAKERETI is a New Zealander of Te Ātiawa, Ngāti Tūwharetoa, Ngāti Rangatahi-Matakore, and Pākehā descent. Her novels include *The Imaginary Lives of James Pōneke* and *Where the Rēkohu Bone Sings*. In 2016, her short story "Black Milk" won the Commonwealth Short Story Prize, Pacific region. She also coedited *Black Marks on the White Page*, an anthology that celebrates Māori and Pasifika writing, with Witi Ihimaera. Her novels, essays, and short stories have won recognition in Aotearoa, and she has been the recipient of several writers residencies and awards. Tina teaches creative writing at the International Institute of Modern Letters, Te Herenga Waka Victoria University of Wellington. She wrote *The Mires* while living on the Kāpiti Coast of Aotearoa New Zealand.

About the Author

[illegible]

A Note on the Cover

Upon receiving the assignment, I did extensive research into the Māori people, as well as all the flora and fauna specific to New Zealand swamps. Each plant and animal represented on the cover is specific to the region and was chosen with care. Throughout the novel, elements of magical realism are woven in as we learn about the characters' deep connections to their ancestors. To portray this on the cover, I utilized an unexpected color palette and layered textures that are meant to create a mystical effect.

—Sarah Kellogg

Here ends Tina Makereti's
The Mires.

The first edition of this book was printed
and bound at Lakeside Book Company
in Harrisonburg, Virginia, in August 2025.

A NOTE ON THE TYPE

The text of this novel was set in Tiempos Text, a modern serif typeface designed by Kris Sowersby in 2010. Striking a perfect balance, Sowersby's design prizes functionality while retaining the elegance of a serif typeface. Tiempos is a robust and clear font, perfect for economic and legible typesetting.

HARPERVIA

An imprint dedicated to publishing international voices,
offering readers a chance to encounter other lives and other
points of view via the language of the imagination.